PENGUIN CRIME FICTION

THUS WAS ADONIS MURDERED

Sarah Caudwell, of Scottish descent, was born in London.
She studied law at Oxford, was called to the Chancery Bar,
and practiced law for several years at London's Lincoln's Inn,
the scene of much of *Thus Was Adonis Murdered*. She is now
a member of the legal section of Lloyds Bank, Ltd. *Thus Was
Adonis Murdered* is her first novel.

Thus Was Adonis Murdered

SARAH CAUDWELL

PENGUIN BOOKS

Penguin Books Ltd, Harmondsworth,
Middlesex, England
Penguin Books, 625 Madison Avenue,
New York, New York 10022, U.S.A.
Penguin Books Australia Ltd, Ringwood,
Victoria, Australia
Penguin Books Canada Limited, 2801 John Street,
Markham, Ontario, Canada L3R 1B4
Penguin Books (N.Z.) Ltd, 182–190 Wairau Road,
Auckland 10, New Zealand

First published in the United States of America by
Charles Scribner's Sons 1981
Published in Penguin Books 1982

LIBRARY OF CONGRESS CATALOGING IN PUBLICATION DATA
Caudwell, Sarah.
Thus was Adonis murdered.
I. Title.
PR6053.A855T5   1982   823'.914   82-12258
ISBN 0 14 00.6310 2

Printed in the United States of America by
George Banta Co., Inc., Harrisonburg, Virginia
Set in Baskerville

To J.G.F.C.G.
for all the letters I've failed to write you

CHAPTER 1

Scholarship asks, thank God, no recompense but Truth.
It is not for the sake of material reward that she (Scholarship) pursues her (Truth) through the undergrowth of
Ignorance, shining on Obscurity the bright torch of
Reason and clearing aside the tangled thorns of Error
with the keen secateurs of Intellect. Nor is it for the sake
of public glory and the applause of the multitude: the
scholar is indifferent to vulgar acclaim. Nor is it even in
the hope that those few intimate friends who have observed
at first hand the labour of the chase will mark with a word
or two of discerning congratulation its eventual achievement. Which is very fortunate, because they don't.

If the events in which Julia Larwood became involved
last September had not been subjected to the penetrating
scrutiny of the trained scholar—that is to say, my
own—well, I do not say it is certain that Julia would even
now be languishing in a Venetian prison. The crime being thought to be one of passion, great lenience might
have been shown; the Italian Government might have
declared an amnesty; the Foreign Office might have done
something. Very possibly. I do say, however, that it was
only as a result of my own investigation that Julia's innocence was conclusively established and that she returned
to England without a stain on her character.

As an instance of what the methods of Scholarship may
achieve, the affair seems not unworthy of some written
record. And you may think, dear reader, that those who
had been able—modesty forbids me to say, if others do
not choose to, privileged—to observe for themselves the
process of my reasoning would have competed in eagerness to undertake the task. How little, if you think so, do

you know the Chancery Bar. Timothy Shepherd—additionally inspired by the reverence which ought to be felt for his former tutor—that is to say, myself—Timothy, you might imagine, would have been delighted by the opportunity. But no—Timothy has a case on the Companies Act coming up in the House of Lords; he is weeks behind with his paperwork; he cannot do it. Selena Jardine, who is fond of Julia and would have been distressed by her prolonged incarceration—no, Selena is engaged in a planning enquiry on behalf of certain objectors to a road-widening scheme; she is months behind with her paperwork; she cannot possibly do it. Michael Cantrip and Desmond Ragwort, of the same Chambers—Cantrip is instructed on behalf of a lady who claims by custom immemorial to be entitled to hang her washing across her neighbour's garden; the neighbour has instructed Ragwort to oppose the claim; they confidently expect the matter to occupy their attention for the best part of term, and that of a High Court Judge for at least a fortnight: no, clearly they cannot do it.

I am obliged, therefore, with some reluctance, to do the thing myself. It means my own work must be laid aside: the day must be deferred to a yet more distant future which sees the publication of *Causa in the Early Common Law* by Hilary Tamar and the appearance in learned journals of such phrases as 'Professor Tamar's masterly exposition', 'Professor Tamar's revolutionary analysis' and so forth. But I am content to make the sacrifice—if I hesitate, it is for fear that some of my readers will suspect that my motive for publication is mere self-advertisement. The danger of incurring so contemptible an opinion has almost deterred me; but I cannot allow mere personal delicacy to deprive the public of a possibly useful and instructive chronicle. I shall set down what happened, as it happened: and if, in the cause of Truth, I am unable to minimize my own achievement,

I hope that the wiser spirits — I refer, in particular, dear reader, to yourself — will not think the worse of me for it.

I had decided to spend September in London — my work on the concept of *causa* required me to study various original documents in the Public Record Office. And Oxford in September is not at all amusing.

I had at first been uncertain where I should stay. For the occasional night or two, I am sure of a welcome at Timothy's flat in Middle Temple Lane. I feared, however, that my presence for a whole month might place an excessive strain on his hospitality. Fortune came to my aid: a former colleague of mine, now the owner of a house and two cats in Islington, had arranged to spend the month in the United States of America and had realized, at a late stage, the difficulty of taking the cats with him to that country — he wrote in piteous terms, begging me to come and care for them. Happy to be of assistance to a fellow scholar, I consented.

On my first day in London I made an early start. Reaching the Public Record Office not much after ten, I soon secured the papers needed for my research and settled in my place. I became, as is the way of the scholar, so deeply absorbed as to lose all consciousness of my surroundings or of the passage of time. When at last I came to myself, it was almost eleven and I was quite exhausted: I knew I could not prudently continue without refreshment.

If, at eleven o'clock on a weekday morning, you leave the Public Record Office, turn right down Chancery Lane and continue past the Silver Vaults to the nearest coffee house, you will generally find gathered there (professional obligations and their Clerk permitting) the junior members of 62 New Square. They are a decorative little group — it would be a difficult taste that was pleased by none of them. Between Ragwort and Cantrip there are certain points of resemblance: they are the same age; of similar height; both thin; both very pale. But it is for those whose pleasure lies in the conquest of virtue that Ragwort's delicate profile and demure autumnal colouring have a most particular charm. Cantrip, in sharp contrast, has eyes and hair of a witchlike blackness, more pleasing to those whose preference is for a savour of iniquity. Selena—I can think of no especially striking feature by which you might distinguish Selena from any other pretty woman in her middle twenties, average in height and roundness of figure, with hair an inconstant shade of blonde; I mean, until she speaks: for her voice is unmistakable, smooth and persuasive, the envy of rival advocates. But until then—well, if you can imagine a Persian cat which has just completed a successful cross-examination, that will give you some idea of her. Timothy, my former pupil, being by some two or three years the senior in call to the Bar, is detained more often than not by the claims of his profession and was absent on the morning of which I write—there is little point, therefore, in my describing him.

They will be debating one of those diverse questions which interest the minds of the Chancery Bar—when to apply by summons rather than by motion, what to do about Ireland, or whose turn it is to pay for coffee.

'Perfectly scandalous,' Ragwort was saying as I entered the coffee house. The object of his disapproval might have been almost anything—Ragwort has such high principles. It turned out on this occasion to be the price of coffee. But he is a young man of graceful manners—on seeing me he ordered another cup, almost without hesitation.

I had feared, in the middle of the Long Vacation, to find Lincoln's Inn deserted. I expressed my surprise and pleasure at finding them.

'My dear Hilary,' said Selena, 'you surely know by now

that in the period ironically called the Long Vacation, Henry allows us to be away from Chambers for no more than a fortnight. Cantrip and I have already taken our fortnights—Ragwort is saving his for the end of the month.'

Henry is the Clerk at 62 New Square. From references which will from time to time be made to him some of my readers, unfamiliar with the system, may infer that Selena and the rest are employed by Henry under a contract more or less equivalent to one of personal servitude. I should explain that this is not the case: they employ Henry. It is Henry's function, in exchange for ten per cent of their earnings, to deal on their behalf with the outside world: to administer, manage and negotiate; to extol their merits, gloss over their failings, justify their fees and extenuate their delays; to flatter those clients whose patronage is most lucrative; to write reproachfully to those who delay payment for more than two years or so; to promise with equal conviction in the same morning that six separate sets of papers will be the first to receive attention. By the outside world, I mean, of course, solicitors: nothing could be more improper than for a member of the English Bar to have dealings, without the intervention of a solicitor, with a member of the general public.

I asked if Timothy's absence, at least, was attributable to pleasure. Selena and Ragwort shook their heads.

'Got nobbled,' said Cantrip.

'Nobbled?' I repeated, a little perplexed by the expression. Cantrip is a Cambridge man—it is not always easy to understand what he says. 'Nobbled? By whom, Cantrip? Or, to adopt the Cambridge idiom, who by?'

'Henry, of course,' said Cantrip. 'Spotted old Tim trying to make a break for it and sent out the guards to head him off. Had him hauled back to the stalag.'

'Cantrip means,' said Selena, 'that as we were leaving for coffee Henry sent a message by the temporary typist that Timothy's presence was required in Chambers. It appears that a rather distinguished firm of London solicitors needs the advice of Chancery Counsel on a matter of some urgency.'

'That's right,' said Cantrip. 'So while we're swilling coffee, poor old Tim is listening to the demented ravings of the senior partner in Tiddley, Thingummy & Whatsit.'

'So you see, Hilary,' said Selena, 'no one's on holiday. Except Julia, of course. She should be in Venice by now.'

'Julia?' I said, much astonished. 'You haven't let Julia go off on her own to Venice, surely?'

'Am I,' asked Selena, 'Julia's keeper?'

'Yes,' I said, rather severely, for her attitude seemed to me to be irresponsible. She likes, I know, to pretend that Julia is a normal, grown-up woman, who can safely be sent round the corner to buy a loaf of bread; but, of course, it is quite absurd. Poor Julia's inability to understand what is happening, or why, in the world about her, her incompetence to learn even the simplest of the practical skills required for survival — these must have made it evident, even in childhood, that she would never be able to cope unaided with the full responsibilities of adult life. She must have been, no doubt, a docile, good-natured child, with a certain facility for Latin verbs and intelligence tests — but what use is that to anyone? Seeking some suitable refuge, where her inadequacies would pass unnoticed, her relatives, very sensibly, sent her to Lincoln's Inn. She is now a member of the small set of Revenue Chambers in 63 New Square. There she sits all day, advising quite happily on the construction of the Finance Acts, and doing no harm to anyone. But to let her go to Venice — I imagined her, wandering alone through those devious alleyways, looking — as, indeed, she does at the best of times — like one of the more dishevelled heroines of Greek tragedy; and I could not forbear to chide.

'Furthermore,' I added, 'it is no use your implying, Selena, that your part in the enterprise was a merely negative one. If you tell me that Julia could have managed to purchase a travel ticket, find her passport, pack her suitcase and catch an aeroplane, all without the aid of some competent adult, I shall be obliged to disbelieve you.'

Selena admitted to having provided such assistance. She had accompanied Julia to a travel agent and had represented, on her behalf, the necessity of a holiday in Venice being arranged at five days' notice. (I did not ask why Julia had made no earlier arrangements — to plan five days in advance is, for her, a remarkable achievement.) The travel agent had found a vacant place on something called an Art Lovers' Holiday. Asked in what manner this differed from other holidays, the agent had explained that it included guided tours of various places of historical and artistic interest: additional tours were available on an optional basis.

'This made,' said Selena, 'a great impression on Julia. If some of the tours are optional, the remainder, she reasons, must be compulsory. For most of the time, therefore, she will not be on her own, but travelling about the Veneto in a group of respectable Art Lovers under the supervision of a qualified guide. So you see, Hilary, that all this alarm and despondency is quite unjustified.'

'You naturally prefer,' I said, 'to look on the bright side. So far as I am aware, however, the qualifications for a guide are not those of a nursemaid or a guardian of the mentally infirm. The poor fellow will take his eye off her for a moment and she will wander off. What then?'

'She will ask the way back to her hotel.'

'She will have forgotten the name of her hotel.'

'We have made her write it down on a piece of paper.'

'She will have lost the piece of paper. She will find herself alone in a strange city. She will not know where she is or what she ought to do.'

'The same thing,' said Selena, 'happens in London at least once a fortnight.'

There was some truth in this. In her native city Julia is still unable to find her way with confidence from Holborn to Covent Garden. Even so—

'Julia,' said Ragwort firmly, 'will not get lost in Venice. I have lent her my guide books, both to Venice itself and to those cities of the Veneto which she is likely to visit. I wasn't always able to get the English version, so one or two of them are in Italian. Still, I don't think it matters— the main thing is that they all have maps in them. Perfectly clear, simple maps. Julia will be able to see at a glance where she is, where she ought to be and how to get from one to the other.'

This was a kindness beyond mere courtesy. Visiting Venice in the previous spring Ragwort had formed a passionate attachment to the city and all connected with it— the guide books were as dear to him as the last mementoes of a love affair. To hand them over to Julia, particularly when one remembers her tendency to spill things—

'I have told her,' said Ragwort, 'that she is to take great care of them and not to read them while drinking gin. Or coffee. Or while eating pizza with her fingers. And I have put brown paper covers on them to protect them on the outside. So it really should be all right.'

'Of course it will be all right,' said Selena. 'And it doesn't matter about some of them being in Italian. Julia speaks very good Italian.'

This opinion of Selena's is erroneous but incorrigible. Selena herself declines to learn any foreign language. Julia, on the other hand, makes her way along the shores of the Mediterranean in the happy belief that everyone still speaks some version of Latin, with the endings of the nouns slurred and a slightly lilting accent: she achieves in this way a sufficient fluency to be regarded by Selena, when they travel together, as the one who speaks the language.

I raised another question which was perplexing me. 'It all sounds,' I said, 'very expensive. How can Julia afford it? I thought that the Inland Revenue had reduced her to destitution.'

Julia's unhappy relationship with the Inland Revenue was due to her omission, during four years of modestly successful practice at the Bar, to pay any income tax. The truth is, I think, that she did not, in her heart of hearts, really believe in income tax. It was a subject which she had studied for examinations and on which she had thereafter advised a number of clients: she naturally did not suppose, in these circumstances, that it had anything to do with real life.

The day had come on which the Revenue discovered her existence and reminded her of theirs. They had not initially asked her for money: they had first insisted, unreasonably but implacably, that she should submit accounts. They had shown by this that they were not motivated by a just and lawful desire to fill the public purse for the public benefit: their true purpose was to make Julia spend every evening for several months copying out the last four years' entries in her Clerk's Fee Book on an old typewriter that did not work properly. I myself am not entirely sure that the age and defectiveness of the typewriter were an essential feature of the Revenue's planning. But Julia was: every time it stuck, her bitterness towards them deepened. The Revenue, on receiving the result of her labours, had uttered no word of gratitude or commendation. They had demanded a large sum of money. More than she had. More, according to her— though I think that she cannot be quite right about this— than she had ever had. More than she could ever hope to have.

In this extremity, she had appealed to her Clerk. Julia's

Clerk is called William, an older man than Henry, and perhaps more indulgent. It took a mere two hours of sycophantic pleading, freely laced with promises of perpetual industry, to secure his assistance. He sent out fee notes, as a matter of urgency, requesting immediate payment from those solicitors who were indebted to Julia for her services.

His efforts raised a sufficient sum to pay the Revenue, but left Julia with nothing to live on. Or at any rate with only so much as might support the bare necessities of life. I did not see how she could afford to go to Venice.

'The unhappy events to which you refer,' said Selena, 'occurred some months ago. That is to say, in the financial year which ended on the fifth of April. On or about that date, the Revenue wrote to Julia, reminding her that they were now entitled to another year's accounts.'

'And Julia was jolly miffed,' said Cantrip. 'Because the way she saw it, she'd done her bit as far as accounts were concerned.'

'But she consoled herself,' said Selena, 'with the reflection that it was only one year's accounts and couldn't be as bad as last time. So she went back to her typewriter and in less than three months prepared her accounts for the previous year.'

'But since,' said Ragwort, 'her income for the previous year included the rather substantial sum raised by William to pay her previous liabilities to the Revenue—'

'She now owes them even more than she did last year. And she's really rather despondent about it. Because it seems to her that every effort she makes to reduce her liability will in fact simply serve to increase it. And it is difficult to point to any fallacy in her reasoning.' Selena gazed sadly into her coffee cup.

'It is still not clear to me,' I said, 'why she now feels able to afford a holiday.'

'It is true,' said Selena, 'that if she takes a holiday, she can't afford to pay the Revenue. But if she doesn't take a holiday she still can't afford to pay the Revenue. On the sheep and lamb principle, she has decided to go to Venice. I think it's very sensible. She will return to London spiritually refreshed and able to cope with life.'

'Spiritually?' said Ragwort. 'My dear Selena, we all know exactly what Julia is hoping to find in Venice, and there is, I regret to say, nothing spiritual about it.' Ragwort's rather beautiful mouth closed in a severe straight line, as if denying utterance to more explicit improprieties.

'After a bit of the other,' said Cantrip. It is a Cambridge expression, signifying, as I understand it, the pursuit of erotic satisfaction.

'Julia has been working very hard all summer,' said Selena, 'and has had few opportunities for pleasure. No one, I hope, would grudge her a little innocent diversion. My only fear is that she may be over-precipitate. I have reminded her that young men like to think one is interested in them as people: if one discloses too early the true nature of one's interest, they are apt to be offended and get all hoity-toity. But we must hope someone takes her fancy in the first day or two, or she may feel she hasn't got time for the subtle approach.'

'How long does she have?' I asked.

'Ten days. But effectively only eight, because two are spent travelling. She gets back to London on Saturday week.'

After a moment's reflection, Selena thought it prudent to qualify her last statement with the words 'Deo volente.' The phrase was intended, no doubt, to allow for some lesser catastrophe than Julia's arrest on a charge of murder.

CHAPTER 2

Despite her professed confidence that Julia would come to no harm, Selena's conversation betrayed, in the days that followed, an unusually anxious acquaintance with those columns of *The Times* which carried the news from Italy. It was full, suddenly, of casual references to student unrest in Bologna; the problems of the Tuscan peach farmers; and the doctrinal innovations of the Vatican and the Italian Communist Party. Happily, it appeared that neither crime nor accident, civil commotion nor natural disaster had impinged on any person answering to Julia's description.

In addition to this negative intelligence, she expected letters. She had impressed on Julia her duty to write daily, for the edification and amusement of those left in Lincoln's Inn.

'You made it clear, I hope,' said Ragwort, 'that the letters should be suitable to be read in mixed company and the activities described of unquestionable decorum?'

'Not precisely,' said Selena. 'I said that what we hoped for was a picaresque series of attempted seductions. I told her we would not insist, however, on their uniform success. I said that on the contrary we might think it inartistic.'

Ragwort sighed.

I had thought Selena optimistic to expect that any letters sent from Venice would reach London before Julia herself; but we were fortunate, throughout the period of which I write, in the efficiency of the postal services. The first of Julia's letters arrived on Tuesday, and Selena, who alone can decipher her writing, read it to us over coffee.

Heathrow Airport.
Thursday afternoon.

Dearest Selena,

'Twelve adulteries, nine liaisons, sixty-four fornications and something approaching a rape' are required of me for your innocent entertainment. Well, you will have to be patient — the aeroplane is not designed to accommodate such adventures. I am beginning, however, as I mean to go on, and in accordance with your own instructions — that is to say, with an exactly contemporaneous account of everything that happens.

It occurs to me that to abide literally by this resolution may have a slightly inhibiting effect on the adulteries, liaisons, etc. In certain circumstances, therefore, I shall hope, as regards precise contemporaneity, for a measure of indulgence — which, since you are the most reasonable of women, I do not doubt to receive.

It is about an hour and a half since you left me at the airport. Things, since you left, have not gone well with me: they have taken me from a place where there was gin to a place where there is no gin, and from a place where I could smoke to a place where I cannot smoke. That is to say, from the departure lounge to the aeroplane. They have also taken my passport.

*

'They can't do that to Julia,' said Selena. 'She is a British subject.'

*

And it's no use your saying, Selena, that I am a British subject and they can't do that to me. They have done. It began with a difference of opinion about my suitcase; I had thought it was hand luggage, which I could keep with me; the stewardess, at the last moment, decided that it was not. Deferring to the expert view, I handed it over, and she pushed it down a sort of chute. Only as it slid, with irreversible momentum, into the bowels of the aircraft, did I remember that my passport is in the side pocket. I shall not see my passport again until I get my luggage back: which will be, if my memory of airport procedure is not at fault, on the other side of the Passport Control Barrier. We have the makings of an impasse.

Too late, too late, Selena, I recall your as always excellent advice, to keep my passport at all times in my handbag. Together with such other essential documents as my ticket, my traveller's cheques, my Italian phrasebook, Ragwort's Guide to Venice and my copy of this year's Finance Act. Will any of these, do you think, be accepted as proof of my identity? Or am I doomed to be shuffled for ever between Venice and London, with occasional diversions, on account of administrative error, to Ankara and Bangkok?

*

'I would not wish,' I said, 'to say that I told you so.'

'The postmark is Venice,' said Selena. 'We may infer that the Finance Act was accepted in lieu of the passport.'

*

And that, I may say, is the optimistic view, assuming as it does that we actually get to Venice. The pessimistic view is that the aeroplane will be hijacked. There is sitting next to me a man of about fifty, of vaguely military appearance, who looks the type for such an undertaking: his suntan is too deep to have been acquired in England; his white moustache bristles piratically; his blue eyes are of a fanatic brightness. And he is wearing Bermuda shorts: these expose to public view his legs, which are hairy and prehensile, like those of a spider. A man who parades such legs as I have described in such clothing as I have mentioned on an aeroplane full of passengers — some of tender years, others perhaps of nervous disposition — that man, you will surely agree, Selena, is capable of any depravity. His hand luggage bears a distinctive label, similar to those given to me by the travel agency, pro-

claiming him to be, like me, an Art Lover. But one cannot be an Art Lover without some minimum of aesthetic
sensibility. That minimum he lacks—for evidence, *vide
supra*. I conclude that he is an impostor.

* * *

'Can't bear spiders, poor grummit,' said Cantrip. 'Did I
ever tell you—?'

'Yes,' said Selena. 'We have heard all about the spider
episode, Cantrip, and we don't want to hear it again. It's
a revolting story.'

'I thought it was rather witty,' said Cantrip.

'I gather,' said Ragwort, 'that Julia didn't.'

'No,' said Cantrip, rather sadly. 'No, she didn't, actually.'

It will not, I hope, be necessary, at any stage in my narrative, to disgust my readers with an account of the spider
episode. I will say only that any exchanges of an erotic
nature between Julia and Cantrip which may hereafter be
referred to may be conclusively presumed to antedate the
incident. Though, in all fairness, it does seem to me that
a woman who retires for the night with Cantrip on the
31st of March in any year, forgetting that the following
day—still, as I have said, I propose to draw a veil over the
whole matter.

* * *

Mind you, Selena, when it comes to looking round for
potential hijackers, I am by no means happy about the
armour-plated matron on the other side of the gangway. I
am suspicious of her coiffure—can any hair grown in
nature be moulded to such iron symmetry? And can any
lady so closely resembling the late Queen Boadicea be
without military aspirations?

I notice with apprehension that she too is labelled as an
Art Lover. Perhaps there is a conspiracy. In furtherance
of some desperate enterprise, a band of ruthless extrem-
ists have disguised themselves as amateurs of the artistic

and historical. I shall look round carefully and see if there are any more of them.

There is another Art Lover's label a few rows back, on the other side of the gangway, attached to the shoulder-bag of a rather pretty girl. Her hair is of the shade which you yourself favoured in the spring — 'Harvest Moonlight', I think, was what the manufacturers called it. She has that ethereal pallor which one associates with idealism: a large proportion of hijackings are committed by idealists.

There is a young man sitting next to her. They seem, though they do not converse much, to be travelling together. If so, then presumably he too is an Art Lover. His face is of the shape known in geometry as trapezoid: rectilinear but not rectangular, being wider at the jaw than across the forehead. His figure is of the same geometric form, but the other way up, being broader at the shoulders than the hips. Still, he is of clean and wholesome appearance and could be quite pleasing to look at; but he has a distrustful, peevish expression, as if on constant guard against someone pulling a fast one.

He is asking the stewardess just how much longer we're going to have to wait here: his manner indicates that he expects an untruthful answer, his accent that he is an American. The proportion of hijackings committed by Americans is also very large.

The only other Art Lovers I can identify are two young men sitting some rows ahead of me. I would not have noticed them; but one has just stepped out into the gangway to allow the other to lift their hand luggage on to the luggage rack. (One is not supposed to put luggage in the luggage rack. They have been reproved by the stewardess.)

The one who did the lifting (up, and, following reproof, down again) is well suited to the task, having the physique of a more than usually muscular ox — rather like that Rugby full-back who was in love with you at Oxford, the reliable-looking one who was always threatening to commit suicide. His face, which was briefly turned in my direction, has a heavy, overcast sort of look, and eyebrows that almost meet. Not my sort of thing at all.

But the other—the one who stood aside to let the lifting be done—he looks like a more attractive proposition. His hair is an even paler shade than the blonde girl's. And he is thin, very thin. He is wearing a rather beautiful wide-sleeved shirt of that coarse muslin material that Ragwort sometimes likes—I think it is called cheesecloth. He has adopted a most graceful and decorative attitude, leaning back against the top of the seat with just sufficient pressure to emphasize the charming hollow of the left hip. But I haven't been able to see his face.

*

'Quite disgraceful,' said Ragwort.

'Taken her mind off getting hijacked, anyway,' said Cantrip.

'Aesthetic considerations,' said Selena, 'have prevailed over concern for her personal safety. It reflects very well on her.'

'Aesthetic, forsooth,' said Ragwort.

*

The captain has announced that we are about to take off. He has recommended us to read the safety booklet. I have done my best; but it is all in pictures, with nothing to explain them. There is a picture of a female passenger sitting upright, then an arrow, then a picture of her leaning forward with her head in her hands. Is the only thing required of me in an emergency to lean forward and put my head in my hands? If so, I shall be equal to it. I may, however, be missing some deeper significance. The artist intends, perhaps, to depict an act of contrition—the lady is preparing to meet her Maker. That is a less agreeable idea.

Some miles above Paris.
Later.

Things are much improved. My lungs have been filled with health-giving nicotine. The due proportion of gin has been introduced into my bloodstream. I have been given food in little plastic trays. I have decided that the Art Lovers are not going to hijack the aeroplane.

The blonde girl, it is true, has still that translucent pallor which I associate with idealism. It now occurs to me, however, that it is more probably due to travel sickness.

The man sitting next to her may indeed be an American; but, though many hijackings are committed by Americans, it by no means follows that many Americans commit hijackings. One must avoid the fallacy of undistributed middle.

The armour-plated matron has vented her martial spirit in complaining to the stewardess about the food. She is displeased with both the quality and the quantity. Her views on the former would make her, one might think, indifferent as to the latter — but not so: she declares it uneatable and demands a second helping.

My spider-legged neighbour, on the other hand, is pleased with everything. This, he says, is the life. 'Got to hand it to the travel agent johnnies,' he says. 'Do a chap proud on a package like this. Good plane, good food, decent-sized noggin to drink, bang-up dish to sit next to. That's the life for Bob Linnaker, all right.'

He seemed to intend a compliment.

'The travel agents,' I said, putting on what I hoped was a Ragwort-like expression, 'had no title to include me in the package. If they claimed to do so, your remedy is under the Trade Descriptions Act.'

At this he laughed immoderately and said that I was a sharp one. I fear I am not perfect in my imitation of Ragwort. I must study carefully, when I return to London, how he achieves that austere narrowing of the eyelids and daunting compression of the lips.

*

'I am afraid,' said Ragwort, 'that Julia, however much she may practise, will never achieve the appearance of truly formidable propriety. Her shape is against it.'

'I think that Julia has rather a nice shape,' said Cantrip. A certain tenderness softened his witch-black eyes: he was no doubt thinking of times before the spider episode.

'Precisely,' said Ragwort, his features composing themselves in that expression of cold decorum which would have been so useful to Julia. 'It is the sort of shape, to put the matter with all delicacy, which gives rise to a misleading inference of sensuality.'

'Not all that misleading,' said Cantrip, continuing nostalgic.

'Most misleading,' said Selena, 'to those most apt to draw it.'

*

As for the two young men, I can tell you nothing more — our relative positions prevent me from observing them. I wish I could see the face of the thin one. The face is for me of the essence of attraction. No matter how graceful the figure, if the face lacks aesthetic charm, I can feel no spark of passion. It is, I know, absurd — you will make fun of me for being a sentimental woman: well, that is how I am, Selena, there is no help for it.

*

'Would one say,' said Ragwort, 'that Julia was sentimental, exactly?'

'Incurably,' said Selena.

*

My neighbour still seems to believe that proximity is the sole condition of friendship. He addresses me as his dear. In reply, I have addressed him coldly as Mr Linnaker; but he is undiscouraged. Actually, he says, it's not Mr, but Major, though he doesn't bother with it now he's in Civvy Street. Anyway, to his friends he's just Bob. This puts me in a dilemma: to call him Bob will seem an admission of friendship, to call him anything else will seem uncivil.

He has also taken to patting my knee. This is making me rather peevish. I try to be tolerant of other people's innocent pleasures; but it is, after all, my knee. Still, it is hardly feasible, when sitting next to somebody on an aeroplane, to move unobtrusively away.

I could try reading the Finance Act. That would surely give an impression of quite implacable respectability. I must, at some stage, give some attention to the Finance Act: I promised William, if he would allow me to go to Venice, that my Opinion on Schedule 7 would be ready within forty-eight hours of returning. Yet somehow, despite the interest of its subject-matter and the elegance of its style, the Finance Act does not at the moment appeal to me.

The only refuge seems to be the lavatory. I don't suppose I can stay there for the rest of the journey—other passengers would become vexed; but it would be a temporary respite from the Major. And I should be able to get a look, on the way, at the face of the thin young man.

*

'The next paragraph,' said Selena, 'is rather difficult to read. The writing, even by Julia's standards, is unusually irregular. She also seems to have spilt gin over it. Do get some more coffee, Cantrip.'

*

Ah, Selena, Selena. 'The face of the thin young man' I have written, as if of some commonplace and worldly thing. How casually my pen first wrote that phrase, not knowing of what it wrote: with what trembling ardour do I inscribe it now. 'The face of the thin young man'—ah, Selena, such a face. A face for which Narcissus might be forsworn and the Moon forget Endymion. The translucent skin, the winging eyebrows, the angelic mouth, the celestial profile — lament no more, Selena, the drabness of our age and the poverty of our arts — over the time that has brought forth such a profile not Athens, not Rome, not the Renaissance in all its glory shall triumph: Praxiteles and Michelangelo kneel in admiration.

I grow too faint with passion to continue. It is a dreadful thing, at such a moment, to lack the benefit of your advice; but I shall post this immediately on arrival, so that you may know as soon as possible of the agitation which now affects my spirits. I remain, in the meantime,

Yours, as always

Julia

PS. The above, I need hardly say, is entirely without prejudice to my devotion to the virtuous and beautiful Ragwort, to whom please convey my respectful regards.

*

'I think Julia's quite struck with this blond chap,' said Cantrip — he is noted for his insight into the feminine heart. 'She hasn't gone on like this about anyone since that Greek barman they took on to help out in Guido's in June.'

'If then,' said Selena. 'I don't think she's mentioned Praxiteles since the out-of-work actor in February.'

'The whole letter,' said Ragwort, 'is perfectly disgraceful. I am very relieved that we have reached the end of it.'

I would not impute to any of my readers a less refined sensibility than belongs to Ragwort, or for any frivolous reason risk offending it. I have none the less thought it right to set out Julia's letter *in extenso*, containing, as it does, descriptions of various individuals who will be mentioned later in my narrative, including her supposed victim.

CHAPTER 3

There was a coolness. Selena said that she did not in the least blame Timothy but added that one might have known how Henry would go on about it. Ragwort was satisfied if the Bar Council saw no objection — and confessed to a little surprise on hearing they had not been asked. Cantrip used the expressions 'blackleg' and 'teacher's pet.'

All this because Timothy was going to Venice — unlike Julia, at someone else's expense. His absence from coffee on my first morning in London had been due, as the attentive reader may recall, to an application for his advice by the senior partner in a leading firm of solicitors. The senior partner — Mr Tiddley or Mr Whatsit, I am not sure which — was one of the trustees of a discretionary trust. 'Quite a nice little trust,' the senior partner had said modestly; worth, on the most recent valuation, just under a million pounds. The principal beneficiary, advised to take certain steps to mitigate his prospective liability to capital transfer tax, had been found recalcitrant. Timothy's assistance was required to persuade him of the seriousness and urgency of the matter.

To do so, moreover, in person. Attempts to explain in writing — and a number of long letters had already been sent on the subject — had been met with an obdurate refusal to perceive the need for action. It happened that the beneficiary, though normally resident in Cyprus, would shortly be going to Venice to settle the affairs of his recently deceased great-aunt, who had made her home in that city: an admirable occasion, thought the senior partner, while his mind was directed to such matters, for him to consider also his position under the English trust, established by his late grandfather. It would therefore be most kind if Timothy—for a fee, it went without saying, which would reflect not only the intrinsic value of his advice, but also the inconvenience to him—'Oh, quite,' said Ragwort—of being absent for several days from London—if Timothy would go to Venice. Timothy, kindness itself, had consented.

'And your accommodation,' said Ragwort, 'will also be in a style commensurate with the value of your advice. Danieli's, I suppose. Or perhaps the Gritti Palace?'

It appeared that the estate of the deceased great-aunt included a little palazzo just off the Grand Canal. The beneficiary had been good enough to indicate that Timothy would be welcome to stay there.

'Most agreeable,' said Selena, wrinkling her nose.

'Delightful,' said Ragwort, raising an eyebrow.

'Makes one sick,' said Cantrip.

The thing that made Selena wrinkle her nose, Ragwort raise an eyebrow and Cantrip sick was not mere envy of Timothy's good fortune. What chiefly irked them was its effect on Henry, who for several days had not ceased to comment on it as an instance of the wonderful rewards heaped on the just—being those who do not spend their mornings drinking coffee—by comparison with the unjust—being those who do. In the eternal struggle of Counsel against Clerks to gain a moment in which the former may call their souls their own, some yards of ground had been lost. Coffees were curtailed, lunches abbreviated, dinner engagements cancelled.

But they are tolerant, good-natured young people in 62 New Square, their minds always open to equitable compromise. Upon Timothy's undertaking that on the eve of his departure, that is to say on Friday, he would buy dinner for all those adversely affected, it was agreed that no more should be said of the matter. I pointed out that I myself had some claim to be among his guests; to which he answered, very nicely, that he had not imagined I could think myself excluded.

We were to meet in the Corkscrew, a wine bar on the north side of High Holborn, popular on the grounds of proximity with the members of Lincoln's Inn. Our entertainment was to include two further letters from Julia, which even Selena, in the conditions obtaining in Chambers, had not yet had time to read.

At seven o'clock, I was the first to arrive. I sat down at one of the little round oak tables and lit the candle provided for its illumination. The bar of the Corkscrew is designed for those who prefer a certain murkiness: long and narrow in construction, it admits, even at noon, the minimum of daylight; most of what does get in is absorbed in the dark ceiling and wood-panelled walls; there is left, after this, just so much as may comfortably be reflected in the surface of a polished table or the glint of a wine glass. To light a candle there is almost in itself enough to inspire in those gathered round it a sense of cheerful conspiracy.

I did not have long to wait for company. Timothy, arriving with Ragwort and Selena, stopped at the bar to acquire a bottle of Nierstein and a bowl of biscuits. The other two joined me at once in the circle of candlelight.

'Why biscuits?' I asked. 'Timothy is just going to buy us an excellent dinner.'

'We'll be eating late,' said Ragwort. 'It's Cantrip's night for reading the *Scuttle*.'

It is thought prudent by the proprietors of the *Daily Scuttle* that their publication, before it goes to press, should be read by a lawyer. They are subject to the endearing superstition that they will protect themselves, by this ritual, against all claims and proceedings for libel, blasphemy, obscenity, sedition, contempt of court, scandalum magnatum or any other crime or civil wrong known to English law. In the evenings this work is contracted out on a freelance basis to various indigent members of the Junior Bar. Though the law of libel and so forth is not peculiarly within the province of the Chancery Bar, the post of Friday reader, for reasons now lost in antiquity, is always held by one of the members of 62 New Square. It is currently occupied by Cantrip. If hunger compelled us to begin dinner without him, good fellowship would not allow us to end it in like manner. We would therefore be dining late. In the meantime, the Corkscrew would enjoy our custom.

It is poignant to reflect that as we sat drinking Nierstein in the convivial quarter-light of the Corkscrew poor Julia must already have been trying to persuade the Venetian police that the presence of her Finance Act at the bedside of the corpse—but I must not anticipate the orderly development of my narrative. We drank untroubled by knowledge of Julia's difficulties: it was the last occasion for some time that we were able to do so.

As to the unhappy consequences of Timothy's going to Venice, no more, of course, was to be said. Still—

'Are you really sure it is proper,' said Ragwort, 'to see the lay client without a solicitor present? To explain, you know, in words of one syllable what you are telling him?'

'And in words of four syllables what he is telling you,' said Selena.

'Quite sure,' said Timothy. 'One's instructing solicitor is, of course, entitled to be present; but he may quite properly waive his rights in the matter.'

'Well, if you say so,' said Ragwort, 'then naturally we accept it. Since you are buying us dinner. But what seems so strikingly unconventional is that you should go to the client. It is surely a long-established rule of etiquette that the client comes to Counsel. It has always been my understanding that only in the most exceptional cases, such as grave disability—'

'My client,' said Timothy, 'does, in a sense, suffer from a disability. He can't face coming to England. He spent his thirteenth year at an English public school and this inspired in him such an aversion to this country that he has since refused to set foot in it.'

'How eccentric,' said Selena. The honey of her voice was seasoned, as it were, with lemon: herself much attached to her native land, she is inclined to take personally any disparagement of it. 'If he doesn't mind living in Cyprus, dodging the crossfire between the Turks and the Greeks, it is quite absurd of him to be afraid of coming to England. And if he is prepared to go to Italy, which, as we all know, is at present in the grip of a vast crime wave—'

'Is it?' said Ragwort.

'My dear Ragwort, of course it is,' said Selena. 'Crime in Italy is a national industry. If an Italian isn't murdering someone in Calabria, it's only because he's too busy kidnapping someone else in Lombardy. Or embezzling public funds in Friuli. Or stealing little-known pictures from churches in Verona. Or burgling the Courthouse at Monza. That, at any rate, if *The Times* is to be relied on, is how they have spent the past week, and we have no reason to think it untypical.'

'My client,' said Timothy, 'is not troubled, as I understand it, by the possibility of being murdered, kidnapped or embezzled. His objection to England is founded on the belief that the temperature never rises above forty degrees Fahrenheit, that the only food available is tepid rice pudding and that the population consists entirely of bullying prefects and ragging fourth-formers.'

'I wonder if it's wise,' said Selena, 'to send you to talk to him, Timothy. You do look very English, you know. You'll probably remind him of his former geometry master and he'll run away and hide.'

I seem to have omitted to give my readers any description of my former pupil. It is true, however, that he does have that long-boned, angular, straw-coloured look which is widely regarded as characteristic of the English-man.

'Precisely what is it,' I asked, 'that you have to persuade him to do?'

'I have to persuade him,' said Timothy, 'to become domiciled in England before the 19th of December of this year.' He leant back comfortably in his chair, not looking like a man discouraged by the difficulty of the task before him. 'On that date, which is his twenty-fifth birthday, the discretionary trust will come to an end. My client, as the only surviving descendant of his late grandfather, will scoop the jackpot. The capital transfer tax payable on that event, if my client is then domiciled outside the United Kingdom, will be something on the order of £450,000. If, on the other hand, he were then to be domiciled in England, tax would, of course, be charged at a concessionary rate under the transitional provisions of paragraph 14 to Schedule 5 of the Finance Act 1975 and he would have to pay only fifteen per cent of that sum.'

'That certainly seems,' I said, ignoring all this talk of Schedules and paragraphs, 'to be a substantial induce-ment. But will it be enough to overcome his repugnance to this country?'

'Oh, my dear Hilary,' said Timothy, smiling at me, 'he doesn't have to come to England. Merely to become domiciled here.'

I perceived with chagrin that I had been led into a trap. Timothy's smile, to a casual observer, might have seemed unobjectionable, even attractive. I, knowing him better, identified it at once as that smile of enigmatic complacency which signifies that he knows something I don't about the law and is going to explain it to me. It would be irritating, heaven knows, in anyone—in a former pupil it is quite intolerable. Though a member of the Faculty of Laws, I am an historian rather than a lawyer: my interest in the principles of English law wanes with the Middle Ages. I do not doubt—for his clients' sake I devoutly hope—that Timothy knows more than I do of modern English law: it is nothing for him to look complacent or enigmatic about.

Still, I remembered that he was buying me dinner. I allowed him, therefore, as he clearly wished to do, to give a little lecture on the law of domicile. The nub of which was, as I recall, that if you are resident in one country but intend to spend your last years in another, you will not necessarily be domiciled in either, but rather in the place where your father was domiciled at the time of your birth. If he, at that time, happened to be in a similar equivocal condition, then your domicile will be that of your paternal grandfather at the time your father was born. And so *ad infinitum*, if Timothy has explained the thing correctly, through any number of ancestors of migrant disposition, till domicile is finally established in the Garden of Eden.

In the present case, however, such extremes were not called for. His client's grandfather, the founder of the nice little trust, had lived all his days in England and shown no desire to wander. The client's father, though serving, when the boy was born, in the British Army in Cyprus, and married to a Greek girl, had written home numerous letters, still extant and available for inspection by the Capital Taxes Office, expressing his ultimate intention to return to England. They had both behaved, from Timothy's point of view, admirably: it was only the client himself who was being difficult.

'But surely,' said Ragwort, 'your task is very simple, Timothy. It is clear that your client has an English domicile of origin. Whenever he is not domiciled anywhere else he will be domiciled in England. If he is resident in Cyprus, all he has to do is form an intention to retire, in his declining years, to some country other than

Cyprus. Paraguay or New South Wales or somewhere. He can manage that, surely.'

'And you will draft a nice letter for him', said Selena, 'explaining his intention to the Capital Taxes Office. One or two little artistic touches, to add verisimilitude, such as the purchase of a grave in the country chosen for retirement—'

'I fear,' said Timothy, 'that my client has behaved foolishly. At the time of the Turkish invasion of the island, when other British residents were making haste to leave, he made several public statements, reported in the Press, declaring with some vehemence that he himself would do nothing of the kind. He would continue, he said, to run the farm which he had inherited from his mother and would devote his life to restoring the island to peace and unity.'

' "Devote his life",' said Selena. 'Dear me, what a very unfortunate phrase.'

'Yes, isn't it? So the Revenue are likely to be a little sceptical about his forming a sudden intention to end his days in Paraguay or New South Wales. No, I am afraid he'll have to sell his house in Cyprus and become resident somewhere else. Somewhere, of course, where he has no intention of remaining permanently.'

It must have been, I think, at about this point that the telephone rang: there was nothing odd about that. The girl behind the bar answered it and called for Timothy: there was nothing odd about that, either—anyone wanting to communicate, at such an hour of a Friday evening, with one of the junior members of 62 New Square would do sensibly to try the Corkscrew. The telephone was too far for us to eavesdrop without effort: we had no reason to think that the effort ought to be made.

I tried, instead, to learn from Selena and Ragwort whether I too, by living in a country I did not mean to stay in and establishing a domicile in one I never meant to go to, could save myself a vast sum in capital transfer tax.

'No,' said Selena.

'No,' said Ragwort.

'Why not?' I asked, rather indignantly.

They pointed out that to save tax of £400,000 I would first have to be the heir to a fund worth a million. I conceded with regret that I was not. Neither was Selena. Neither was Ragwort. It seemed — for we had no doubt that in intellect, charm and beauty we were all more deserving than Timothy's client — an extraordinary oversight on the part of Providence.

Timothy, concluding his telephone conversation, looked a little less cheerful than when it had begun; but he paused at the bar to buy another bottle of Nierstein.

Returning to the table, he refilled Selena's glass. This, as it turned out, was a pity. Then he filled his own. Ragwort and I were left to fend for ourselves: a trifling discourtesy, but not like Timothy. I began to think that something must be wrong.

'That was Cantrip,' said Timothy, sitting down and addressing himself to Selena. 'I'm afraid it sounds as if Julia's in a spot of trouble.'

'She can't be,' said Selena. 'She's still in Venice. I mean, I dare say she could be, but Cantrip couldn't know about it.'

'Cantrip, you will remember, is working in the News Room of the *Scuttle*. The News Room is equipped with a number of teleprinter machines, which produce a continuous print-out of the reports coming in from the various international news agencies — Reuters and so on. The process, I gather, is nearly instantaneous: once a report is telephoned through to the agency, from anywhere in the world, it's only a few minutes before it's on the teleprinter.'

'Yes,' said Ragwort, 'we know that. But what could Julia do that would interest an international news agency?'

'They seem to think,' said Timothy, looking apologetic and still addressing Selena, 'that she's stabbed someone. Fatally.'

It was, as I say, a pity that he had so recently refilled Selena's glass, for she now released her hold on it and it dropped, almost full, on to the hard composite floor.

'I'm sorry,' said Selena. 'How very clumsy of me. I don't think, Timothy, that I have correctly understood you. What exactly do you say it said in the agency report?'

'So far as I can discover,' said Timothy, 'that an English tourist has been found stabbed to death in a hotel bedroom in Venice. And that a member of the same group, Miss Julia Larwood of London, barrister, has been detained by the police for questioning.'

'Nonsense,' said Selena.

'I know,' said Timothy, still looking apologetic. 'But that seems to be what it said in the report.'

'They didn't say,' asked Ragwort, 'who's supposed to have been stabbed?'

'No. I suppose they're waiting to tell the next of kin, if there are any. But it sounds as if it must have been one of the Art Lovers.'

'Timothy,' said Selena, 'are you sure it isn't one of Cantrip's frightful jokes?'

'Quite sure, I'm afraid. Cantrip's jokes, though admittedly frightful, are not as frightful as that. Besides, if it had been a joke, he would have been trying to sound serious. He wasn't: he was trying quite hard to sound casual. He was still in the News Room, you see. I was rather confused at first. He began by asking me if I knew a bird called Julia Larwood and I said of course I knew Julia, what on earth was he talking about. To which he replied that he didn't think I did, but he thought it was worth asking because his News Editor had suddenly got interested in her. So I gathered then that something odd was happening.'

'Are we,' asked Ragwort, 'going to do anything, in particular?'

'We're meeting in Guido's, as arranged. Cantrip will be keeping an eye on the teleprinter, of course, and if any more news comes through before ten o'clock he'll tell us about it.'

It is difficult, on such an occasion as I have described, to know on precisely what note to resume the conversation. We were silent for several moments.

'Dear me,' said Selena eventually. 'What a very good thing, after all, Timothy, that you are going to Venice tomorrow.'

CHAPTER 4

Guido's is not the nearest restaurant to the Corkscrew, nor the most economical in that vicinity. The superiority of its menu, however, is sufficient compensation for the short walk down Holborn Kingsway and round the back of the Aldwych Theatre; and Timothy was paying the bill.

It was not yet nine o'clock: we could not expect Cantrip for at least an hour. I proposed that in the meantime, and while eating our asparagus, we should proceed, as previously intended, with the reading of Julia's letters. Though they might throw no direct light on the stabbing incident, it would, I suggested, be useful for Timothy, before plunging *in medias res* on Julia's behalf, to be as well-informed as possible of the antecedent events.

The first began ominously.

Hotel Cytherea,
Venice.
Late on Thursday night.

Dearest Selena,

I have news of a most shocking nature to impart to you.

You will scarcely believe it. If anyone else had told me, I should not have believed it myself. 'No, no,' I should have cried, 'it is not possible. The monstrous cannot disguise itself in an angelic mask. Reason and nature prohibit it. The deformity of the mind would necessarily distort the perfection of the profile. The depravity of the soul would infect with some hideous blemish the smoothness of the complexion. No, it cannot be.'

*

'I suppose she's referring,' said Timothy, 'to the young man she admired so much on the aeroplane. But this is evidently written only a few hours later — what can have happened in the meantime that Julia finds so shocking? She is, after all, a tolerant woman.'

'To a fault,' said Selena.

*

But it is no use writing to you in this haphazard incoherent fashion, beginning at the end and ending God knows where. I will proceed clearly and chronologically, beginning at the beginning.

The beginning was not altogether auspicious, owing to my separation from my passport. We were fortunately met at the airport by our courier, a haggard, aquiline, fragile-nosed Venetian lady, who told us that her name was Graziella. It took Graziella a mere ten minutes to understand my difficulty, explain it to the Customs officer and secure my lawful entry to Italian soil. In the meantime, however, the other Art Lovers were obliged to wait for us in the motorboat which was to transport us across the lagoon to Venice. By the time we joined them, there were signs of restiveness.

The armour-plated matron, in particular, who was sitting next to the beautiful young man, made some rather wounding remarks about total imbeciles with no consideration for other people. She may not, perhaps, have intended me to hear them; but she much underestimates, in that case, the carrying power of her voice.

So fearful was I of incurring yet further disapproval, so intent on the composition of some soothing apology, that while getting into the boat I somehow missed my footing. My entry into the vessel was accordingly at an angle rather obtuse than perpendicular to the quayside and at a speed rather rapid than graceful. In short, I fell in head first.

This caused the armour-plated matron to make certain further comments reflecting on my sobriety. Still more regrettably, it enabled the Major, on the pretext of breaking my fall, to gather me in a tenacious embrace, uttering as he did so loud cries of 'Whoops-a-daisy.'

By a further stroke of misfortune, my handbag, in consequence of my over-rapid descent, had become unfastened and its contents had dispersed themselves about the floor of the boat. Anxious to be as little obliged as possible to the Major for the assistance which he offered in their recovery, I set about collecting them with, as I now realize, imprudent haste and insufficient thought for the effect on my balance of an attitude of semi-genuflection. Impatient, no doubt, of further delay, the boatman now cast off. The sudden movement threw me against the side of the vessel, and brought the wooden bench, fitted thereto for the repose and comfort of passengers, into collision with my nose. My nose began to bleed.

I was thus compelled, after all, to be obliged to the Major, *videlicet* for the loan of his handkerchief. He took the occasion to pat me here and there, and seemed inclined to offer me his shoulder to bleed on. I explained to him that it was essential, when suffering from a nosebleed, to lean backwards rather than forwards, and that if he did not object to my first soaking his handkerchief in the lagoon the bleeding would stop very shortly. 'Attagirl,' said the Major, patting me again and adding that he liked a woman with pluck.

I considered the advantages of bursting into tears: not only would it have relieved my feelings but also, apparently, discouraged the Major's admiration. Looking about me, however, I felt that I would not have a sympathetic audience. It seemed possible, moreover, that the Major would change his mind and discover a preference for the weeping and womanly. I judged it better to keep a firm hold on the remnants of my sangfroid. Settling myself as far as possible from my fellow passengers, I leant back with my eyes closed and the Major's sea-soaked handkerchief pressed firmly against my nose.

I could not feel I had made a favourable impression.

*

'Julia did very well,' said Selena, 'not to fall into the lagoon. How beastly of that woman to suggest she'd had too much to drink.'

'Most uncharitable,' said Ragwort. 'Julia, as we all know, needs no assistance from alcohol to make her trip over things.'

*

Graziella, as we crossed the lagoon, gave a most instructive account of the history of Venice from its foundation in the fifth century to the defeat of the Frankish Invasion in the ninth. I was not, however, in any condition to attend to it as I should have done, or to observe the many features of artistic and historical interest which she pointed out to us. When at length I thought it prudent to remove my nose from the handkerchief, the crossing was almost completed. I looked up and saw Venice, floating on the water.

Venice, as one sees from the map in Ragwort's Guide, consists essentially of three large islands, though subdivided by canals into a great many smaller ones. Two of the three lie curled together, divided only by the Grand Canal, in an embrace of such Gallic sophistication as to prevent my pursuing further the anatomical analogy. To their left, excluded from their intimacy, the long thin island of Giudecca stretches out alone, a parable in geography of the hazards of a *partie à trois*. For consolation, like a divine hot-water bottle, it has at its foot the little island of San Giorgio Maggiore.

The church of San Giorgio, therefore, and a little afterwards that of the Salute, rising on the left at the entrance to the Grand Canal, are the first of the great religious buildings of Venice to offer themselves to the admiration of the tourist. That they are to the honour of exclusively Christian deities seems by no means certain: there is a too Eastern voluptuousness in their swelling domes, a too Athenian elegance in their Palladian façades. They seem designed for travellers who would wish, on setting forth, to murmur a prayer to Allah as well as to Saint George; or who, giving thanks for a safe home-coming on the wide steps of the Salute, would include a word or two to the goddess Aphrodite.

With the palaces along the Grand Canal there is no such ambiguity. They, one does not doubt for a moment, were built entirely to the greater glory of their owners, in a single-minded spirit of keeping up with the Foscari. If one façade has two tiers of columns and carved stonework, the one next to it has three; the one opposite has columns even more delicate; the stonework of the next is pierced and drawn in a still more intricate embroidery. So that one almost expects, seeing them reflected in the water, to find there too some further embellishment.

I experienced, as we travelled through this great corridor of mirrors, the emotion I had last felt during the transformation scene of the pantomime, when taken to it, at the age of seven, by my maternal grandmother. She took me again when I was eight, for my maternal grandmother was always very kind to me; but by then I was less easily impressed. The pleasure was one, therefore, that I had not looked to feel again.

Turning off to the right somewhere after the Accademia Bridge, we disembarked at the landing stage of the Cytherea.

'Signore, signori,' said Graziella, 'dinner will be at eight o'clock. If you will come to see me before then in the reception area, I will explain to you about our excursions. You have plenty of time to wash and repose yourselves; but dress is quite informal.' She glanced at me, however, in a way which suggested that the management of the Cytherea, broad-minded though it might be, would prefer to draw the line at mud-stained trousers and a blood-spattered shirt.

We retired, as instructed, to wash and repose ourselves. I directed my mind, while so engaged, to the subject of the beautiful young man, lamenting once more the absence of your own always admirable counsel. Deprived of it in fact, I sought it in hypothesis: 'If Selena were here,' I asked myself, 'what would she advise?'

I answered without hesitation that you would recommend a pragmatic approach: not to base my plans on some theoretical first principle, but to examine the situation as it was and see what advantage could be taken of it.

This naturally led me to think of canals. We were in a city full of canals. How could this circumstance be turned to my advantage? One possibility would be to fall into one and be rescued by the beautiful young man. That, I thought, would surely lead to something. There was, however, a flaw in this scheme: I might fall into a canal, but the young man might not rescue me.

Another possibility would be for the young man to fall into one and be rescued by me. That seemed even more certain to lead to something. But I saw that this scheme also was by no means foolproof. The only way of ensuring that he fell into a canal would be to push him into it:

unless this could be done with extraordinary discretion, the enterprise might well prove self-defeating. Nor was I entirely confident that once I had got him into the canal I would be able to get him out of it again.

*

'Timothy,' said Selena, 'Cantrip did say "stabbed", didn't he?'

'Oh yes,' said Timothy, ' "stabbed" was certainly the word.'

*

To be perfectly candid, Selena, I was not wholeheartedly enthusiastic about any plan involving my immersion in a canal. Though beautiful, they are not, at close quarters, appetizing: it seemed to me that what they would certainly lead to would be a nasty cold, complicated, possibly, by some unpleasant virus.

I concluded that you would advise me to have nothing to do with canals, but to concentrate on the opportunities offered by the hotel itself. The Art Lovers are accommodated in an annexe, surrounded by canals on three sides and joined to the main hotel by a little bridge. On the fourth side it adjoins another building, forming part, as it were, of the same peninsula; but this has nothing to do with the Cytherea and there is no way through to it. The bridge is accordingly the only means of access. The rooms on the first floor are occupied by the Art Lovers, those on the second, apparently, by members of the hotel staff. The ground floor is used merely as a sort of entrance hall, where the chambermaids sort the linen and so forth.

I contemplated with some satisfaction the possibilities offered by this arrangement. I had only to get rid of the other Art Lovers and the hotel staff and find some means of barricading the bridge—and I should have the lovely creature entirely at my mercy, without means of escape. Unless, of course, he were to jump out of the window into the canal, in which case I would be obliged, albeit reluctantly, to revert to the plan previously mentioned. Though certain points of detail remained to be worked out, it was in a mood of some optimism that I went down to dinner.

I remembered that I had at least the benefit of your advice on general strategy. It is your view, as I understand it, that when dealing with young men one should make no admission, in the early stages, of the true nature of one's objectives but should instead profess a deep admiration for their fine souls and splendid intellects. One is not to be discouraged, if I have understood you correctly, by the fact that they may have neither. I reminded myself, therefore, that if I could get the lovely creature into conversation, I must make no comment on the excellence of his profile and complexion but should apply myself to showing a sympathetic interest in his hopes, dreams and aspirations. Little did I know, Selena, how fearful were those dreams, how sinister those hopes, how altogether unspeakable those aspirations.

*

'Dear me,' said Timothy. 'What can he have done?'

'It would be very helpful,' said Ragwort, 'if this young man turned out to have a serious criminal record. It would make him a natural suspect for—any unpleasantness which may have occurred.'

'Most helpful, certainly,' said Selena. 'Though whether Julia, in such a case, would have expressed herself in quite those terms—still, no doubt we shall see.'

*

The dining-room of the Cytherea occupies a corner at the junction between two canals, so that one may eat by a window looking out on one and adjourn for offee to a terrace at the side of the other. The terrace, in fact, faces the annexe in which we are accommodated

The management, it seemed to me, had done rather

badly about the seating arrangements. They had put the beautiful young man and his travelling companion at a table with the armour-plated matron. They had put the pretty blonde girl at a table with the trapezoid young man. They had put me at a table with the Major.

'Care to join me in a bottle of plonk, m'dear?' asked the Major. The notion of joining the Major in anything was repugnant to me; but I felt I could not civilly refuse. He studied his Wine List with the furtive squint which has characterized the English abroad since the decline of the pound sterling: it comes of comparing prices while pretending to study the vintage. He suggested that the Colle Albani sounded like a decent little wine. Confirming, by a similar surreptitious glance, that it was two hundred lire less than anything else available, I concurred in his choice.

'Comfy little billet, this,' said the Major. I did not dispute it — the standards of the Cytherea seemed to me to be luxurious. 'Been in worse quarters than this in my time, I can tell you, m'dear,' he continued, undiscouraged by my agreement. 'I remember the troopship I went on to Tripoli in '48—'

From this starting point, he launched adroitly into an epic of military reminiscence, beginning shortly after the Second World War and ending—no, I fear it has no ending, or, if it does, that I have not yet heard it. It included a number of anecdotes designed to illustrate the proposition that the Major had 'always been a bit of a japester.' There was one, as I recall, about hijacking a tramcar in Alexandria in '49 and another about the introduction of a goat into the nurses' quarters in Limassol in '52.

I began to be very worried about Desdemona. We are given to understand that Othello's courtship of her consisted almost entirely of stories beginning 'When I was stationed among the Anthropophagi—' or 'I must tell you about a funny thing that happened during the siege of Rhodes.' The dramatist Shakespeare would have us believe that she not only put up with this but actually enjoyed it: can that great connoisseur of the human heart really have thought this possible?

'And what do you do now, Bob?' I asked, several eternities later, hoping for a change of subject.

He told me that on leaving the Army he had found himself with a few bits and pieces which he had picked up as souvenirs here and there on his travels. Thinking that these objects might be of interest to the public, he had been inspired to invest his gratuity in the purchase of a junk shop in Fulham. (He used the expression 'junk shop' as if referring modestly to a rather superior antique-dealing establishment: I suspect that it is, in fact, a junk shop.) Some of his friends had also found themselves with bits and pieces similarly picked up here and there in the course of their military careers: these had been added to his stock in trade. The bits and pieces proving more valuable than expected, the business had prospered. I would think it, he said, a funny job for an old soldier, but it suited him. He now reverted to reminiscence, telling me of various pranks and japes by which the bits and pieces had been acquired.

'I suppose we ought to ask old Eleanor Frostfield to join us for coffee,' said the Major, as the meal drew at last to its close. 'Bit of a bore running into the old girl, but I'd better do the dutiful.'

Eleanor Frostfield proved to be the armour-plated matron. I had noticed no sign of any acquaintance between her and the Major; but they know each other, it seems, in the way of business, Eleanor being the owner, by inheritance from a deceased husband, of a firm of art and antique dealers.

I fell in very cordially with his suggestion, for it seemed to me that any invitation to Eleanor must in all courtesy be extended to the two young men at the same table. In the end, since it hardly seemed kind to exclude the remaining pair of Art Lovers, all seven of us adjourned to the terrace together. In the course of arranging this, it was discovered that the beautiful young man was Ned; that his broad-shouldered friend was Kenneth; that Eleanor was Mrs Frostfield; that the pretty blonde girl was Marylou Bredon; that the young man with her was her husband Stanford; that the Major was Bob to his friends; and that I was Julia Larwood. I already knew, of course, that I was Julia Larwood, and the others, I dare say, also knew who they were; but there is presumably some sense in which the sum of human knowledge was increased.

The Major, once our coffee had arrived, tried to go on telling me about a merry prank by which he had become the owner of a twelfth-century Greek icon, formerly the property of a monastery near Paphos. Fortunately, he was interrupted by Kenneth, who told him, in a Scots accent heavy with disapproval, that he shouldn't have done it; and went on to deplore the damage done to the artistic inheritance of Cyprus by a succession of occupying armies. This did not silence the Major for long; but it diverted his attention. Kenneth became the audience for a series of further anecdotes, illustrating the hardships of military life not known to young men of Kenneth's generation.

Eleanor and Marylou were sitting next to each other. I settled myself on a footstool at their feet, and thought that I should try to eradicate the unfortunate impression I had earlier made on Eleanor. I remembered that I had seen the name of her firm quite recently, on a capital transfer tax valuation obtained by clients of mine. This gave me some straw for the bricks of flattery.

'I shall not venture,' I said, 'to open my mouth in Mrs Frostfield's presence on any subject connected with the arts. I expect you know, Marylou, that Mrs Frostfield is a director of one of our leading firms of experts in antiques and the fine arts.'

It worked like a charm. Insofar as a woman so closely resembling the late Queen Boadicea can be said to simper, Eleanor simpered. 'Really,' she said, 'Miss Larwood exaggerates. We're not Christies or Sotheby's, you know.' But she made being Christies or Sotheby's sound rather over-flamboyant.

She melted to such an extent as to ask my own profession. I answered that I was in practice at the Revenue Bar; but the name of her firm was naturally familiar to me, since clients of mine with important collections to be valued for tax purposes so frequently had recourse to the expertise of Frostfield's. There is no bond like that of mutual clients: we were thereafter as Ruth and Naomi. Well yes, Selena, I do exaggerate — but at least we were 'Julia' and 'Eleanor'.

I remarked on the coincidence of her being acquainted with the Major. It seems, however, that it is not really surprising. The travel agency which arranged our package has close connections in the world of art and antiques and long experience of making business travel arrangements for those concerned with it.

'Business travel?' I asked. 'You are not simply on holiday, then?'

'My dear Julia,' said Eleanor, with a certain coyness, 'for accounting purposes, of course, it has to be business travel. You will be the first to appreciate that with our penal system of taxation —'

'Do you mean,' asked the enchanting Ned, taking part in the conversation for the first time, 'that you put your holidays down as a business expense for tax purposes?'

'My dear boy, of course,' said Eleanor benignly. 'Everyone does.' It was not for me to strike a discordant note by suggesting that such a practice fell on the wrong side of the delicate line between legitimate avoidance and illegal evasion.

It is ironic to reflect that I congratulated myself, as I sat there on the footstool, on the pleasantness of my situation. The soft night air was warm against my cheek; the stars were shining in a velvet sky; the canal was lapping gently against its banks; the Major was telling someone else about the troopship. What more could a woman ask for, to be perfectly contented?

Except, of course, the favours of the lovely Ned. The time had come, I felt, to show an interest in his hopes, dreams and aspirations.

'And you, Ned,' I asked, 'are you professionally involved in the fine arts?' I prepared to give sympathetic encouragement to a boyish ambition to discover a lost Giorgione or something like that.

'No,' said the lovely creature. 'No, actually, I'm a lawyer, like you.' Less romantic, but easier — one could spend many happy hours discussing recent decisions of the Court of Appeal. 'That is to say, I took my degree in law. I am not in private practice.'

'Ah,' I said, 'you have gone into industry.'

'No,' he said, looking at me demurely under his beautiful eyelashes. 'No, not precisely. I am employed by the Department of Inland Revenue.'

My pen as I write these dreadful words falls trembling from my petrified fingers. I am left with hardly the strength to sign myself

Yours, as always,
Julia.

CHAPTER 5

Few of my readers, I imagine, subscribe regularly to the *Scuttle*: it is not a journal designed for the cultivated taste. Some, however, may on rare occasions have been

moved to seek further details of the supermarket corruption scandal or the political vice link probe promised by
its towering headlines. They will then have discovered
that housewives in East Dagenham have been offered
more trading stamps with a purchase of McCavity's
strawberry preserve than with the equally wholesome and
delicious confection produced by the factories of
McGonegal: that, by the stringent ethical standards of
the *Scuttle*, is a corruption scandal. They will have read
that a back-bench Member of Parliament has had dinner
in the company of a girl employed two doors away from a
Soho nightclub: that is the political vice link. Such
readers will sympathize with my own feelings on hearing
that the monster of depravity pre-figured in Julia's letter
was, after all, nothing worse than a poor, harmless,
necessary Civil Servant. 'Well, really,' I said.

'My dear Hilary,' said Selena. 'You do not seem to
appreciate the intensity of Julia's feelings towards the
Department of Inland Revenue. She is under the impression that it is a vast conspiracy having as its sole objective
her physical, mental and financial ruin. Her feelings at
finding them suddenly in her midst are expressed with
remarkable moderation.'

'It's disappointing,' said Ragwort, 'that the young man
has not turned out to be a homicidal maniac. But it can't
be helped.'

'I wonder what's happened to Cantrip,' said Timothy.
'They usually let him go by this time.'

It was growing late. The steady filling of Guido's tables
was a sign that in theatres in the neighbourhood final cur-
tains had begun to fall. We asked for our second course.

Cantrip arrived simultaneously with the *escalope de
veau*. His hair and eyes looked blacker than ever, his complexion paler; his fingertips too were slightly blackened
from flicking through damp newsprint: he looked like an
invitation card for a rather frivolous wake. He took out

and placed on the table a strip of paper, evidently torn from the teleprinter.

VENICE 22.30 HOURS LOCAL TIME 9.9.77
VICTIM OF HOTEL STABBING NAMED BY POLICE AS
EDWARD WATSON 24 OF LONDON INLAND REVENUE
EMPLOYEE BRITISH WOMAN TOURIST STILL HELD FOR
QUESTIONING

'Chap who got done in was a chap from the Revenue,' said Cantrip.

'Oh dear,' said Ragwort, looking sombrely at Cantrip.

'That's what I thought,' said Cantrip, looking glumly at Ragwort.

'If Michael and Desmond are going to talk piffle —' said Selena. The use of their Christian names was a sign of her utmost displeasure.

'She was jolly miffed about that last assessment,' said Cantrip.

Selena began carefully cutting her *escalope* into very small pieces, looking like a Persian cat which had unexpectedly found itself in low company.

'Few people,' said Timothy, 'are delighted by their tax assessments.'

'Precisely,' said Selena. 'Properly regarded, the news is most encouraging. A man from the Revenue might be murdered by anyone.'

'Let us,' continued Timothy, 'be sensible. None of us, surely, can seriously believe that Julia has stabbed anyone. It's not simply a question of character, it's a matter of competence. Even if she wanted to, which she wouldn't, she wouldn't have the faintest idea how to do it.'

'That's true,' said Cantrip, looking more cheerful. 'I hadn't thought of that.'

'So I don't doubt that the whole thing is simply a

mistake and in the long run we can sort it out. It would be rather nice, though, if we could get it cleared up before there's been too much publicity. It's not the sort of thing that's good for one's practice.'

'That,' said Selena, 'is certainly a point. Once solicitors start thinking of Julia as liable to intermittent fits of homicidal mania, they may begin, however irrationally, to question her soundness on the Taxes Acts. Will there be anything in tomorrow's *Scuttle*?'

'Not a chance,' said Cantrip. 'I told them it was all incredibly libellous and too *sub judice* for words. Which it may be, for all I know. Anyway, they've dropped it like a hot potato.'

'Oh, well done, Cantrip,' said Selena.

'And I rang a chap I know at the news agency and asked him if he'd noticed they'd got a story pouring out over the teleprinters which would land them with a fantastic claim for damages. And he hadn't, so he was jolly grateful to me for telling him. That's why they're not mentioning Julia's name any more.'

Mollified by these achievements, Selena summarized for Cantrip's benefit the contents of the previous letter before proceeding to the next.

Terrace of the Cytherea.
Friday evening.

Dearest Selena,

I have found a convenient place in which to enjoy undisturbed the pleasures of writing to you and of drinking Campari before dinner. One corner of the terrace is divided from the rest by a little trellis, over which there grows some kind of vine or similar shrub. The vine or similar shrub is not, by the highest standards of horticulture, doing terribly well; but it is enough to screen one from observation by anyone coming on to the terrace whom one might wish to avoid. As it might be, the Major.

There is also a clear view of the bridge to the annexe, so that one is aware of the approach from that direction of anyone whom one might wish, by apparent accident, to meet. As it might be, the lovely Ned.

The discovery of Ned's appalling profession has made me, as you may imagine, implacable in my resolve. Have the Revenue, in their demands on my time, my energy and my meagre earnings, been deterred by any sentiments of pity or remorse? No. Shall I, if Ned's virtue were the dearest jewel they own, show more forbearance in pursuit of it? No, I shall not. 'Canals if necessary' is my watchword now.

It was in this frame of mind that I woke to greet the morning, personified by a waiter bringing coffee and rolls. (He is a rather pretty waiter, young and very thin, with shy dark eyes, like those of a gazelle; but my heart is set on the enchanting Ned and I took no notice of him.) On beginning to dress, however, I met with a setback.

Graziella had asked us, since the day's excursion was to include places of divine worship, to refrain, if female, from wearing trousers, if male, from wearing shorts. I had been disposed to welcome any prohibition designed to protect the public from the sight of the Major's legs. For myself, I foresaw no difficulty in complying, for I have with me two skirts of suitable length for the daylight hours. One has a few small cigarette burns and the other has lost the button which ought to secure the waistband; but these seemed minor defects, not calculated to offend the devout.

To make a final choice between them, I consulted the looking-glass, assisted in a critical examination of my appearance by the sunlight pouring in from the window behind me. It was thus that I discovered that neither, in these conditions, has the opacity required for perfect decorum. In the dim interior of the churches they would be unobjectionable; in the sunlit exterior, however — you will see the difficulty.

But I was not dismayed. I remembered that while I was packing you had advised me—foreseeing, it may be, with wonderful prescience, this very contingency—to take a petticoat. There was some difficulty, you may recall, in finding one which would not, if extracted from my suitcase and waved in the air by an over-zealous Customs officer, expose me, by its grubby and ragged condition, to the censure of my fellow passengers; but our searches were at last rewarded by finding a perfectly clean one, almost unworn.

I remembered, when I put it on, why it was almost unworn. It is the one I bought last January in a sale, and which turned out, when I got it home, to be four inches longer than any of my skirts.

*

'One can't think of everything,' said Selena.

'No, of course not,' said Timothy.

*

Someone once explained to me that this sort of thing is all due to the Second Law of Thermodynamics, which requires that everything shall tend towards Chaos. One cannot struggle for ever against the laws of physics: I began to think it might be best, however compulsory the excursion, to return to bed and read the Finance Act, very quietly, until someone came and told me what to do. Someone, in the end, usually does.

Before I could give effect to my indecision, there was a knock on the door: Marylou had come to make sure I was ready for the excursion. I told her of my difficulty.

'Julia, honey,' she said, 'couldn't you just cut four inches off the hem of your slip?'

'That,' I said, 'would be a most ingenious solution. But impracticable. One would need a pair of scissors.'

'No problem, honey,' she replied. 'I have my dressmaking scissors in my room.'

Off she went to fetch them, and, on her return, sheared away, in a matter of moments, the four inches of material which had divided me from the presentable.

It was thus, after all, only a few minutes after half past eight that we arrived in the entrance hall to begin our excursion round Venice.

*

'Interesting,' said Ragwort.

'Interesting?' said Cantrip, almost choking on his steak Diane. 'Interesting? Absolutely sickening is what I call it. I don't know what it is about Julia. She only has to sit back and look helpless—which, God knows, I admit she is— and some misguided girl turns up and starts taking care of her. It's just like a baby cuckoo. What a baby cuckoo does is get itself hatched in someone else's nest. Then it just sits there with its beak open, looking hungry. And the birds the nest belongs to, instead of chucking it over the edge, get this irresistible urge to shovel food down it. Same effect as Julia has on girls. And what's more, they're usually jolly attractive girls, who ought to have something better to do than collect worms for Julia.'

'The ways of Nature,' said Selena, 'are indeed very wonderful.'

'What I thought interesting,' said Ragwort, 'was the dressmaking scissors. There are, of course, various sizes and types of scissors used in dressmaking. But one could not conveniently use a small pair to cut off the hem of a petticoat—it must have been a proper pair of tailor's scissors. With long blades. Quite long and quite sharp. And pointed, of course, at the ends. You did say "stabbed", didn't you, Cantrip?'

*

There were no defaulters among us except Ned's large friend Kenneth. The rest of us, in a group which also included a score or so of foreign Art Lovers, followed obediently in the footsteps of Graziella. Graziella takes conscientiously her duty to instruct us in the general and artistic history of Venice: I feel that she may require us, at the end of the holiday, to take an examination in these subjects. I listen to her, therefore, with the utmost attention, for I would not wish in that event to disappoint her.

The excursion began in the Piazza San Marco, described by Napoleon as the finest drawing-room in Europe. This showed, said Graziella, that Napoleon was a very silly man, because the Piazza is not in the least like a drawing-room: in reality, though certainly spacious and elegant, it is the forecourt to St Mark's Basilica, designed to permit the visitor, before admiring in detail the church's rich mosaics and luxurious columns, to appreciate as a single unity the grandeur of its incomparable façade. We duly appreciated the façade.

The Venetians, it seems, adopted St Mark as their patron saint in the ninth century, at which time the mortal remains of the Evangelist were reposing in Alexandria. To demonstrate their piety, the Venetians sent out a body-snatching expedition, which abstracted the sacred corpse from its resting-place and brought it back through Customs packed between two sides of pork, so discouraging investigation by the fastidious Muslims.

This reminded the Major of a funny thing that happened to him in the Lebanon in '52. I began to worry about Desdemona again.

Having secured the body, they spent three hundred years building a church to house it, during which time they pillaged the Levant for suitable building materials. In the meantime, they lost the corpse; but they did not allow this to discourage them. The opportunity to put the finishing touches to the masterpiece came in 1204, when they more or less hijacked the Fourth Crusade. The Crusaders had meant to go to Jerusalem; but the Venetians, who were providing the transport, said about halfway across the Mediterranean that it would be a better idea to go and sack Byzantium. So they went and sacked Byzantium; as a result of which the Venetians acquired an empire in the Eastern Mediterranean and the four horses of antique bronze which stand on the balcony of St Mark's Basilica.

From there we went on to the Doges' Palace. Graziella instructed us to note the development, as thereby exemplified, from the Gothic to the Renaissance style, and gave us a little lecture on the Venetian constitution. She spoke of it tenderly: it had been, it seems, a splendid constitution, full of senates and committees and checks and balances and other things delightful to the political theorist.

'If it was that fine,' said Stanford, 'why didn't it last?'

'It lasted six hundred years, signor,' said Graziella. 'And when it was quite worn out and would not work at all any more, it was exported, of course, to the United States of America.'

Stanford's expression, as I have mentioned, is habitually that of a man who suspects that somebody is going to pull a fast one: it now became that of such a man finding his suspicions confirmed. Marylou looked at him as if judging him to have committed some regrettable public blunder; and further marked her displeasure by keeping to my side, rather than his, during the remainder of our time in the Doges' Palace.

Regard for historical truth compelled Graziella, when we came to the room of the Council of Ten, to make some mention of the methods by which that body, during the Middle Ages, had preserved the security of the Most Serene Republic. She spoke rather vividly of the dark proceedings, the whispered evidence and unappealable judgements to which that graceful room must be presumed a witness. Marylou was much distressed — as I thought, she is an idealist.

'I can't believe it,' she said. 'Julia honey, do you believe anyone could do such awful things in such a lovely room?'

'I can believe anything,' I answered, 'when a young man with such a beautiful profile as Ned's turns out to be a tax-gatherer.'

'Are you suggesting,' asked Ned— by whom, of course, I made sure to be overheard— 'that my Department is to be compared with the Council of Ten?'

'No,' I said, with the bitterness of experience, 'it is infinitely worse.'

You may perhaps feel, Selena, that I departed a little in this conversation from the policy you have recommended. My remark was made, however, with great severity—I hardly think you should count it as a compliment. Besides, since I have paid more attention to Marylou than to anyone else, I am rather hoping that both Ned and the Major may now suspect me of a certain unorthodoxy in erotic preference: the former will be lulled into a false sense of security and the latter will be discouraged. I feel I may risk a compliment or two.

*

'It's too bad of Julia,' said Ragwort. 'Her preferences, as is all too well known, are as orthodox as anyone's. If not more so.'

'Absolutely,' said Cantrip.

'Never mind,' said Selena, 'no one takes Julia seriously.'

*

The last visit of the morning was to a small glass-works, where we were to observe, said Graziella, the traditional and historic art of glass-blowing. I was feeling inclined, by this time, to take a keener interest in the traditional and historic art of putting bubbles into Campari soda, but I did not venture to say so.

Soon, however, like the first rumblings of a zinc thunder-sheet, there began to be murmurs of complaint from Eleanor. It wasn't, she said, good enough: what we had been promised was a guided tour of sights of artistic and historical interest; instead of which, we were made to spend half the morning being dragged round a glass-factory. This was not mere incompetence, but contrived deliberately: the object was to make us buy at an inflated price the probably inferior products of the factory and so enable that woman (*videlicet* Graziella) to pocket a handsome commission.

These complaints were initially addressed to me — we are, you will remember, as Ruth and Naomi. It seemed clear, though, that they represented merely a limbering up for a direct attack on Graziella. I considered the prospect of spending the next eight days caught in the crossfire between these two formidable women — its frightfulness spurred me to action.

'Eleanor,' I said, 'I have not your stamina. I was thinking of slipping away and having a coffee in the Piazza. If you're really not keen on the glass-blowing, perhaps I could persuade you to keep me company?'

Eleanor would naturally have preferred to stay and have a row with Graziella; but she could not, with much colour of politeness, say so. I bore her off in triumph, congratulating myself on my stroke of diplomacy. Buying Eleanor coffee, even in Florian's, seemed a small price to pay.

Our conversation turned to the subject on which we are most in sympathy — that is to say, the wickedness of income tax. Such phrases as 'penalizing achievement,' and 'petty-minded persecution,' soon filled the air of the Piazza.

Descending, in due course, from the general to the particular, Eleanor sought my views on what might be done to mitigate her own liabilities. Her position is very pitiful: though her share of profits from Frostfield's is received as director's remuneration and treated, therefore, as earned income, and her other investments have been selected for capital growth, her top rate of tax is 90%.

*

'May I infer,' I asked, 'that Mrs Frostfield is in comfortable circumstances?'

'You may infer,' said Timothy, 'that her income is somewhere between £20,000 and £25,000 a year.'

'And if,' said Selena, 'a substantial proportion of that is derived from growth investments—'

'You may conclude,' said Ragwort, 'that she could, without undue personal sacrifice, have paid for her own coffee. Even in Florian's.'

*

I did my best to be helpful; but Eleanor seems already to be excellently advised—every suggestion I put forward is reflected in her existing arrangements. I had almost despaired of assisting her when it struck me that she was quite perfect for the penniless husband scheme. Or rather, vice versa.

'Eleanor,' I said, so excited that I spilt my Campari soda, 'am I right in assuming that you are free to marry?'

'My dear Julia,' she said, emitting a noise like a baby xylophone, intended, I gather, to express amusement, 'if you are advising me to find myself a rich husband—'

'No, no,' I cried. 'Certainly not. You must find yourself a husband with no money at all.'

I went on to explain to her the consequences of marriage, which are, of course, that the earned income of the female spouse may be treated as hers for tax purposes, just as if she were a separate person, but her investment income is treated as the income of her husband. It follows, as we all know, that if the parties to a marriage have both earned and unearned income they should arrange for the earnings to be those of the wife. It also follows that a single lady with income from both sources should take immediate steps to acquire a penniless husband.

Presented, free of charge, with this elegant and ef-

ficient tax-saving scheme, requiring no expensive docu-
mentation and not attracting stamp duty, you will imagine that Eleanor wept tears of gratitude and offered to
buy me another Campari soda. You will be wrong.

'Really, Julia,' she said, repeating the xylophone effect,
'you seem to take a very cynical view of marriage.'

I am, as you know, Selena, by no means cynical, being
on the contrary sentimental to a fault; but if people are
going to let sentiment interfere with their tax planning,
there is no helping them.

*

'Julia's scheme,' said Ragwort, 'makes no allowance for
the cost of keeping the husband.'

'It is clearly envisaged,' said Selena, 'that the husband
would undertake those functions — as of gardener, chauf-
feur and general handyman — for which a woman in
Eleanor's position would otherwise expect to pay on a
commercial basis.'

There followed a digression, while my companions
discussed the merits of the penniless husband scheme.
Knowing nothing of such matters, I am unable to report
it in detail: should any of my readers be able to put it to
personal advantage, they will perhaps think it proper,
when next in the Corkscrew, to offer Julia a glass of wine.

*

I asked Eleanor if she did not find it a little unnerving
to have among our travelling companions a member of
the Department of Inland Revenue.

'Ned? Oh, my dear Julia,' said Eleanor, 'of course not.
He's a friend of Kenneth's.' I looked, I suppose, baffled.
'You do know who Kenneth is?'

I mumbled an embarrassed negative — not to know who
Kenneth was seemed to be a solecism, but one I could not
remedy.

'Oh, my dear Julia,' said Eleanor, with a further
xylophone imitation, 'Kenneth Dunfermline. One of our

most promising young sculptors.'

'Oh, really? How very interesting—I didn't realize,' I said, trying to disguise the fact that the name was unfamiliar to me. 'Even so, Eleanor, I am by no means persuaded that friendship with a sculptor, however distinguished, will prevent a man from the Revenue from behaving like a man from the Revenue. I don't think that I myself would be inclined, in such company, to mention, for example, that I was putting down my holidays as a business expense.'

On this point, however, it appears that Eleanor's strength is as the strength of ten, because her heart is pure: she really is here for business purposes. An English lady of substantial means and excellent taste, a life-long collector of antiques and objets d'art, and a resident of Venice for the past thirty years, has recently made the transition to Paradise: her collection is expected to be of considerable importance. The object of Eleanor's journey is to take an early view of it, in the hope, I gather, of arranging a private purchase of those items which interest her: once they go to auction, she says, the prices will become ridiculous. She has asked the Major if he is here for the same purpose and it appears that he is. Neither of them, therefore, is in Venice for pure pleasure: their designs are on the furniture and effects of the late Miss Priscilla Tiverton.

*

'Well, I'm damned,' said Timothy. 'They're pillaging the estate of my client's great-aunt.'

CHAPTER 6

It was not, after all, such a very remarkable coincidence. The funeral rites of the rich are a signal for vultures to gather: among whom one may class, with all respect, antique dealers and the Chancery Bar.

This observation was not well received. Timothy suggested, a little waspishly, that if I thought so ill of his source of income I might not wish him to buy me a brandy. I reassured him on this point.

Some of my readers, it occurs to me, may divert their idler moments by reading detective fiction: a pastime sometimes conducive to over-fanciful speculation. For their benefit, I should at once make it clear that the late Miss Tiverton had died, so far as is known, of entirely natural causes; that the designs of Mrs Frostfield and the Major on her collection of objets d'art did not cause or contribute to the crime of which Julia was suspected; and that the choice of Timothy to advise in connection with her brother's trust fund was — save to the extent that there may be seen in his presence at the right place at the right time for the purpose of our investigation the hand of a benevolent and all-seeing Providence — was save to that extent the purest coincidence.

It was getting quite late. Those theatre-going patrons of Guido's who had lingered to see in the flesh the originals of the autographed portraits on the walls were beginning to be rewarded. Our brandies arrived. Selena continued her reading of Julia's letter.

> My room at the Cytherea.
> Sunday evening.
> I hope there is not going to be any unpleasantness — I mean I think there is. At any rate, no one can say it is my fault — I mean they will certainly say so. Well, I will describe to you in full the events of the weekend: I leave it to you to judge whether I have at any stage or in any particular done more than politeness and good nature required of me.
> On Saturday morning, sitting on the terrace in the cor-

ner previously described, I was reflecting on my proposed pursuit of Ned and wondering, rather anxiously, whether it might cause distress to his friend Kenneth. I would be reluctant — for I am well-disposed towards artists — to do anything which might give pain to one. That there is an attachment one can hardly doubt, but whether it is a deep and sincere attachment, of the kind which makes people upset, or of a merely frivolous nature, I cannot at present be certain. I reasoned, however, as follows:

(1) either Kenneth is deeply and sincerely attached to Ned or he is not;

(2) if he is not so attached, then my pursuit of Ned will cause him no distress;

(3) if he is so attached, then either the attachment is reciprocal or it is not;

(4) if it is reciprocal, Ned will reject my advances and my pursuit of him will accordingly cause Kenneth no distress;

(5) if it is not reciprocal, Kenneth will suffer distress whether or not I pursue Ned;

(6) if Kenneth will suffer distress whether I pursue Ned or not, my pursuit of Ned cannot be the cause of Kenneth's distress;

(7) it is therefore logically impossible for my pursuit of Ned to cause Kenneth distress.

I had taken up my pen to report to you this example of the usefulness of logic — without which I might have come to an altogether different conclusion — when I saw that Marylou had come on to the terrace. She is by no means one of those whom I would wish to avoid: I emerged from the cover of the vine or similar shrub.

'Are you,' I asked, 'waiting for your husband?'

'My husband,' said Marylou, 'has gone to Verona for the weekend to stay with a business associate.' She made the expression 'business associate,' which I would previously have thought innocuous, sound decidedly

pejorative. She didn't make 'husband' sound all that flattering, either. Wondering if these were discreet American
euphemisms for some unmentionable debauchery, I
made noises of sympathetic enquiry.

Stanford is employed by the English subsidiary of an
American engineering firm. He is, it seems, one of those
abrasive, dynamic young executives who refuse to take
holidays unless calculated to further their acquaintance
with those useful in business. Still, after a campaign of
several months, Marylou had at last persuaded him to
take her on a genuine private vacation—one, that is to
say, during which Stanford would devote to her his whole
time and attention and she, in her turn, would not be
obliged to make polite conversation with the wives or
other relatives of his customers and colleagues. Or so,
poor girl, she had believed. At the last moment before
their departure, he had disclosed to her his acceptance of
a weekend invitation from an important customer in
Verona. Justly indignant at his duplicity, she had refused
to go; but now she had no one to look at Venice with
her.

I suggested, naturally, that we should explore it
together, and asked if there was anything in particular
that she would like to see.

'I saw a divine set of embroidered table linen when we
went to the Rialto yesterday,' said Marylou. 'But I didn't
have time to buy it. Could we go back there? Or is it too
far?'

I assured her that it was not. Although the distance
from St Mark's to the Rialto represents nearly half the
length of the Grand Canal, it is, by land, a mere five
minutes' walk.

That, at any rate, is the impression given by the map in
Ragwort's guide book. There is a strange lack of correspondence between places as represented by maps and
places as they actually are. Setting forth on a route which

should lead one, according to the cartographer, to one's objective in square F11, one suddenly finds oneself outside a church which he assigns to square M3. If, as in Venice is always the case, the church contains two Bellinis and a Giorgione, it is hardly possible for the Art Lover to pass by without a glance.

Our progress towards the Rialto was therefore erratic. Our passage across it was no less dilatory. Of the two rows of shops which line the ancient bridge, none could complain of lack of patronage. It was not only the set of table linen: it was, in the end, three sets of table linen; it was lace shawls; it was leather purses, elaborately decorated; it was little glass mice, holding orchestral instruments; it was many other things of pleasure and delight, all described by Marylou as perfectly divine and not really expensive. Graziella had told us of the great days of Venetian commerce, when all the money in the world was said to change hands on the Rialto: it appeared Marylou's ambition to restore them single-handed.

We came at last to the far bank of the Grand Canal and the district known as the Dorsodouro. Seeming rather to welcome the student than the tourist, it is altogether different from that of St Mark's. There is in the very air an almost Attic saltiness, reminding one that here indeed is one of the historic centres of the European intellect, the nursery of the Renaissance, the acropolis of free thought against the pedantry of Popes and the tyranny of princes. Here the great Aldus—

'That's not what Graziella said yesterday about the Council of Ten,' said Marylou, the confidante of these reflections.

'Graziella,' I replied kindly, 'was talking yesterday about the Middle Ages. I am now speaking of the Renaissance, which is entirely different. And I should mention, Marylou, that to interrupt Counsel, when fairly launched on a nice piece of rhetoric, is the exclusive prerogative of the judiciary—and in them to be discouraged.'

I had forgotten that Americans always think one means what one says. To my dismay, she began to apologize. I added at once that she was a dozen times prettier than the entire High Court Bench, and might interrupt me whenever she pleased. But she seemed unpersuaded. By way of further assurance, therefore, I kissed her on the nose. This occurring outside the Casa Rezzonico occasioned some mockery from the passing Venetians; but in all good nature, Selena, what less could I have done?

*

'No good will come of this,' said Ragwort.

'It was only on the nose,' said Selena.

*

We had lunch in the restaurant recommended by Ragwort, off the Campo San Barnaba, where a vine-tree has spread its branches to make a roof over the garden. They fed us on vegetable soup and omelettes and gave us cold wine in a china jug. I hoped, with these diversions, that Marylou might forget her matrimonial discontentment. Not so, however.

'Julia, honey,' she said, somewhere around the second *grappa*, 'do you think that marriage can be a valid interpersonal relationship in a life context?'

'I am not well qualified to judge,' I answered cautiously. 'I am not a marrying woman.'

'I guess you'd think it intrusive,' she said, 'if I asked why not.'

'By no means,' I said hastily; but explained that there was no one with whom I would contemplate such an arrangement except my learned and elegant friend, Desmond Ragwort,

*

'Well, really,' said Ragwort.

*

who had, however, rejected my honourable proposals.

'You mean you asked him and he said no?' said Marylou.

I confirmed that that was indeed the case. She was shocked at such heartlessness and undiscernment and displayed, warm-hearted girl, such sympathetic indignation on my behalf

*

'It's a bit much,' said Ragwort.

*

that I felt obliged to point out, in extenuation of Ragwort's offence, that any virtues I possess are not of a domestic nature. This, however, did not placate her. If, she said, all Ragwort wanted was someone to keep the house clean and give him a nice time in bed

*

'From Julia of all people,' said Ragwort.

*

then he was not worthy of me: a woman of my intellect and personality, she said, needed someone who would appreciate her as a person, not merely a household object.

*

'Do have some brandy, Ragwort,' said Selena. 'You'll feel much better.'

*

It was a day of many and diverse pleasures. The best of which was the discovery, on our return to the Cytherea, of the lovely Ned sitting all alone in the bar. Alone and discontented: Kenneth, it seemed, had been busy all day with something serious and artistic; Ned, deserted, had wandered round Venice with no one to talk to and been very bored. He was sadly looking forward to an equally tedious Sunday.

Well, Selena, one has not a heart of stone. Marylou and I, having already agreed to spend Sunday morning together at the Lido, invited Ned to join us. If he had been a plain young man, we could hardly have done otherwise.

On Sunday morning, therefore, I rose in a mood of optimism — I had great hopes of the Lido.

'The signorina is very happy today,' said the pretty waiter who brings my breakfast.

'Who could fail to be happy,' I answered, 'who is given breakfast by a young man with such beautiful eyes?' My linguistic ability was not equal to expressing this in Italian, nor his to fully understanding it in English; but he gathered, sufficiently to look pleased, that a compliment was intended.

Arriving first on the terrace, where we had arranged to meet, I settled down in my usual corner. In consequence of this, I came to overhear a most peculiar conversation, or rather fragments of one, between Eleanor and Kenneth Dunfermline. I will report it in as much detail as I can manage and see what you make of it.

They came together on to the terrace and sat down at a table at the other end of it. I stayed where I was, concealed by the vine or similar shrub. That I might have the embarrassment of overhearing them did not occur to me, for anything said in normal tones would not have been audible. I had not allowed for the resonance of Eleanor's voice in moments of irritation.

For a few minutes, indeed, they talked quite quietly and peaceably, so that I heard nothing. Then I heard Eleanor say, 'It's no use blaming me, Kenneth. Of course I thought he knew about it — I wouldn't have mentioned it otherwise.' Then Kenneth said something I didn't hear, which seemed to soothe her a little. The next thing I heard her say was, 'Well, I've warned you about him and that's all I can do. As long as you keep it properly locked up while he's anywhere about the place, you shouldn't have anything to worry about.'

I at first assumed, I don't quite know why, that she was talking about the Major. The Major strikes me, for some reason, as the sort of man in whose vicinity it might be prudent to lock up the spoons. It seems, however, that I must have been wrong about this, because soon afterwards I heard her say that someone called Bruce had stolen an armchair and a rococo looking-glass which she rather liked. I concluded that Bruce, whoever he is, must have been the subject of her previous warning.

I cannot imagine, however, what Kenneth could have in his possession of sufficient value to be in danger of theft—unless, of course, one counts the lovely Ned. So it all seemed rather odd; but not nearly as odd as the next part.

Built, as I have mentioned, like an ox, Kenneth had hitherto displayed a corresponding placidity. Soon after the reference to Bruce, however, he seemed to become enraged. He rose from his chair and stood in front of Eleanor, head down and shoulders forward as if about to charge. Indignation now made him, too, sufficiently resonant to be audible to me. I cannot attempt a verbatim account of his remarks: the general burden was that Eleanor didn't own him, that he wasn't employed by Frostfield's and that she'd already had her money's worth out of him. Something, too, about not letting down his friends to please her.

After which he left the terrace, evidently in dudgeon. Eleanor, to my relief, left soon afterwards, saving me the embarrassment of discovery.

Don't you think it extraordinary, Selena, that Eleanor and Kenneth should in two days have reached a sufficient intimacy to have a row? Rancour, I have always supposed, is the fruit of long acquaintance. But you, with your usual agility of mind, may perhaps arrive at some reasonable explanation.

*

'I like the Bruce chap,' said Cantrip.

'You mean,' said Ragwort, 'that you see him as a kindred spirit?'

'No, I mean I like him for the murder. I think he did it.'

'With respect,' said Timothy, 'are you not theorizing a little in advance of the evidence? A single mention of his name in an overheard fragment of conversation—'

'Jolly significant, though. Because now we know that this sculptor chap's got something valuable with him. And we know this Bruce chap knows he's got it. And we know it's the sort of thing this Bruce chap will go to any lengths to get hold of. We don't know what it is, of course. I expect it's some more of this rocky cocoa stuff, if that's what Bruce goes in for. Is rocky cocoa valuable?'

'One imagines,' said Ragwort, 'that a good piece of genuine rococo furniture would command an attractive price.'

'Right. So what the Bruce chap does is hang around the Cytherea till he thinks there's no one about. Then he weasels into the annexe with a view to knocking off the rocky cocoa armchair or whatever it is. Only the chap from the Revenue comes back unexpectedly and catches him at it. Threatens to call the fuzz. The Bruce chap pleads with him a bit, I expect, says he's got a wife and five children and so on and they've got no armchairs to sit on. But it's no good, because chaps from the Revenue are specially trained not to listen to hard-luck stories. So the Bruce chap gets desperate and stabs him. I like it, myself. What do you think?'

'I think,' said Selena, 'that we'd better go on and find out what this unpleasantness is that Julia is worried about.'

*

Marylou and Ned joining me soon afterwards, we took the *vaporetto* across the lagoon to the Lido. There we swam very energetically and drank a good deal of Campari soda. That, I mean, was the sum of our joint achievements: Marylou and Ned did most of the swimming and I drank most of the Campari. Ned, when disrobed, is a fraction more muscular than I had imagined, but not distastefully so. And not at all hairy, which was a great relief to me.

I begged them both to avoid sunburn. It would be disgraceful, I said, to take out with me the two most beautiful people in the Cytherea and bring them back looking like boiled lobsters.

'Only in the Cytherea?' asked Ned, looking reproachful.

'In Venice,' I said. 'On the whole coast of the Adriatic.'

'Why not the whole Mediterranean?' he asked, still not satisfied. But I was not to be drawn into such gross exaggeration.

I did not forget to show an interest in Ned's hopes, dreams and aspirations. I asked if he really intended to spend all his days in the service of the Revenue, sending ever more menacing letters in ever more buff-coloured envelopes. 'Surely,' I said, 'it is a very soul-destroying occupation?' This seemed to me to be rather subtle.

'I don't know,' answered Ned. 'Perhaps there'll suddenly be some amazing transformation in my circumstances. My friend Kenneth has plans to make both our fortunes.'

Encouraged, however, to speak more of these, he said, 'Oh, they won't come to anything. You know what artists are like. I take Ken's plans as seriously as your compliments, Julia. No, I expect I'll stay with the Revenue.' He even seemed a little irritated at having mentioned any alternative: I therefore felt no obligation to pursue the subject further.

*

'Don't you think,' said Selena, 'that that is also a significant conversation?'

'Well,' said Timothy, 'he was right, in a way, about the
sudden change in his circumstances. But presumably he
wasn't thinking of being murdered, poor boy. What have
you in mind?'

'I was remembering,' said Selena, looking dreamily into
her empty brandy glass, 'the efficiency of Eleanor's tax-
planning. Still, perhaps I am being fanciful — let us continue.'

*

We had lunch in the open, under a blue canopy in the
elegant avenue which leads from the beach to the
vaporetto station. Afterwards, we returned across the
lagoon: Graziella had instructed us on no account to miss
the Historic Regatta. This is an annual pretext for the
Venetians to dress up in Medieval costumes and glide
along the Grand Canal under gold awnings, in barges
shaped like lions and dolphins.

The pressure of the crowds gathered to watch the spectacle brought me into closer proximity with the lovely
Ned than could otherwise have been achieved. This, with
the heat and the wine I had drunk at lunch, induced in
me a certain dizziness: I was hard put to it to refrain from
any open advance.

I did consider, indeed, whether I should try fainting, as
recommended by the dramatist Shakespeare. It seemed to
me, however, that unless Ned felt obliged to carry me all
the way back to my room at the Cytherea nothing of
substance would be achieved by this. He does not seem to
me the kind of young man who would readily undertake
such a task.

*

'I don't believe Shakespeare told Julia to try fainting,' said
Cantrip. 'He's dead.'

'She is referring,' said Selena, 'to his early poem "Venus and Adonis". Julia read it at an impressionable age and has since regarded it as a sort of seduction manual.'

'It is a most indelicate work,' said Ragwort. 'Not at all suitable reading for a young girl.'

'It's hardly Julia's fault,' said Selena. 'They told her at school that Shakespeare was educational.'

'As I recall,' I said, 'the methods employed by the goddess in her pursuit of Adonis, though forceful, achieved only limited success. Doesn't Julia find that discouraging?'

'No,' said Selena. 'No. On this point alone, she believes that Shakespeare has been less than candid. She is persuaded, you see, that the poem is based on personal experience. The historical evidence shows that he yielded.'

*

We returned, therefore, in the usual way to the Cytherea—that is to say, with no one carrying anyone else. Ned went off to rest before dinner.

'Julia, honey,' said Marylou, 'you must let me fix that skirt.'

At some stage of the afternoon the hem of my skirt had come down. It is in the nature of hems to come down; and Marylou is of the school of thought which holds that they should be put up again. We accordingly adjourned to her room, where she keeps her sewing things, acquiring en passant from the bar a bottle of Frascati.

We sat on the bed, drinking Frascati, she sewing and I watching her sew. She displayed a great interest in life at the English Bar, and I was happy to gratify her curiosity. I gave her, I think, a pretty fair and balanced picture. That is to say, I did not dwell exclusively on the forensic triumphs attributable to my own skill and brilliance, but mentioned also the forensic disasters brought about by the idiocy of my lay client, the incompetence of my instructing solicitor or the senile dementia of the tribunal hearing my case. It was, in short, a very similar account to what she would have got from any other member of our profession.

'Julia, honey,' she said, 'I think I ought to oversew the hem of your slip.'

The lower edge of my petticoat, since its abbreviation, inevitably lacked its original smoothness. The defect was latent: but for my taking my skirt off to allow her to sew the hem, Marylou herself would not have remembered it. Still, it is curiously pleasant to watch someone engaged for one's benefit on some delicate domestic task: with only formal protest I surrendered the petticoat.

I seem to have given her an unduly rosy picture of life at the Bar. 'I wish I'd done something like that,' she said, rather wistfully. 'I wish I'd done something valid and meaningful, instead of just getting married.'

I assured her that celibacy was not a prerequisite to practice at the Bar: I suggested, indeed, that a husband might prove a great comfort in those moments of stress and anxiety which are unavoidable in our profession.

'Not if the husband was Stanford, honey,' said Marylou. 'Stanford is not the kind of husband who would be supportive to me in a self-actualizing role. Stanford does not care about me as an individual person.'

I said — what else could I say? — that if Stanford did not adore her he was both a fool and a scoundrel; and I could not easily believe so ill of him.

'No, honey,' said Marylou. 'He adores the way I look and the way I dress and the way I keep house and the way I organize parties. He does not adore me as a person. He does not care about me as a person. If my husband cared about me as a person, he would not have come to Venice with me and then gone to Verona for the weekend to stay with a business acquaintance.'

She then burst into tears.

I was much distressed by this and did not know what to

do. Still, it is common knowledge that those who weep do not wish to do so *in vacuo*, but on a convenient shoulder: I proffered my shoulder and Marylou wept on it. 'There, there,' I said, or words to the like effect.

It will be clear to you from the foregoing that the reasons for my being on Marylou's bed in a fairly small quantity of underwear and holding her head on my shoulder were of the most innocent nature imaginable. I do quite see, however, that it was perhaps not the best moment for Stanford, returning from Verona, to walk, without knocking, into the bedroom. The scene was open to misconstruction: from Stanford's expression it was clear that he misconstrued.

Still, he did not, while I remained present, actually say anything. I was hopeful that by the time we all went down to dinner Marylou would have persuaded him of the absolute purity of her motives and my own. From the way Stanford looked at me over dinner, however, I fear this is not the case. I hope, as I say, that there will be no unpleasantness.

I was so put out by all this that when the Major suggested cutting a rug together some evening I was not immediately able to think of an excuse and have, in principle, agreed.

I excused myself from coffee on the grounds of a headache, seeking in the privacy of my room the consolation of reporting to you the difficulties in which this leaves me

Yours, as always,

Julia.

*

'It does seem extraordinary,' said Ragwort, 'if anyone was going to murder anyone, that no one murdered Julia. One's glad they didn't, of course.'

CHAPTER 7

It was now very late: even the actors were leaving.

'We'd better go,' said Timothy. 'Selena, do you still feel like driving me to Heathrow tomorrow?'

It had been arranged, earlier in the week, that Selena should drive Timothy to the airport, arriving there in time to coincide with Julia's return. The rest of us, thinking to spend in convivial reunion the hours between Julia's arrival and Timothy's departure, had intended to include ourselves among her passengers. It was agreed, in spite of the altered circumstances, that these arrangements should stand.

'I say, Ragwort,' said Cantrip. 'You know what you said about no one murdering Julia — you don't think it's one of those mistaken identity things, do you? I mean, you don't think someone meant to murder Julia and got the Revenue chap instead?'

I pointed out that to murder, in mistake for Julia, a thin young man with fair hair would require a peculiarly myopic assassin.

'Might have been dark,' said Cantrip. 'And we don't know whose room it happened in — the report just said "in hotel bedroom." Suppose the chap from the Revenue was in Julia's bed —'

'That,' said Ragwort, 'is a possibility which, regrettably, we cannot altogether discount. But wouldn't Julia have been there with him?'

'Temporarily absent,' said Cantrip. 'In the loo or somewhere.'

'I'm rather doubtful,' said Timothy, 'about the timing. You rang the Corkscrew at about twenty past eight, Cantrip. So I take it the news must have been on the teleprinter by quarter past. If the murder happened after dark, I wouldn't have thought it was possible.'

'Don't know,' said Cantrip. 'Depends what time it gets dark in Venice.'

Timothy paid the bill. We rose to leave.

'By the way,' said Selena, 'if you don't mind, I'd still like to get to Heathrow in time to meet the flight Julia should have come back on.'

'Yes, of course,' said Timothy. 'If it turns out she's on it after all —'

'That, certainly, would be a great relief. But if she isn't, then I think, you know, in the light of what Cantrip's just been suggesting, that I'd like to be sure that all the other Art Lovers are.'

It was thus at a comparatively early hour on Saturday morning, considering the lateness of our retirement, that Selena collected me from my borrowed residence in Islington. She had received, but not yet had time to read, a further letter from Julia, evidently posted on Wednesday. She proposed, by reading it aloud, to improve the otherwise idle hours at Heathrow.

Taking my place beside her, I resigned myself to being driven through the traffic of North London at the pace she describes as brisk. Still, we arrived without accident at Middle Temple Lane.

Timothy had already spoken by telephone to Julia's travel agents. They had confirmed that their customer, Miss Julia Larwood, was experiencing certain difficulties with the Venetian police, but were happy to reassure him that she was not actually in custody: she had merely been asked to surrender her passport and not to leave the Veneto. Arrangements were being made for her accommodation. Relieved, I dare say, to find that they were not solely responsible for the poor creature, they had given Timothy the name and address of their representative in Venice — that was to say, Graziella — and had promised that she would give him every possible assistance in his efforts on Julia's behalf.

To save Selena an unnecessary detour, Cantrip had offered to make his own way to Ragwort's house in Fulham, where we would collect them both. It had not been, perhaps, a wholly altruistic offer: Ragwort is known to make excellent breakfasts. Indeed, I had rather hoped — but Cantrip had already finished the scrambled eggs, and Selena did not think we had time for coffee.

Ragwort and Cantrip joined me in the back seat of the vehicle and we continued westwards, Selena negotiating with wonderful insouciance — I suppose that is the expression I am looking for — the series of roundabouts which seems designed to prevent the motorist, once in London, from ever leaving it.

Cantrip had also been making telephone calls. Claiming the privileges of a part-time employee, he had used the information service of the *Scuttle* to find out the time of sunset in Venice. It was eight o'clock.

'In that case,' said Timothy, 'the mistaken identity theory must be out of court, mustn't it?'

'Local time,' said Cantrip. 'The Italians are an hour ahead of us. So by London time it would only be seven. And then I rang this chap I know at the news agency and asked how long it would take for a story like that to get on the teleprinter. I said I'd got a bet on about it. And he reckons they've got a chap in Venice who's hot stuff newshoundwise, so once someone called the fuzz it'd be on the wire in an hour or so.'

'Still cutting it fine,' said Timothy.

'Not that fine,' said Cantrip. 'Look, the way I see it is this. Friday evening, about quarter to eight Italian time. This American bird and her husband changing for dinner. There's a row — you know, starting with an argument about who left the top off the toothpaste or something and going on from there. And as you'd expect, Julia's name crops up. "And on Sunday afternoon," says Stanford, "when I found you and Julia lying on the bed in a newt-like condition, don't you tell me she was just explaining an interesting point of Chancery procedure. Pigs might fly," says Stanford. "There were goings-on going on." And Marylou says all right, if that's his attitude, she is happy to say that she and Julia actually spent the whole afternoon in nameless debaucheries —'

'We are given to understand,' said Ragwort, 'that that is not the case.'

'That wouldn't stop her,' said Cantrip. 'I mean, when a girl's having a row with her husband, she's not going to admit that all the years they've been married she's been absolutely faithful to him — too humiliating. So they always say they've been having it off with someone else, even when they haven't. Of course,' he added with some bitterness, 'this often causes a lot of distress and embarrassment to innocent third parties. But they don't think about that.'

'We defer to your experience,' said Ragwort, 'as a potential co-respondent.'

Cantrip construing this remark as offensive, there ensued a scuffle.

'Please,' said Selena, 'this isn't Monday morning in the Companies Court.'

'Sorry,' said Cantrip. 'Where was I? Oh yes — Marylou says that as a matter of fact Stanford is quite right and she spent Sunday afternoon in bed with Julia. Going on to say that if he really wants to know this was about seventeen times more fun than anything along similar lines with Stanford. Good exit-line, so she sweeps out of the matrimonial bedroom and goes down to dinner. And Stanford, in a frenzy of jealous passion, seizes the nearest weapon—the dressmaking scissors or whatever—and goes off to Julia's room to avenge his honour.'

'Surely not,' said Selena.

'No use your saying "surely not" like that—Americans get jolly steamed up about these things. Meanwhile Julia's lured the chap from the Revenue to her bedroom—made a lot of wild promises, I expect, about submitting her returns on time and so on—and had her way of him. Feeling, in consequence, all bright and breezy and full of the joys of spring—you can defer to my experience on that, too, Ragwort—she is now having an invigorating shower. Singing, I dare say.'

'Singing?' said Ragwort, apparently deeply shocked.

'Well, she thinks it's singing, poor grummit. Her voice doesn't actually go up and down much the way it's supposed to, but you can't tell her that. Anyway, it doesn't matter whether she's singing or not, the point is she's having a shower. And the chap from the Revenue is still lying on the bed. Enter Stanford, in a frenzy of jealous passion as aforesaid. It's just got dark, but he doesn't turn the light on, because he wants to creep up on Julia without her knowing. He's a simple-minded sort of chap, the way these executives mostly are, and he thinks whoever's in Julia's bed must be Julia. So he stabs the chap from the Revenue. Exit Stanford. Julia comes out of the shower, still singing, I expect, and goes over to the bed with a view to burbling a few affectionate words at the Revenue chap—"How about a swift drink?" or something. And after a bit she notices there's a lot of blood about the place and the chap seems to be dead. She screams—well, she makes a sort of gargling noise, the way she does with spiders—and goes out into the corridor. Where shortly afterwards someone finds her pootling up and down saying "I say, there seems to be a corpse in my bed." Enter the fuzz and arrest her. And that could all happen in a lot less than ten minutes, so there'd be plenty of time for the agency chap to have it on the wire by quarter past eight London time.'

We considered this Jacobean sequence. Selena relaxed her usual pressure on the accelerator and surrendered to a taxi her position in the fast lane.

'I was under the impression, Cantrip,' said Timothy, 'that you regarded Bruce as the principal suspect — the man Eleanor was talking about.'

'Yes,' said Cantrip, 'but I didn't know then that Julia'd been found in a compromising situation with the American bird. My money's on Stanford now — I don't mind an each-way saver on the Bruce character. Who are you backing, Ragwort?'

'I am not addicted,' said Ragwort, 'to the vice of gambling. But it seems to me that this mistaken identity idea is an unnecessary complication. I would have thought the girl herself was a more likely suspect.'

'The American bird?' said Cantrip. 'Why?'

'Let us by all means accept,' said Ragwort, 'that Julia's relationship with this girl was of pellucid innocence. From Julia's point of view. It will not have escaped your notice, however, that the chain of events which led to Julia being in a state of deshabille on Marylou's bed, with Marylou's head on her shoulder — and our knowledge of anatomy, assisted, in Cantrip's case, by personal recollection, reminds us, in this connection, that Julia's shoulder is an area closely adjacent to Julia's admirable bosom — that each of that chain of events was initiated by Marylou?'

'She only offered to mend Julia's skirt,' said Cantrip.

'Oh, quite so,' said Ragwort. 'There is a perfectly inno-cent explanation for everything she did and it is of course our duty, as Cantrip so rightly points out, to assume, if we possibly can, that it is the correct one. Were we, however, briefly to be dispensed from that charitable obligation —' Ragwort leant back and gazed up at the roof of the car with a very spiritual expression, probably wasted on it.

'Let us grant ourselves,' said Timothy, 'a hypothetical dispensation.'

'Ah well, in that case, as I have already suggested, one might see what she did in a rather different light. And it would then be material to notice that Julia's own behaviour, as described by herself, could have been construed as not wholly discouraging. She had paid the girl compliments. She had kissed her on the nose outside the Casa Rezzonico. She had talked to her about the Renaissance and the Chancery Bar. There had been, in short, nothing in Julia's manner to indicate that she would recoil from an advance with loathing and abhorrence. If, indeed, that is what she would have done.'

'If you mean,' said Selena, stepping rather severely on the accelerator and overtaking the taxi again, 'that Julia is not the sort of woman who would wantonly wound anyone's feelings, particularly those of a girl who had been kind to her and was alone and friendless in a strange country—'

'Of course,' said Ragwort, 'that is exactly what I mean.'

'So the way you see it,' said Cantrip, 'this American bird got a lech for Julia and fancied her chances?'

'I would not have expressed it,' said Ragwort, 'with quite such felicity. But that is the essence of what I am suggesting. And if Marylou is a romantic sort of girl, who might take such an attachment seriously, then it seems not impossible, if she discovered Julia's interest in the man from the Revenue, that she might make use of her dressmaking scissors to dispose of her rival.'

'Doesn't work,' said Cantrip. 'Because whoever did in the chap from the Revenue left things set up so that Julia got clobbered for it. I mean, either they wanted her to get clobbered or they didn't mind her getting clobbered. If the American bird was keen on Julia, she wouldn't have done that.'

'Oh?' said Ragwort, looking at Cantrip in great surprise, 'Oh, don't you think so? I cannot pretend, of course, to your worldly experience; but I would rather have thought it was p ecisely what she might do.'

The tedium of securing a parking space at Heathrow and of the checking-in procedure I have fortunately no need to share with my readers. When it was done with we managed to find a table in one of the airport bars overlooking the area into which passengers from Venice would emerge to find transport.

'Selena,' said Timothy, 'what was it you were saying last night about Eleanor Frostfield?'

'Oh,' said Selena, casually, 'there were one or two things about Eleanor which I thought quite interesting. The first was the excellence of her tax arrangements. She has taken, it appears, every step Julia can think of to minimize the claims of the Revenue on her personal income — every step, that is, except marriage to an impecunious husband. One may perhaps find it a little surprising — or one may not, I leave it entirely to you —' Selena spread one hand in a gesture illustrating the liberality with which she offered us this choice — 'that a woman so admirably advised should allow such a defect in her arrangements to go unremedied. Then there's this matter of the row with Kenneth Dunfermline. The sort of row, as Julia rather perceptively remarks, which usually occurs only between persons on terms of some intimacy. One gathers,' she added, as off-handedly as a Persian cat not noticing the cream, 'that Kenneth is an artist. It is, of course, a notoriously unremunerative profession.'

'I say,' said Cantrip, 'are you suggesting that Eleanor and this Dunfermline chap are married to each other?'

'My dear Cantrip, I am suggesting nothing. I am merely drawing attention to one or two matters of possible interest. If they seem to you to point to any particular conclusion—' she spread both hands, in a gesture of even greater generosity.

'But if they were married,' said Cantrip, 'why were they pretending they'd only just met?'

'I don't think they were,' said Selena. 'Julia assumed they didn't know each other because they weren't sitting together on the plane. Everything after that suggests at least an acquaintance. A marriage, if one of mere fiscal convenience, they might well choose not to publicize; but that's another matter.'

'Even if you were right,' said Timothy, 'would it get us anywhere?'

'No,' said Selena, absentmindedly, 'no, I suppose not. But one can't help thinking, can one, about that conversation between Kenneth and Eleanor, when he seems to have been insisting on carrying on with some plan or other against her wishes. Some plan involving a friend of his. And at the Lido, Ned says that Kenneth has plans to make both their fortunes. It rather sounds, doesn't it, as if Kenneth were engaged in some kind of commercial enterprise which he expected to be profitable—and in which, for some reason, Ned was an essential participant. Of course,' said Selena, in a manner so casual as to suggest that she had almost lost interest in the subject, 'if Eleanor had married Kenneth for reasons of fiscal advantage and he were then, after all, to earn a large sum of money, the effect on her tax position would be quite catastrophic.'

The suggestion that Eleanor Frostfield had done away with Ned to safeguard the marginal tax advantage of a hypothetical marriage to Kenneth Dunfermline may seem to my readers, seeing it in the coldness of print, too fanciful to be entertained for a moment. My readers, however, have not been exposed to the oblique seductiveness of Selena's advocacy.

'My dear Selena,' said Timothy, 'it is a most attractive

and ingenious hypothesis. It might even, I suppose, be right. But would you care to estimate my chances of persuading the Italian police that it is probable? No, Selena, it won't do. Remember, we don't have to find out who did the murder—all that matters as far as we're concerned is satisfying the police that Julia didn't. But if I do have to start suggesting alternative suspects, I'd rather it was someone reasonably obvious.'

'By all means,' said Selena. 'But there isn't anyone obvious.'

'Oh surely,' said Timothy. 'Statistics show, I gather, that if one is going to be murdered it will probably be by one's spouse or lover. Presumably there's no doubt, in Ned's case, that that means Kenneth Dunfermline? It's difficult to imagine any other reason why two such dissimilar young men should be travelling together.'

The possibility that Kenneth had committed the crime had long since occurred to me. But I had misgivings: Venice is a sophisticated and cosmopolitan city—her police force, I felt, would not take a less than worldly view of Ned's connection with Kenneth, nor would they be unfamiliar with the criminal statistics. I feared, if they did not regard Kenneth as the obvious suspect, that they must have some excellent reason not to suspect him at all.

The public address system announced the arrival of the flight from Venice. We began to give closer attention to the stream of returning passengers.

'They won't be out for ages,' said Cantrip. 'They'll have to hang about for their luggage to come through on that turntable thing.'

But it was only a few minutes later that we caught sight of a rather subdued little group which seemed to correspond to Julia's description of the Art Lovers: a handsome, middle-aged woman, whose figure had that unyielding symmetry achieved only by a substantial corset; a muscular young man, sombre of feature; a pretty girl with pale blonde hair; and, close beside her, another young man, square-shouldered, who gave the impression of a certain aggressiveness towards the world.

'I say,' asked Cantrip, 'do you think that's them?'

'Certainly,' said Selena. 'Those labels on their hand luggage — they're the same kind as the travel agents gave Julia. But where's the Major?'

'I think,' said Timothy, 'that the Major must have undertaken to act as porter. If he's collecting all their suitcases from the conveyor belt, that would explain how the rest of them have got through Customs so quickly. It looks as if they're coming up here to wait for him.'

The Art Lovers came up the staircase and through the door of the bar. At our first unobstructed view of the American girl, Ragwort gave what sounded almost like a whistle. We regarded him with surprise: Ragwort is notoriously unsusceptible.

'The dress,' said Ragwort, 'is Yves St Laurent. The shoes and handbag are Gucci. The scarf is Hermès. And if that young woman,' said Ragwort, admiration for her elegance contending with puritan disapproval of its cost, 'is wearing a penny less than six hundred pounds on her back, I'll be — I shall be very much surprised.'

The Art Lovers sat down several tables away, too far for us to hear any conversation between them. Not that it would have been informative: apart from telling Stanford what they would like from the bar — at any rate, he went off there and returned with a tray of drinks — they hardly exchanged a word: it was plainly not a festive gathering.

Better placed than they for this purpose, we perceived before they did the arrival in the area below of a tall man pushing a loaded baggage trolley: he was deeply sun-tanned; he had a white moustache; he was wearing Bermuda shorts.

'Ah,' said Cantrip, 'there's the Major.'

The scholar must miss no occasion for acquiring knowl-

edge, no matter how suddenly and briefly it arises.
'Quick, Cantrip,' I said, 'get down before them and see if
you can get their addresses from the luggage labels. Pretend you think your suitcase might be on the Major's
trolley.'

For any enterprise savouring of the illicit, Cantrip is the
man. He did not pause to argue the proprieties. By the
time the Major's waving hand had attracted the attention
of his fellow Art Lovers, Cantrip, slipping like a needle
through the crowd, was already crouched beside the
trolley.

The Major said something. Cantrip said something.
Watching, we followed without difficulty the gist of their
remarks: the Major was telling Cantrip that his suitcase
was not on the trolley; Cantrip, with a nicely judged
impression of imperfect sobriety, was insisting on making
sure.

The first of the Art Lovers to join them was Kenneth
Dunfermline, who showed a perfect indifference to their
argument. He took the suitcase offered him by the Major
and walked rather slowly away. He was a powerfully built
young man, and the suitcase not unduly large: the weight
of it, I thought, unless filled with granite, could not alone
account for his dragging step and the weariness of his
movements. But whether it was grief alone or some yet
greater burden that weighed so heavily on the sculptor's
muscular shoulders — that was a question beyond Scholarship to determine.

The next to reach the trolley was Eleanor Frostfield.
Again, though we could not hear what was said, Eleanor's
opinion of drunken young men who had mislaid their luggage, and apparently could not even remember whether
it was a pigskin suitcase or a canvas holdall, was entirely
clear to us. Cantrip, looking apologetic, persisted in his
search.

Eventually, though glancing back suspiciously, the

Major lifted two suitcases from the trolley and escorted Eleanor towards the taxi rank. Cantrip, completing his researches, sensibly continued to wander in apparent search for his luggage. He was scribbling surreptitiously on the cuff of his shirt — a sacrifice on the part of the *homme bien soigné* which might not, I think, have been made by Ragwort.

The return of the Major from the taxi rank coincided with the Americans' arrival beside the trolley. Stanford was already carrying a valise, presumably containing his wife's Venetian acquisitions; but he lifted, without apparent difficulty, two large pigskin cases and carried them towards the exit. Marylou lingered to say something, no doubt a few words of thanks and farewell, to the Major. Then she followed her husband. The only luggage remaining on the trolley was a large, rather battered suitcase and a small canvas holdall: the Major, after a few moments, picked them up and walked briskly away. Cantrip returned to the bar.

'Did you get all the addresses?' I asked anxiously.

'Yes,' said Cantrip. 'And I saw something jolly funny, too. Bet you can't guess.'

'Don't let us guess,' said Selena. 'Tell us.'

'You know that holdall thing the Major went off with? Well, it's not his. It belongs to the Revenue chap.'

'How very odd,' said Selena. 'Are you sure?'

'Of course I'm sure. It had his name on the label. Edward Watson, with the same address as the sculptor chap. And what I think is,' said Cantrip, striking an uncharacteristic note of high morality, 'when a chap's been done in, it's a bit off for some other chap to start nicking his luggage.'

CHAPTER 8

Reflecting on the curious conduct of the Major, justly condemned by Cantrip as unbecoming to an officer and gentleman, we made our way to the airport restaurant and there ordered lunch. Selena, as she had promised, read to us the most recent letter from Julia.

> My room at the Cytherea.
> Monday night.

Dearest Selena,

I do not for a moment question the excellence of your advice — it is as religion with me. I do rather wish, however, that I had asked you just how long one is supposed to keep up this hopes, dreams and aspirations business. You will recall that I have, effectively, only eight days in Venice, of which four have now elapsed. Should it turn out that the process of lulling into a false sense of security requires a minimum of a fortnight — but no, if it were so, you would have told me.

What I mean is that a point presumably arrives at which one stops admiring the young man's fine soul and noble intellect — or rather, of course, still admires them tremendously, but admits that one's admiration is tinged with just the faintest *soupçon* of carnality. And the question which perplexes me is how I am to know, in relation to the enchanting Ned, when that point has been reached.

The trouble is that in spite of my efforts I feel he may already have some suspicion of the nature of my interest in him. He will have become accustomed, in the course of his distasteful employment, to thinking the worst of everyone. It would, moreover, be typical of the practice of the Revenue to let me spend a great deal of time and effort admiring his soul and intellect without intending it to do me any ultimate good. If my fears on this point were to be well-founded, then, it seems to me, I might as well abandon subtlety altogether and adopt the more forthright and vigorous approach recommended by the dramatist Shakespeare. On the other hand, I would not wish to prejudice, by precipitate action, any good I may already have done myself by my restraint.

This morning I began to wonder if it might not be sensible, rather than spend a holiday altogether unenlivened by the pleasures of the flesh, to try my luck with the quite pretty waiter who brings my breakfast. There is something in his manner which suggests that his favours would be less hard to come by than those of the enchanting Ned: one would not, I think, have to talk much about his soul.

And yet afterwards, as we travelled peacefully along the Brenta towards Padua, with the wake of the boat tumbling the reeds at the waterside, I was so moved by the beauty of the surroundings and of Ned's profile that I felt I would willingly devote the whole week, even if in vain, to undivided pursuit of him. Well, Selena, you will mock me again for being incurably sentimental.

The purpose of the excursion down the Brenta, from the point of view of the Art Lover, is to observe and appreciate the development of the Palladian villa. In the sixteenth century, it seems, all the Venetians decided to go and live in the country. This was due, I suppose, to the republication, as part of the Renaissance, of Horace's Epistles, in which the poet speaks highly of the simple rustic life. Feeling that if they were going to live the simple life they ought to do the thing properly, the Venetians looked round for someone to build them villas as similar as possible to that occupied by Horace. Andrea Palladio, therefore, then a rising young architect, went out and bought a book by the Roman author Vitruvius, also republished as part of the Renaissance, and read the chapter on building villas. That, at least, is what he meant to read: as it happens, misled by the obscurity of the Latin, he actually read the chapter on building temples. This explains why the Veneto is full of villas looking more or less like the Parthenon, with the addition of the usual domestic offices.

From what one might call the social point of view, the day was not a success. Whenever I managed to draw Ned away from the main body of Art Lovers, with a view to admiring his soul and intellect, the Major would appear suddenly out of nowhere, crying 'Jumping Jiminy, this place is quite something, isn't it?' In the end I abandoned the unequal struggle.

Marylou's husband still regards me with an unfriendly eye and seemed to be steering her away from me — I was hardly able to talk to her at all. I was obliged, on the other hand, to talk a great deal to Eleanor, who still has hopes of having a row with Graziella. She had two complaints about the excursion: first, that we had not visited enough villas; second, that we had arrived too late in Padua to appreciate the artistic glories of that city. I pointed out in vain that to remedy either of these shortcomings would of necessity aggravate the other. To distract her from any direct conflict with Graziella, I had to keep talking about the Trade Descriptions Act all the way back to Venice. This was rather wearing: it might have been less so if I actually knew anything about the Trade Descriptions Act.

The Major's conversation at dinner followed, to begin with, its usual pattern, save that his anecdotes tend now to be couched in the form of useful advice, designed to assist me in various difficult situations: 'The thing to do, if you're stranded on shore after hours in Valletta —' 'What you want to remember, if you're running low on water in the Western Desert and Johnny Arab's getting a bit edgy —' I attended as little as possible, and went back to worrying about Desdemona. In certain predicaments, I may well regret this.

Towards the end of the meal, however, he raised an entirely different subject. Leaning towards me and shielding his mouth, as one wishing to speak in confidence, he asked me if I remembered the French chappie Graziella had been talking about. He proved to be alluding to the late King Henri III of France, mentioned by Graziella as having visited the Villa Malcontenta on his return from Poland in 1583. She had further mentioned that his reign had been of short duration, attributing this to the aversion felt by his subjects to his effeminate habits.

'Don't know if you followed,' said the Major, 'what she said about his effeminate habits?'

'I gathered,' I said, 'that the practices which attracted an unfavourable press consisted of something more than an excessive use of eau de Cologne on the handkerchief.'

'Well—' the Major appeared embarrassed. 'Word to the wise and so forth. Nod's as good as a wink. No names, no pack drill.'

'Yes?' I said, trying to be helpful.

'Saw quite a lot of that sort of thing in the Army, I'm afraid. Courts Martial and so forth. Got to know the signs. Well—just between you and me and the gatepost, m'dear, I wouldn't be surprised if young Ned over there was a bit that way. No names, no pack drill—don't want to say anything against the lad. Just—not the sort of chap I'd want to share a tent with. Hope you don't mind my mentioning it, m'dear.'

I was not unduly surprised by this suggestion: it is almost invariably the first thing said about men with profiles by men without profiles. Indeed, it is a benevolent dispensation of Providence that those who express most dread of an unorthodox advance are usually those whom Nature has most effectively protected from any risk of one. Still, the remark placed me in a dilemma. Principle required me to say that it was, if true, no matter for criticism; expediency, on the other hand, urged me to impress on the Major my invincible prudishness. Seeking an answer which should reconcile the two:

'Unless you suppose me,' I said coldly, 'to have designs of some sort on the young man, I cannot imagine why you should think the question of any interest to me. I would very much prefer not to discuss the matter.'

'Sorry, m'dear,' said the Major. 'Just thought — well, thought you might be getting a bit smitten with him. Wouldn't like to see you pick a wrong 'un.'

'My dear Bob,' I said, raising a Ragwort-like eyebrow, 'I am most obliged to you for your concern. But I am not a swooning adolescent — I am a grown-up woman in practice at the English Bar.'

I was rather pleased with this, since there is, after all, a sense in which it is actually true. The Major was abject in his apologies. Allowing myself to be only somewhat mollified, I excused myself from coffee and came back to my room, to enjoy in privacy the pleasures of writing to you. The others having already withdrawn, the Major was left to entertain Eleanor Frostfield. You may think this a bit hard on Eleanor; but if she ever finds herself running low on water in the Western Desert, at least it won't be my fault if she doesn't know what to do about it.

I shall not post this tomorrow morning but shall wait to see if anything of interest occurs during the excursion to Verona. We had the choice between the full day excursion tomorrow, which includes Asolo and Vicenza, and the afternoon excursion on Friday. Hearing Ned sign on for the longer one, I naturally did likewise. Unfortunately, the Major has done the same. Still, perhaps the Major will miss the coach somewhere and be left stranded. Or perhaps Ned and I will both miss the coach somewhere and be left stranded together — that would be even better.

*

'I say,' said Cantrip, 'you don't think the Revenue chap
made a pass at the Major and the Major, in defence of his
honour—'

'No,' said Ragwort.

'Oh, all right,' said Cantrip.

> Terrace of the Cytherea.
> Nearly lunch-time on Wednesday.

It has been known in times past, Selena, when others
have spoken disparagingly of men, suggesting that they
are as a sex altogether worthless and contemptible, for me
to offer a word or two in their defence. I have been heard
to say tolerantly that some of my best friends are men,
though if I had a daughter I might not wish her to marry
one. Not any more, Selena. Henceforth, when the subject
of men arises, look for me among those most absolute in
condemnation. They are a deplorable sex. Let me tell you
what happened on the excursion to Verona; and what
happened afterwards.

Graziella, for some reason, was not available to accompany the excursion: we were dependent for guidance on
the coach driver, who did not feel the same anxiety for
our intellectual improvement: he confined himself, in
each of the places we visited, to setting us down in the
main square and telling us at what hour he intended to
take us up again.

It fell to me, in these circumstances, to act as interpreter for Ned and the Major, neither of whom speaks
any Italian. I myself am not the linguist you are kind
enough to think me; but I can ask the way with
reasonable conviction and usually understand at least
some of the answer. Moreover, by the grace of Ragwort, I
was in possession of guide books to all the towns we were
to visit, so that I was also able to act as guide.

At Asolo I did rather well. The foreign Art Lovers,

despite the heat, went rushing off up the hill to look at the Castle; but I, from my perusal of the guide book, was able to tell my companions that we were already in the very square in which the poet Browning had been inspired to write his celebrated poem 'Pippa Passes'— the one, if my memory serves me, in which there was joy in the morning.

'This charming and picturesque little town,' I said, 'due, no doubt, to being built on a steep hillside, has evidently escaped the attention of developers since the Middle Ages. We may safely assume it to be much as it was in Browning's day. It seems probable, therefore, that he wrote the poem to which I have referred on the terrace of that rather attractive café, refreshing his Muse, I expect, with a Campari soda or something like that. By doing likewise, we may be able to recreate something of the experience which inspired his immortal lines.'

In Vicenza I did rather badly. If you ever happen, Selena, to be in the main square of Vicenza and want to get from there to the Olympic Theatre, final masterpiece of the architect Palladio, do not rely on Ragwort's guide book. If you do, you will find yourself, before you discover your mistake, halfway down the road to Milan, trying to explain what it was about the Church of Saints Felix and Fortunate that made you think it worth a detour. You will also find yourself having to walk two miles back in the blazing heat to get to the Theatre. If you were not an Art Lover, you might decide at that stage to give the Theatre a miss; but my conscience would not stretch so far — besides, I had told them we were going there.

*

'My guide books,' said Ragwort, driving his fork rather crossly into one of the scampi which the airport restaurant had obligingly just unfrozen for him, 'all contain excellent maps, all perfectly clear and accurate and straightforward. If Julia can't tell the difference between left and right —'

'No, of course not,' said Selena kindly, 'not your fault in the least,. Ragwort.'

*

After all this, the enchanting Ned refused to be pleased with the Theatre. It is a most attractive building, designed with great ingenuity to persuade one, when in the auditorium, that one is in an open air theatre somewhere in ancient Greece. I invited my companions to admire this masterpiece of deception. Ned declined.

'I don't like it,' he said. 'I don't like looking down streets that aren't there. I don't like looking at the ceiling and thinking it's the sky. I don't like all this make-believe.' There is no pleasing some people.

In Verona I did superbly. By that time I had worked out the strategy for the successful guide. It's no use looking through the guide book for something interesting and then trying to get there: it may turn out to be miles away. No, the thing to do is to discover where one is to start with and then find something in the guide book which says that it's interesting — much inconvenience may thus be avoided.

By looking round a bit during lunch I established that we were in a restaurant near the corner of the Via Oberdan. Identifying the place on the map, I was pleased to see that there were several blobs of brown colouring in close proximity: brown blobs indicate artistic significance. There were, it is true, other blobs of brown some inches away. Pursuant, however, to the policy mentioned above, I ignored them.

After lunch, therefore, I was able with perfect confidence to lead my companions to the Piazza dei Signori and the Piazza dell' Erbe and to point out to them those architectural features of the Palazzo del Capitano and the Palazzo dei Ragione which the guide book considered deserving of attention. The information I gave them may not, I admit, have been in every detail entirely accurate,

for the guide book was in Italian: my knowledge of Italian
architectural terms is sketchy, you might say non-
existent, as is also indeed my knowledge of English architectural terms. My translation was therefore a trifle
emancipated.

We continued to the Cathedral, where I had a further
inspiration. Verona lies in a more or less semi-circular
loop of river and we had set out from the approximate
centre—from the point, I mean, equidistant from each
point on the bank: according to the laws of geometry, it
seemed to me, we should be able, by walking along the
bank and taking, when we chose to do so, a turning
perpendicular to it, to return, without retracing our
steps, to our point of departure.

Knowing how infrequently in the real world things
obey the laws of mathematics or any other logical system,
I would not, perhaps, but for the wine we had drunk at
lunch, have ventured to put this theory to any empirical
test; but Verona showed a proper respect for the laws of
geometry. Leaving the Cathedral, we walked some distance along the bank, observing on our left the grandeur
of the view across the river and on our right a row of
antique shops, of professional interest to the Major; then,
turning off at right angles to the river, we proceeded, so
far as possible, in a straight line; and found ourselves, just
as Euclid would have expected, back in the main square.

I was astonished at my success. I had taken my companions on exactly the tour I had planned and had
thrown in for good measure the Churches of Saint
Anastasia and Saint Nicholas, which had presented
themselves in our path. In the latter, I had even managed
to identify the Madonna and Child by Tiepolo, highly
spoken of by the guide book, but treated by the Church
with a rather cavalier lack of distinction. It seemed unwise to attempt to improve on my achievement.

'You will observe,' I said, 'that this spacious and

elegant square is amply furnished with open-air cafés, in which the traveller may find rest and refreshment. Shall we avail ourselves of this circumstance?'

'If you'll excuse me, m'dear,' said the Major, 'I think I'll just pop back and have another shufti at those antique shops.'

'Are you sure you won't get lost?' I asked. Much as I would have liked to lose the Major, I felt responsible for him.

'Trust an old campaigner to get back to base,' said the Major cheerfully.

And off he went, leaving me alone with Ned. We sat down together, under the shade of an awning, in one of the cafés previously mentioned.

The time had come, I felt, to talk about Catullus: Verona, you will recall, is the poet's birthplace. If I could not manage, by judicious quotation from the most ardent of lyric poets, to indicate the warmth of my feelings, there was, I thought, no hope for me. With no need on this subject to resort to the guide book—his work was the chief comfort of my susceptible adolescence—I spoke sympathetically of his attachment to Clodia, severely of her unkindness. Ned chose to defend her.

'I don't see why you think,' he said, 'that she ought to have been so grateful for having all this poetry written to her. I expect your friend Catullus got more fun out of writing it than she did out of reading it—she'd probably rather have been taken out to dinner or something.' And more to the like effect.

'Ah well,' I said at last. 'It is natural that you should take her side. Your own experience, no doubt, is all of being the object of passion, rather than of suffering it.'

'I don't know why you suppose,' he said, looking down demurely in such a manner as to display the full luxury of his lovely eyelashes, 'that I am the object of so much admiration. Or that I am always indifferent to it.'

The reappearance at this stage of the Major, who could perfectly well have gone on wandering round antique shops for another half-hour, seemed singularly ill-timed. If the maps he had purchased, supposed to be of anti-quarian interest, turned out to be fakes, it would be, I felt, a deserved consequence of his over-hasty selection.

'Don't let me interrupt,' said the Major. 'Can see you two were having a good old chinwag.'

'I was complaining,' I said, 'of the way I am treated by the Inland Revenue.'

'Julia doesn't think,' said Ned, 'that we are fair to her.'

'Oh no,' I said, 'I didn't say that. I could never say, Ned, that you were anything but fair. What I am com-plaining of is not your fairness: it is your coldness, your lack of feeling, your indifference to human suffering.'

'Ah well,' said the Major, 'only doing your job, of course. I'm sure the little lady doesn't mean it personally, do you, m'dear?'

'I'm afraid she does,' said Ned. 'But I hope to persuade her to think more kindly of us.'

My confidence in Catullus seemed vindicated, for this was not a remark, you will surely agree, Selena, which a well-brought-up young man could make without intend-ing some encouragement. Nor, as you shall hear, was this the only cause given me for optimism.

We continued to sit in the café, reviving ourselves with coffee for our homeward journey. The Major was greatly pleased with his maps, and would have liked to show them to us; but they had been carefully rolled and wrapped and he felt it unwise to undo them. Fearing that the maps would put him in mind of some incident in his military career, I agreed hastily that it would be most imprudent.

'Julia,' asked Ned, after a few minutes, 'did you know you had a smudge of ash on your cheek?'

'I didn't know,' I answered. 'But I readily believe it.' If

one smokes French cigarettes, it is usual, after an hour or two, to get a certain amount of ash on one's face.

'If you'll excuse me—' he said. He rose from his chair and took a clean handkerchief from his pocket. Then he leant over me, and, resting his left hand lightly on my shoulder, gently brushed the ash from my cheek.

This produced in me, as you will imagine, Selena, a passionate agitation, gravely affecting my breathing and heart beat. Yet it was of the most pleasant and hopeful kind, for I could not suppose that any young man, unless utterly heartless and lost to all sense of shame, could conduct himself in such a way towards a woman whose advances were unacceptable.

'Excuse me, m'dear,' said the Major. 'Just off to inspect the jolly old ablutions.'

'When we get back to Venice,' I said, taking advantage of his temporary absence, 'instead of paying the exorbitant prices which they charge in the bar of the Cytherea, why don't you come and have an aperitif in my room? I've got some brandy I bought in the duty-free shop.' If I had misconstrued his behaviour, I thought, he could always say that he didn't like brandy before dinner.

'I'd love to,' answered Ned. 'How kind of you, Julia.'

You will imagine with what impatience I now looked forward to our return; how bitterly, though silently, I cursed the late arrival of the coach driver; with what equal fervour, though in equal silence, I urged him to drive back at all speed along the *autostrada*. Nor, during the drive to Venice or our brief journey by boat to our hotel, was there anything in Ned's smiles or amiable manner to warn me of the unspeakable treachery he was proposing to commit.

We arrived at the landing stage of the Cytherea.

'How about a snifter in the bar?' said the Major.

'You're forgetting, Bob,' said the enchanting Ned, sharing between us a smile of angelic sweetness, 'Julia has kindly invited us to drink brandy in her room.'

O Perfidy, thy name is man. They are, as I have said, a deplorable sex, and never again shall you hear me speak well of them. If I could think kindly of one, it would be of a young man of obliging disposition, such as Cantrip. Cantrip, you may say, has his faults; but at least he can be prevailed on to engage in a health-giving frolic without expecting one to talk for weeks on end about his soul. Cantrip, so far as I am aware, has never claimed to have such a thing.

*

'I jolly well do have a soul,' said Cantrip.

'Well, don't tell Julia,' said Selena. 'It'll only upset her.'

*

I am old enough, I hope, to bear philosophically a reverse in the lists of Aphrodite; but to be obliged, in addition, to offer the Major the hospitality of my room, not to speak of large quantities of my duty-free brandy, was more than I could easily endure. By the time the long day was over, I was too shattered in spirit to take up my pen to write to you: I sought consolation in the Finances Act.

After a morning of looking at churches, I have returned to the Cytherea for lunch. I shall have the company, it seems, of the beautiful but perfidious Ned—I have just seen him coming across the bridge from the annexe. Let him not look to me for kind words or compliments—I shall upbraid him for every infamy committed by his Department since the institution of income tax.

In a mood, as I have indicated, of the most bitter misandry, this leaves me

Yours, as always,
Julia.

'Julia is being unreasonable,' said Ragwort. 'The young man gave her no encouragement beyond mere civility.'

'There is,' said Selena, 'a postscript.'

Wednesday evening.

The deed is done—Clarissa lives. No time to write more.

Yours, as always,
Julia.

'Who,' said Cantrip, 'is Clarissa?'

'Clarissa,' said Ragwort sadly, 'is the eponymous heroine of the celebrated novel by Mr Richardson. The phrase used by Julia is that, if my recollection serves me, in which the villain Lovelace announces his conquest of her long-defended virtue.'

'I say,' said Cantrip, 'do you mean Julia's scored with the man from the Revenue?'

'It would seem so,' said Timothy. 'I hope that's not going to complicate things. They're calling my flight—I'd better go. I'll ring you tomorrow, Selena, as soon as I know anything definite.'

I hope my farewells to Timothy did not seem unduly off-hand. All my goodwill went with him; but I was a little preoccupied—I had remembered something curious about the news from Italy.

CHAPTER 9

Between the best of friends a difference of opinion may arise. So it was with Selena and myself on the matter of Sunday. It seemed to me plainly convenient that I should spend the day at Selena's. Thus Timothy, when he telephoned, would have the immediate benefit of my advice.

'I'm sorry, Hilary,' said Selena. 'I have an Opinion to write on the Settled Land Act. I can't spend the day in cooking and idle gossip.'

She was quite wrong in supposing that she would have been put to any trouble for my entertainment: the tastes of the scholar are simple to the point of austerity. An omelette of some kind for lunch, with a salad and a few new potatoes; for dinner, a plain grilled sole, perhaps with a caper sauce—

'No,' said Selena. 'Moreover, I have plans for the evening which do not admit of the presence of a third party.'

In that case, naturally, there was nothing more to be said. Selena has an amiable arrangement for the weekends with a young colleague of mine: I would not for the world encroach on the pleasures of either. I spent Sunday, therefore, in Islington, conversing with the cats and reading back copies of *The Times*: both, in their way, instructive occupations.

Selena telephoned me at half past six. Timothy's news, so far as it went, was, she felt, satisfactory. He had not yet seen Julia—accommodation had been found for her in the little resort of Chioggia, on the other side of the Lagoon—but would be dining with her that evening. His client, having chosen to make the journey from Cyprus by sea, had become unwell during the journey and had fortunately not yet recovered.

'Fortunately?' I said, with a touch of severity.

'One wishes him, of course, no harm.' The smoothness of Selena's voice was not impaired by the intervening telephone wires. 'It does seem convenient, however, that Timothy is free for the time being to pursue his enquiries on Julia's behalf without having to initiate his client into the mysteries of Schedule 5 to the Finance Act 1975.'

'Have his enquiries made any progress?'

'He hasn't managed to see Graziella yet or talk to the police. But he's been in touch with a man at the British Consulate who seems to know something of the matter. So far as one can tell at present, there's nothing solid against Julia at all. It's just that she made a rather unfortunate first impression on the police. They knew from the start, you see, about her exchanges with the young man from the Revenue: the whole affair was apparently common knowledge among the staff of the Cytherea, from the management to the chambermaids. So when they began to question her and she said she'd never heard of him, they found her attitude suspicious.'

'I can see that they might,' I said. 'Why did she say that she'd never heard of him?'

'My dear Hilary, it's quite understandable. They obviously told her that they were enquiring into the death by violence of a Mr Edward Watson. It doesn't immediately occur to one that a person referred to as Edward is someone one knows as Ned. And Julia, naturally, wouldn't know his surname.'

'Would you care,' I asked, 'to justify the adverb?'

'How could she have known his surname? Eleanor Frostfield doesn't seem to have mentioned it when she introduced them. How do you suggest that she could afterwards have discovered it? Would you expect her, in the middle of telling the young man about his beautiful eyelashes and quoting Catullus, suddenly to ask his surname? Going on, perhaps, to demand such further particulars as his place of birth, his mother's maiden name and the number of his passport? Of course not. Still less can you imagine that Julia would stoop, in search of such information, to questioning their mutual acquaintances or prying through the young man's correspondence. My dear Hilary.' Her voice seemed to melt in a delicate mixture of amusement and reproach: an effect, I am told, which has caused a number of her opponents, realizing the absurdity of their submissions, to settle hastily over the luncheon adjournment on terms favourable to her client.

'My dear Selena,' I said, 'you quite persuade me that no woman of breeding and refinement could be expected to know the surname of any young man whom she was trying to seduce. I hope that Timothy will be equally successful with the Italian police. Was there anything else that made a bad impression on them?'

'Well—' said Selena. 'They seem to have got rather excited about Julia's Finance Act. I'm sorry, Hilary, I'll have to go—there's someone at the door.'

I saw no prospect, until I knew why Julia's Finance Act had disturbed the equanimity of the Italian police, of giving my attention to the concept of *causa*. On the following morning, therefore, I proceeded directly to 62 New Square. Not pausing to announce myself in the Clerks' Room, I climbed the stone staircase to the second floor. Being occupied for the purposes of their profession by the younger members of the Chambers, the second floor is commonly referred to as the Nursery. The Nursery comprises three rooms, of varying sizes: I shall not delay my narrative to explain the finely balanced considerations of decorum, convenience and seniority by virtue of which Selena has the small one to herself, Ragwort and Cantrip share the large one and Timothy occupies the one of intermediate size.

For conversation, their natural tendency is to gather in the large one. I found Selena already there, repeating to Ragwort and Cantrip the news from Timothy which she had given me on the previous evening.

'Selena,' I said, 'what's all this about the Finance Act?'

'Ah yes,' said Selena. 'The Finance Act. It appears that a copy of this year's Finance Act, inscribed with Julia's name and professional address, was found a few feet away from the corpse.'

'Oh, strewth,' said Cantrip.

'Dear me,' said Ragwort.

'The Italian police,' continued Selena, 'with childish naïveté, took this to be a clue. As your own more sophisticated minds will immediately perceive, it is, of course, nothing of the kind. One cannot infer Julia's presence from the presence of her Finance Act.'

'Indeed not,' said Ragwort. 'Any more than one could infer, from the presence last Thursday fortnight in Lower Liversidge County Court of a copy of Woodfall on Landlord and Tenant, clearly inscribed with my name, to indicate that it was my property, purchased out of my own resources, that I myself was appearing before that learned and august tribunal; or that I was absent from London; or that, being in London, I had no need of the volume in question for the purpose of advising my clients. It can merely be inferred that certain members of these Chambers—'

'I said I was sorry,' said Cantrip. 'There's no need to keep on about it.'

'That certain members of these Chambers,' continued Ragwort, 'whose names I shall not mention because they have apologized and I, as was my duty, have forgiven them, have very little notion, when it comes to books, of the difference between meum and tuum.'

'Exactly,' said Selena. Cantrip, overcome by the joy of Ragwort's forgiveness, said nothing.

'Have you,' I asked, 'heard anything more from Julia?'

'As a matter of fact,' said Selena, 'there was another letter this morning. I was just going to read it.'

> Terrace of the Cytherea.
> Thursday evening.

Dearest Selena,

My letters to you—are they mere ephemera, stop-gap economies for telephone calls? Or are they to serve, in half a century's time, when you are retired from high judicial office and I, too improvident to afford retirement, still pursuing the vain chimera of paying the last year's income tax, am advising my clients from the comfort of a Bath chair — are they to serve then as a journal or memoir, when we seek diversion in reminiscence? If so, it would be absurd, though nothing I now write can reach London before me, to end the correspondence with yesterday's letter. The postscript, it is true, will tell us that I had my way. But when you ask me how I achieved it, I shall have forgotten; and when I ask you whether I enjoyed it, you will be unable to remind me; and when we say to each other that surely there was some curious and interesting sequel, but cannot quite remember what it was, there will be nothing to recall it to our ageing memories. For the avoidance of which and the resolution of all doubts, I shall continue to write until tomorrow evening.

My postscript may have occasioned you some surprise, following, as I recollect, a passage in which I spoke with some bitterness of Ned's behaviour and announced my intention to upbraid him severely. On the way to lunch, however, I happened to call to mind some advice once given me by my Aunt Regina, who told me that the surest way to a man's affections was to let him think he knew more about something than you did. It seemed worth trying — my Aunt Regina must be regarded as an authority on such matters, for she has had four husbands; though I cannot actually recall her thinking that any of them knew better than she did on any subject whatever.

On the previous evening, as I have told you, I had sought consolation in the Finance Act: Schedule 7 seemed a suitable subject for Ned to know more about than I did. Finding, as I had hoped, that we were the only Art Lovers present at lunch, I turned the conversation to the question of income tax.

'I suppose,' I said, 'if Eleanor is hoping to persuade your Department that she is in Venice for business pur-

poses, she might as well take the matter to its logical conclusion and claim relief under Schedule 7 of this year's
Act on the proportion of her earnings attributable to
work done abroad.'

'Yes,' he said, 'but she'd have to spend at least thirty
days of the year working abroad.'

'Oh,' I said, 'I expect she could manage that. She'd
have to remember, of course, that she could only count
days devoted to the duties of her employment. If she spent
a week overseas and rested on the Sabbath, only six days
would count.'

'No, Julia,' he said, 'you're thinking of the Bill. They
amended it on its way through Parliament. If you're
abroad for at least seven consecutive days which taken as
a whole are substantially devoted to the duties of your
employment, they all count, even if you take a day off.'
This was said with such charming modesty and so little
arrogance at finding me in error that I almost felt a
qualm of conscience; but I remembered his treachery of
the previous day—my heart was hardened and I kept my
course.

'Nonsense,' I said firmly. 'The Act says that a qualify-
ing day is a day substantially devoted to the performance
of the duties of the employment. What you mean is, I
suppose, that your Department has decided to make an
extra-statutory concession, legislating by way of Press
release. To the burden of penal taxation there is now
added the tyranny of secret law-making—as it is, when
one cannot advise one's clients without ferreting through
correspondence columns for proclamations of Revenue
policy.'

My indignation almost caused me to forget the business
in hand; but Ned brought back my attention to it by
repeating, rather crossly, that the day-off-abroad pro-
vision was not embodied in a Press release but in the Act
itself.

'My dear Ned,' I replied, 'I am prepared to bet you a bottle of wine that it isn't.'

'By all means,' he said. 'But I'll have to wait for my wine until we get back to England. We can't settle it without a Finance Act.'

'We can settle it right away,' I said. 'I have the Finance Act in my room.'

And thus it was that the beautiful Ned returned with me across the bridge to the annexe.

It is a great advantage in an enterprise of this nature to know that one's room will have been cleaned and tidied. How often has some promising pursuit been brought to a standstill by my recalling the chaos and squalor of my bedroom? I looked with gratitude, therefore, as we went through the entrance-way to the annexe, at the little group of chambermaids, as pretty as a flock of angels in some Renaissance painting, who gather there to rest in the afternoon. They smiled at me, I thought, with an eye of complicity, as if knowing and approving my purpose. We went up the staircase and came to my room.

'Sit down,' I said, 'while I find my Finance Act.'

There being nothing else to sit on — the chair by the dressing table was occupied by a pile of clothes — he sat down on the bed, on the edge nearer to the door. I was careful, having found my Finance Act, to hand it to him from the other side of the bed, thus drawing him down from a perpendicular to a horizontal position — lying, that is to say, across the bed, rather than sitting on the edge of it. I sat down beside him on the edge further from the door.

'Show me,' I said, 'this mythical amendment.'

It is hardly possible, when two people are sitting on the same bed and trying to read the same copy of the Finance Act, for all physical contact to be avoided. I, indeed, made no attempt to avoid it; but neither, it seemed to me, did Ned. This gave me some encouragement   one would not wish, as a woman of principle, to impose attentions actually distasteful.

The advice of yourself and my Aunt Regina, excellent as both had proved to be, could take me, I felt, no further—it was time to put complete reliance in that given by the dramatist Shakespeare. Leaning across Ned's shoulders, I rested my hand on the area of the bed which lay on the further side of them. So that when, in due course, he looked up from the statute to say, with forgivable complacency, 'Here you are, Julia—sub-paragraph (b) of paragraph 2 of the Schedule,' he found himself, as it were, encircled.

'Why, you are perfectly right,' I said, 'and I owe you a bottle of wine. But I hope you are too kind to insist on immediate payment.'

'Oh, Julia,' he said, opening his eyes very wide with reproach, 'how can you be so shameless?'

'Ah, Ned,' I answered, 'because you are so beautiful.' And met with no further resistance.

*

'It just shows one,' said Ragwort sadly, 'how dangerous it is to gamble. Even when one knows one is right.'

'Come off it,' said Cantrip. 'Going off with Julia to her bedroom in the middle of the afternoon—you can't tell me he didn't think she'd make a pass.'

'Quite so,' said Selena. 'But the charge is not one of ravishment.'

*

Delicacy precludes any more detailed account of the afternoon. This letter may be read in the presence of the virtuous and lovely Ragwort—one would not like to make him blush. That is to say, one would like very much to do so—nothing could be more delightful. But I shall resist the temptation. I shall merely say that the dramatist Shakespeare, in imputing to the forthright and vigorous approach a merely limited success, was shown to have been less than candid.

Afterwards, as is the way with beautiful young men when they wish to show in spite of the evidence that they are not creatures of easy virtue, the lovely Ned put on an expression of prim decorum, as one disapproving of all that has occurred and accepting no share of responsibility for it. Such a look, at such a time, inspires a particular tenderness; for after the horse has been persuaded to bolt, the careful locking of the stable door is extraordinarily endearing.

'Julia,' he said, 'you will keep quiet about this, won't you? I wouldn't like Ken to know about it.'

I assured him that he might count on my discretion. I had already established, as you know, that it was logically impossible for Kenneth to be distressed by anything that might occur between Ned and myself; but Kenneth, being an artist, has perhaps not studied logic and is unaware of the impossibility.

The great danger of such an episode is the sense which it induces of benevolent euphoria, the consequences of which are almost always disastrous. After washing and changing for dinner, I had made my way to the bar of the Cytherea with a view to consuming a refreshing Campari soda and writing you a full account of my success. There, however, I found the Major, looking dejected and reading *The Times*.

My sympathies were aroused. The Major, after all, had no doubt come to Venice hoping, just like me, for a little innocent entertainment, but unlike me had failed to find it. I felt I should do what I could to raise his spirits. In a sense, it is true, it was his own fault: any hopes he might have had of success had been reduced, by his wearing of Bermuda shorts, from the small to the minuscule. On the other hand, I thought, it might be argued that it did him credit to wear a garment which so immediately revealed the frightfulness of his spider-like legs: an unscrupulous

man would have tried to keep them concealed until the
point at which a well-bred woman would feel embarrassment at withdrawing in revulsion.

'Cheer up, Bob,' I said briskly. 'The news can't be that
bad.'

'Just looking at the jolly old investments,' said the
Major. 'I've saved a quid or two from time to time and a
chap I know told me to buy some shares. Down again as
per usual. Got to expect it, I suppose, with this Socialist
shower running the show.'

*

'The Major,' said Selena, 'must have been singularly
unlucky in his choice of investments. The Stock Market is
at its highest for five years.'

*

I pointed out that the decline in his investments would
give him an excellent opportunity to establish a loss for
capital gains tax purposes; but he seemed unwilling to
perceive the advantages of this. Having undertaken,
however, the task of cheering him up, I persisted with it
until dinner, sparing only a moment to add a postscript to
my letter to you and consign it to the evening post.

My efforts to improve the Major's spirits were rewarded
with such success that by the end of dinner he raised
again the matter of the rug-cutting expedition. This put
me in a dilemma. The only places I had seen where there
might be dancing were nightclubs which looked to me
formidably expensive; if I permitted the Major, in such
an establishment, to bear the whole expense, it would be
so enormous as to place me under obligations of an
unmentionable nature. To avoid this, I should have to
contribute equally; but to spend a large sum of money in
order to shuffle round an over-crowded room in
distasteful proximity to such a man—well, there were
limits to my benevolence.

'Bob,' I said, 'you can't really want to spend the evening in a stuffy nightclub. I have noticed a most attractive little bar only a few minutes away, where we could sit out of doors and drink coffee and *grappa* — don't you think that would be much more amusing?'

The bar to which I actually took the Major may not have been quite the bar to which I had intended to take him. Any route one follows in Venice is of necessity devious: alleyways which seem to lead in one direction, finding themselves interrupted by an unexpected canal, turn round and go somewhere entirely different; it is always possible — but never certain — that the bridge you are crossing is the same bridge that you crossed five minutes ago. Still, whether it was the right bar or the wrong bar, it was a perfectly good place to drink *grappa* and coffee.

Perceiving that we were close to the Teatro Fenice and somehow feeling that the responsibilities of guide still rested on my shoulders, I was anxious to tell the Major something of the building's history and significance; but Ragwort's guide book was unhelpful.

'You will observe,' I said, 'that the date over the door is 1792. We may confidently assume, therefore, that the Theatre was the scene of very few of the comedies and musical entertainments for which Venice was celebrated in the eighteenth century. Beyond that, I can tell you nothing: the guide book refrains from any account of it.'

'Never mind, m'dear,' said the Major. 'Can't always rely on guide books, can you?' His tone was sombre, as if the remark had some deeper, possibly metaphysical significance. 'Still,' he added, 'not your fault, m'dear.'

Among the many defects in the state of things which people have from time to time considered to be my fault — but which you have always kindly explained were not my fault at all — the inadequacy of guide books has not so far been included. Still, I answered that it was kind of him to say so.

He continued to speak of his financial position, giving me to understand that in spite of the decline in his investments he had done not too badly for himself and was quite comfortably fixed. I made congratulatory comment.

I would think it odd, he said, that he had never married. I did not in fact think it at all odd—the statistical chances against any woman being prepared to endure both the hairiness of his legs and the tedium of his conversation seemed to me to be negligible. I did not express this view, but said sympathetically that the military life must be difficult to combine with the domestic.

'That's it, m'dear,' said the Major. 'All right for the chap, but no life for the little woman. Ends in heartbreak—seen it often. And since I've been in Civvy Street—well, I've often thought I'd like to settle down. But it's no good if it's not the right woman.'

I agreed that it was undoubtedly better to be married to no one than to someone uncongenial.

'Well, m'dear,' said the Major, 'how about it?'

I did my best to misunderstand. No use—it was a proposal of marriage.

If the survival of the human species were to depend on an act of physical conjunction between the Major and myself, then I suppose—while reserving the right, should the contingency actually arise, to consider the matter further—I suppose that in that event I should somehow bring myself to it. Once. Not twice. No, Selena, I am sorry, but even with the future of the species at stake, I really think not twice: you could not reasonably expect it of me. The institution of marriage, I have been led to believe, involves the occurrence of such acts on a regular and frequent basis. Marriage to the Major is a concept to make the blood run cold.

I had expected, at worst, some overture of a manifestly improper nature, such as might be rebuffed by adopting a Ragwort-like manner. For responding, however, to a proposal of marriage, the conduct of Ragwort affords no useful precedent. The ungoverned merriment with which he habitually receives such an offer is all very well with a friend and colleague, but would be excessively wounding in reply to a comparative stranger. I made some disjointed remarks to the effect that it was kind of him to ask me but marriage was not a habit of mine.

'Know I'm rushing my fences a bit, m'dear,' he said. 'Don't expect you to decide at once. But I'd better warn you, an old soldier doesn't give up easily when he's set his mind on something.'

The stars continued to shine in the velvet sky; but my spirits were enveloped in a cloud of sudden gloom.

The making of the proposal, albeit unaccepted, appeared in the Major's opinion to entitle him, on wishing me goodnight, to embrace me, though a well-judged movement of the head enabled me to reduce the unpleasantness of the whole thing to a rasping of my cheek. The emery-board texture of his chin put me in mind by contrast of the alabaster smoothness of Ned's. I remain very worried about Desdemona.

*

'Why,' asked Ragwort, 'couldn't she just say "No"?'

'They told her at school,' said Selena, 'that she must avoid hurting people's feelings.'

'One sometimes feels,' said Ragwort, 'that Julia took her education altogether too literally.'

*

Today, therefore, my principal objective has been to avoid the Major. I should have liked to have another disagreement with Ned about the Finance Act; but I think I can hope for no further success in that quarter. Seeing the lovely creature on the terrace this morning, I reminded him that I owed him a bottle of wine.

'It is an obligation,' he answered with great coldness,

'that I shall be quite happy to forget.'

From which I concluded that he is still set on proving himself not to be a young man of easy virtue and that it would accordingly take a full week of admiring his soul to prevail on him again.

In case I have anything to add, I shall not post this until tomorrow evening; though I do not suppose, since tomorrow is our last day in Venice, that anything will happen of sufficient interest to deserve reporting to you.

*

'The remainder of the letter,' said Selena, 'is written, therefore, on the day of the murder. Would this be a convenient moment to adjourn for coffee?'

CHAPTER 10

Cantrip appeared thoughtful: he had conceded without even formal argument that it was his turn to buy the coffee.

'I say,' he said, as he brought it back to our table, 'you know this bird Desdemona that Julia keeps on about? She married this chap Othello and he got the idea she was having a bit on the side. So he did her in.'

'I think,' said Selena, 'that we are all reasonably familiar with the unfortunate events described in the tragedy of *Othello*.'

'Well, I'm jolly familiar with them,' said Cantrip, 'because Julia took me to see it once. And I said afterwards I thought it was pretty silly, because the Othello chap's meant to have done frightfully well in the army and be a wiz at strategy and all that. And in that case, he wouldn't be the sort of twit who thought his wife was having it off with someone else just because she lost her handkerchief. And Julia didn't agree. Well, what she actually said was that I was a semi-educated flibbertigibbet whose powers of dramatic appreciation would be strained to the utmost by a Punch and Judy show on Brighton Pier in the off season. So I biffed her with my umbrella. And she tried to biff me with her handbag. But she missed, of course — you know what she's like.'

Evidently lost in the tenderness of this recollection, Cantrip fell silent. The sweep of black hair across his pale forehead gave him a romantic look, as of some poet or artist dying young in the nineteenth century. The events described had taken place, I suppose, before the spider episode: after it Julia would not, I think, have sought to return his biff.

'Did this literary discussion,' asked Selena, 'at any stage return to the merely verbal?'

'Oh, rather,' said Cantrip. 'You see, the way Julia saw it was that a chap who'd spent all his life in the army was just the sort of chap to get a bee in his bonnet about pure womanhood and so on, because he wouldn't get the chance to find out that women were more or less like any-one else and he'd start getting all idealistic about them. So as soon as he found out Desdemona wasn't perfect — I mean, the first time she spilt coffee or dropped cigarette ash on the carpet — he'd start feeling all disillusioned and thinking she'd betrayed his ideals. And after that, making him think she was having it off with some other chap would be absolute child's play.'

'It is, I suppose,' said Ragwort, 'a not unconvincing view.'

'You bet it's not unconvincing. Because when I started thinking about it I realized it was just what happened to my Uncle Hereward. My Uncle Hereward spent the best years of his life in the Army, serving Queen and Country in distant outposts of Empire, and when he came out he was so far round the twist he was practically invisible. With special reference to women. He's got this idea that when he went into the Army women were all pure and un-attainable and when he came out they weren't. And instead of being pleased, he's as miffed as a maggot about it.'

'My dear Cantrip,' said Selena, 'are the psychological difficulties of your relative in any way material to our present problem?'

'Well, of course they are, or I wouldn't be telling you about them, would I? The point is that this Major of Julia's is the same type as Othello and my Uncle Hereward. And Julia, poor grummit, with a view to discouraging his advances, has been setting herself up as a leading contender in the pure womanhood stakes. As a result of which, the Major thinks she's the woman he's been looking for all these years and asks her to marry him.'

'Oh dear,' said Selena.

' "Oh dear" is right. And since Julia doesn't want to hurt his feelings by saying no, she wouldn't marry him if he was the last man on earth, he probably thinks she's more or less engaged to him.'

'No one,' said Selena, 'could be as idiotic as that.'

'You haven't met my Uncle Hereward. Well, if that's how the Major sees things, and then he finds out about Julia and the chap from the Revenue, with particular reference to last Wednesday afternoon, what's he going to do about it?'

'I suppose,' said Ragwort, 'taking Othello as his model, that he would have murdered Julia.'

'Ah,' said Cantrip, 'that just shows you're not as familiar with *Othello* as I am. If you'd been to the thing and sat all the way through it the way Julia made me do, you'd remember that before he did in Desdemona he took out a contract on this other chap he thought she'd been having it off with.'

'Cantrip is reminding us,' said Selena, fearing that our

grasp of the Cambridge idiom might not be sufficient to enable us to follow this explanation, 'that prior to strangling
his wife Othello gave instructions to his subordinate for
the murder of Michael Cassio, his supposed rival in her
affections.'

'Right,' said Cantrip. 'So if Julia wasn't around, the
Major would have done in the chap from the Revenue.'

'I do not recall,' said Ragwort, 'that Othello completed
his revenge by stealing Cassio's holdall. One feels that the
dramatist would have thought it something of an anti-
climax.'

'Never mind about the holdall,' said Cantrip. 'I expect
it had incriminating evidence in it or something. Apart
from that, the two cases are practically identical—even
the handkerchief business.'

'I don't suppose,' said Selena, 'that the handkerchief
which the Major gave Julia was woven by a two-hundred-
year-old sibyl from the silk spun by sacred silkworms. If it
had been, the Major, being a dealer in antiques and
objects of virtue, would hardly have given it to Julia to
stem a nosebleed. Shall I read the rest of her letter?'

> Terrace of the Cytherea.
> Friday morning.

I have a rather curious, possibly even sinister, incident
to relate to you. One might call it, perhaps, the
Phenomenon of the Recurring Major. Before coming to
it, however, I should mention, by way of prelude, an
episode which occurred at breakfast time.

I don't know if you have ever noticed, Selena, how after
a few months of doing without the pleasures of the flesh
and being more or less resigned to it—of thinking, that is
to say, that it would be nice if they were available but that
since they are not one had better get on with construing
the Taxes Acts—how, after such a period, an interruption of the celibate life tends rather to stimulate than

allay the appetite. It is, I have found, the same with strawberries: during the winter I am not subject to any overpowering desire for them; but when I eat my first strawberry of the season and am reminded by direct experience of their warm yet uncloying sweetness and their yielding firmness between one's teeth, then I can by no means content myself with one, or two, or even three, but go on eating them with immoderate greed until the bowl is empty or forcibly taken from me.

Thus, when I woke this morning, I began to reflect on the unlikelihood of any further success with Ned, and on the prettiness of the waiter who brings my breakfast. The travel agents did say, after all, that service was included.

The procedure for taking advantage of Italian waiters—equally applicable, so far as I am aware, in other areas of the Mediterranean—does not merit any long exposition. It consists chiefly of staying in bed until they bring one's breakfast and then smiling benevolently. Waiters, generally speaking, seem not to mind being taken advantage of.

It is to be remembered, however, that they are an overworked and exploited profession, who have to spend much of their energies running to and fro carrying drinks and so on, so that the duration of the pleasure given is not always commensurate to the enthusiasm with which it is offered. If the coffee brought me by the pretty waiter had been cold by the time he left, I should have been willing, in the particular circumstances, to forgive him; but my forgiveness was not called for. Still, one must not be ungrateful—strawberries are strawberries.

I come now to the curious and possibly sinister incident.

For the reasons indicated above, it was rather later than usual—though not so much later as I could have wished—that I was ready to leave my room. On opening my door, however, I observed that the corridor contained the Major. Fortunately, he did not see me, being at that moment in the act of closing the door to his room. To avoid meeting him being at present one of my chief objects, I withdrew again to my room and lit a Gauloise. When I had smoked half of it, I thought it must be safe to leave.

The Major was still in the corridor and was still closing a door. Well, you will say, Selena, that there was nothing very startling about that — he had forgotten something, you will say, had gone back to his room for it and was now leaving for a second time. I do not think, however, that your hypothesis is tenable; for it seemed to me that the door he was closing on this occasion was not that of his own room — it was that of the adjoining room, which is occupied by Ned and Kenneth Dunfermline. Much perplexed, I withdrew again and smoked the rest of the Gauloise. Then, with the utmost caution, I looked out again into the corridor.

The Major was still in the corridor. He was still closing a door. This time, if my observation by now was at all to be relied on, the door of his own room.

Much shaken, I withdrew yet again and consumed in two gulps what remained of my duty-free brandy. The liquid which saw Napoleon across the Russian Steppes did not fail me — when next I opened my door, the corridor was empty. Without further untoward incident, I made my way to the terrace.

The incident I have described seemed to me extraordinarily disquieting. I could think of no sensible reason for the Major to spend some ten minutes rigidly posed in the attitude of one closing a door. The likely explanation, I felt, was that the suggestion of marrying him had had such traumatic effects on me as to induce a series of paranoid hallucinations: whenever I opened a door, I would imagine, unless previously fortified by brandy, that I saw the Major closing one. This, with brandy the price it is, would be an inconvenient affliction.

*

'Odd,' said Selena. 'It looks as if the Major went into the room occupied by Ned and Kenneth and stayed there for about five minutes. After that, evidently, he went back to his own room and stayed there for another five minutes or so before finally going out. I wonder why.'

'It is possible,' said Ragwort, 'that he visited the other room with the consent of the occupants. But the timing seems a little furtive—it sounds, doesn't it, as if he had waited until everyone else in the annexe could be expected to have left their rooms and gone about their lawful business—all those, that is to say, who were not conducting themselves disgracefully with the domestic staff. Don't you think that it sounds like a first attempt to steal whatever was in the holdall?'

'No,' said Cantrip, 'what I think it sounds like is Othello looking for Desdemona's handkerchief.'

'You are suggesting,' asked Selena, 'that the Major, entertaining some suspicion of Julia's dealings with Ned, was searching Ned's room for corroborative evidence?'

Cantrip nodded.

*

My intention in going on to the terrace had been to write to you immediately of this disturbing experience. I was diverted from my purpose, however, by the discovery there of the lovely Ned, leaning in a graceful attitude against the balcony which divides the terrace from the canal.

This was not altogether a piece of good fortune, for he was looking more beautiful than ever. The sunlight catching his pale hair, his white shirt a little open to show the smoothness of his neck, his translucent skin warmed by eight days in Venice—if he reminded one before of something by Praxiteles, one thought now that the artist had cast his work in gold. The effect was to inspire in me as ardent a passion as I had felt when I first saw him on the aeroplane. It seemed to me, after all the trouble I had been to, that Wednesday afternoon had done me no good at all. Well, I suppose that is not strictly true — it is always better to have had Wednesday afternoon than not to have had Wednesday afternoon; but I could find in myself none of that quiet contentment which one looks for as the consequence of an achieved desire.

'You appear,' I said, 'at some risk of falling into the canal. Do at least avoid the danger of looking at your reflection in it. Remember Narcissus.'

At this he smiled and looked pleased; but I was prevented from further compliment by the arrival on the terrace of Marylou, free, for once, of matrimonial surveillance.

'I haven't seen you two in days,' she said, sounding reproachful.

'The loss is ours,' I answered, 'rather than the fault.'

'Anyway,' she went on, 'I hope you're both coming on the trip to Verona this afternoon. Stanford didn't want to go, because he's already been to Verona. But I told Stanford no way was I going to miss seeing Verona just because he'd been there at the weekend seeing a business acquaintance.' Her tone suggested no improvement in her opinion of such a person. 'And I don't figure we'll be seeing the same things he saw over the weekend. He won't have looked at anything historically relevant, not unless you count a ten-year-old bottle of rye. I mean, Stanford is not exactly aesthetically aware. He is a fine person in many ways — but when they dished up aesthetic awareness, I guess that Stanford just wasn't holding his plate out. So I hope you're both coming this afternoon?'

'No, I'm afraid not,' answered Ned. 'Ken's going. But Julia and I both went on Tuesday.'

She expressed her disappointment with flattering exaggeration, and asked if we had enjoyed Verona.

'Very much,' answered Ned. 'Graziella wasn't able to

come with us, so Julia acted as guide.'

'Oh, I wish I'd been with you,' she said. 'I think Julia'd be a just marvellous guide.'

'Oh yes,' he said, with great demureness, 'she is. Excellent. She takes one to all the places one ought to go to. And sometimes,' he added, with even greater demureness, 'to places one ought not to go to.' And thinking, no doubt, that this could not be improved on as an exit line, he excused himself from our company and left the terrace.

I was still not able to write to you immediately of the Phenomenon of the Recurring Major, for Marylou persuaded me to go with her on a shopping expedition. It seemed to me that on the Rialto she had already acquired in wholesale quantities every form of merchandise that Venice offers to the discerning tourist; but she assured me that this was not the case.

As a result of this diversion, it was not until midday that I was able to return here and write to you of my disquieting experience. Even now, I have not escaped interruption. My secluded corner of the terrace has been taken over for the purpose of an assignation. I am left exposed to enquiry from all the tourists who pass to and fro in the lobby of the Cytherea and for some reason look on me as a likely source of information: three large German matrons, wearing identical straw hats, have asked me the way to the ladies'; an earnest young Englishman has asked me to point out the house where Byron lived; a party of French schoolgirls have asked me which *vaporetto* will take them to the Lido. I have responded sympathetically, if not accurately, to all these enquiries. You will therefore forgive, I hope, the disjointedness of my narrative.

Before going to lunch, I shall have to return to my room to get the guide book to Verona — having confessed to Marylou that it was the foundation of my success there, I felt obliged by courtesy to offer it to her for this after-

noon's excursion. I have explained to her that it is Ragwort's and she must be very careful of it.

On leaving my room again, I shall be circumspect but
not fearful. Writing to you has persuaded me to look on
the bright side: I now realize that to see the Major when
he isn't really there must at least be preferable to seeing
him when he is really there. If, however, there is any
repetition of the Phenomenon, I shall report it forthwith
by way of postscript.

Terrace of the Cytherea.
Friday evening.

Men, Selena, are very odd creatures — I shall never
understand them. There seems to be in their conduct no
reason or consistency of purpose — they are blown like
feathers this way and that on every changing breeze of
mood and fancy, so that it is quite impossible to predict,
on any rational basis, what they will do next. Delightful,
of course, in some ways, but confusing. Take, merely as
an example, the enchanting Ned, with whom I should
have said this morning that there was not the slightest
chance — well, I will tell you everything, just as it happened.

Having returned to my room to fetch the guide book to
Verona, I left it again without misadventure — that is to
say, without seeing the Major in fact or fantasy: I concluded with relief that the affliction had been temporary.
Coming downstairs again, I found myself crossing the
bridge back to the main part of the hotel only a few paces
behind Ned and Kenneth. As seemed natural in the circumstances, I said 'hello' to them, patting Ned on the
elbow — a gesture, I think, of no greater intimacy than
one Art Lover might in good fellowship show towards
another.

Ned's reaction to this was most extraordinary. He turned
round towards me very sharply and violently, almost as if

preparing to defend himself against some physical attack, and said, in a tone of disproportionate ill-temper, 'For God's sake, Julia, don't do that.' This seemed an absurdly exaggerated response: he could hardly suppose that I would choose such a time and place for an improper advance; besides, his reaction was more appropriate to an attack on his life than on his virtue.

*

'Dear me,' said Ragwort. 'How very interesting. We can assume, I suppose, that the young man would not immediately have realized who it was who had touched him on the elbow?'

'Certainly,' said Selena. 'And when a man seems at lunchtime to be in fear of his life and is found murdered before dinner, one is disposed to think that there must be some connection.'

*

I apologized for having startled him.

'Don't take any notice,' said Kenneth, evidently embarrassed by Ned's abruptness. 'He's just started worrying about tomorrow's flight. He gets very nervous about flying, don't you, Ned?'

'Yes,' said his friend. 'Yes, horribly, I'm afraid. I'm sorry, Julia — I didn't mean to snap at you.'

Looking at him more closely, I was inclined to believe that this was indeed the reason for his curious behaviour, rather than anything specifically to do with me. He was very pale and showed every sign of nervousness. I noticed with great distress that the perfection of his chin was marred by a strip of adhesive plaster.

'Ned,' I cried, unable to conceal my anguish at this aesthetic catastrophe, 'what have you done to your face?'

'My hand was shaking so much I cut myself shaving,' he said. 'Isn't it silly? Do I look very awful?'

'No, no,' I said, 'no, of course not.'

I filled the time it took us to reach the dining-room

with reassurance and compliment; but Ned's nervousness seemed unabated—I noticed that he ate no lunch and even spilt some of his wine. Still, though concluding that there had been nothing personal in his response to my greeting on the bridge, I would not have given a lira for my chances of further success with him.

Graziella arrived, as we were finishing lunch, to round up in time for a two o'clock departure those Art Lovers who were going to Verona—that is to say, Kenneth and the two Americans. Kenneth hesitated, and seemed to be asking Ned if he minded being left alone; but eventually, patting him on the shoulder and suggesting that he should lie down for a while, he followed Graziella out of the dining-room. Ned and I were the only Art Lovers remaining—Eleanor and the Major had been absent from lunch. Coming over to my table, Ned suggested that we should have coffee together on the terrace.

'Well,' I said, as we drank our coffee, 'this is our last afternoon in Venice—how are you proposing to spend it?'

'I'm still not feeling terribly well,' he answered. 'I think I'd better do as Kenneth says—take a siesta.'

'What a pity,' I said, 'that you won't allow me to share it.' I entertained, as I have said, no hope of getting anywhere with this suggestion—I made it rather as a matter of form, not wishing Ned to think that the strip of adhesive plaster so detracted from his appearance that I could easily refrain from making an advance.

And for all the world as if he knew no better than a young man brought up to serve breakfasts rather than tax assessments, as if no wounding remarks had been made about obligations which he was happy to forget, as if my approach on the bridge had been a matter for satisfaction rather than alarm—'Why not?' he answered.

Men, Selena, are very odd.

We returned across the bridge to the annexe, smiled on again by the pretty chambermaids, and went, this time, to Ned's room rather than mine.

If he felt any modest reluctance to yield again so soon and with so little intervening commentary on his soul and intellect, it was, I am bound to say, most admirably dissimulated, for he devoted himself to the enterprise with great energy and apparent enthusiasm. To such an extent, indeed, that if I were the woman to call a truce with the Revenue — but never let it be said. Such exertion, in the heat of a Venetian afternoon, ends unhealthfully in sleeping between damp sheets. Ah Selena, when in our age I complain of my rheumatics, remind me how pleasantly I earned them.

When I woke up it was past six o'clock. Ned, lying beside me, still looked so peacefully asleep that tenderheartedness prevented me from waking him. Not wanting him to think, however, that I valued him so little as to leave entirely without ceremony, I scribbled my name and address and a few discreet words of affection on the inside cover of my Finance Act and left it, by way of souvenir, on the table beside the bed.

After this, having washed and changed for dinner, I came down to the terrace to write to you of the oddness of men. I am back in my usual corner: the vine or similar shrub has thus protected me from any obligation to converse with Eleanor or the Major, both of whom have returned to the annexe in the past half-hour — they have been having a last rummage, I suppose, among the personal effects of the late Miss Tiverton.

I shall have to stop soon for lack of light: the sun has just set and the only lamp on the terrace is designed more for romantic atmosphere than serious illumination.

Besides, it seems to be time for dinner: the pretty chambermaids have scattered — no doubt to turn down counterpanes and so forth — and those of the Art Lovers who went to Verona have returned and are on their way back to the annexe. I shall go to dinner and post this on the way—I am feeling, for some reason, extraordinarily hungry.

Yours, Selena, as always,
Julia.

'Poor Julia,' said Selena. 'I do hope she got something to eat before people started arresting her.'

CHAPTER 11

By approaching from the south-west rather than more directly from the north-east, going quickly down the steps into the basement area of 60 New Square, sidling past the dustbins with one's back to the wall as far as the rear entrance of 61 and then running fast, but very quietly, up six flights of stairs, it is generally possible, if Henry has not set a typist on special sentry duty, to reach the second floor of 62 without observation from the Clerks' Room. The time taken to read Julia's letter was thought to make this the expedient route for our return to Chambers.

'And in a minute or two,' said Selena, settling herself in the large leather armchair bought second-hand for fifty pence by Ragwort and Cantrip to add a touch of luxury to the room which they jointly occupy, 'when we have got our breath back, we shall ring through to the Clerks' Room with some casual enquiry about our arrangements for the afternoon. And Henry, sounding reproachful, will say that he thought we were still at coffee, having not seen us return. And we will say good heavens, no, we've been back for ages.'

'Will he,' I asked, 'believe you?'

'His state of mind,' said Selena, 'may not be quite what a purist would refer to as belief. He will hardly venture, however, to suggest outright that we are lying. You'd better do it, Ragwort—you do it best.'

The choice of Ragwort was a happy one. Had it been Cantrip or Selena whose enquiry about their afternoon engagements had been interrupted by an indignant interrogation as to their whereabouts for the past half-hour, during which Henry had been looking for them everywhere, either, no doubt, would have managed to sound surprised; but they would not, I think, have been able to mingle with their surprise the delicate suggestion which Ragwort achieved of superhuman patience taxed to its limit by Henry's folly in contriving to look for them at precisely those infrequent moments when they were absent from their rooms.

'Well, Henry,' said Ragwort at last, with a forgiving sigh, 'I suppose you had some reason for looking for me?'

'Young lady to see you, Mr Ragwort,' said Henry. 'She said it was personal.' His voice, clearly audible at the other end of the internal telephone line, was lugubrious. There are, no doubt, many reasons for which a young woman might call on a young man in Chambers and say that the matter was personal: there is only one which occurs to a barristers' Clerk. 'And of course, sir, if you'd told me there might be a young lady turning up wanting to see you, I'd have known how to deal with her. But you hadn't, sir, so I didn't.' If Ragwort, in addition to wasting in idle dalliance time which could more profitably have been devoted to his paperwork, had compounded his error by failing to inform his Clerk of the progress, regress and termination of the liaison, he could not expect Henry to protect him, as Henry would otherwise have done, from the distressing and scandalous scene which must now ensue.

'I see,' said Ragwort. 'So how did you deal with her, Henry?'

'I put her in the waiting-room, sir, and said I'd try to find you. I said I'd seen you go to coffee but you'd be bound to be back soon, sir, knowing how busy you were and with those papers promised for Tancreds first thing tomorrow.'

'Quite so,' said Ragwort. 'Did you happen to ask her name?'

'No, Mr Ragwort. I didn't like to do that, seeing she said it was personal. I wouldn't want you to think that I was prying into your personal affairs, Mr Ragwort.'

'Ah, how very discreet of you, Henry. Well, perhaps you could ask someone to show her up here.'

Ragwort suggested that the rest of us might like to withdraw to Timothy's room.

'Not likely,' said Cantrip. 'If you've been trifling with this bird's affections and now she's coming home to roost, we jolly well want to know about it.'

'I've been doing nothing of the kind,' said Ragwort. 'I haven't the faintest idea—'

'Well, Henry thinks you have. And if she's going to cut up rough about it, you'll need us here to give you moral support.'

'I am obliged to you,' said Ragwort, 'for your concern, but—'

'Lady to see you, Mr Ragwort,' said the temporary typist, opening the door to admit the visitor and so pre-empting further argument. Ragwort rose and extended his hand.

'Mr Ragwort?' asked the girl shyly, in accents which my memory identified as those of West Virginia. 'How do you do? Of course, you won't know who I am.'

She was, as it happened, quite wrong about that. Her pale blonde hair, her graceful figure, the elegance of her mode of dress, so muted as to suggest at first impression a curiously seductive dowdiness—all these were easily remembered; and it was only forty-eight hours since we had seen her at the airport. Not thinking it tactful to allude to that occasion, we allowed Marylou to introduce herself.

Ragwort no longer wished us to withdraw. He was inclined to think, as my readers may recall, that Marylou was a murderess; and her canvas-coloured leather shoulder-bag looked large enough to contain a quite workmanlike pair of dressmaking scissors. Much as he might admire her elegance, he did not wish to be left alone with her — he made haste to effect introductions.

Marylou, on the other hand, though she acknowledged these very prettily, showing a charming deference to my professorship, had clearly envisaged a private interview. Taking the chair offered her, she looked round at us diffidently, as if uncertain how to explain her presence.

'I'm sorry to intrude on you like this,' she said. 'I know you must all be very busy. But I was rather hoping, Mr Ragwort —'

'It may perhaps be of assistance,' said Ragwort, plainly anxious to forestall any express request for privacy, 'if I mention that we are all very old friends of Julia Larwood. With whom, I believe, you are also acquainted.'

'Why yes,' she said, 'how did you know?'

'Julia has written to us from Venice,' said Ragwort. 'She mentioned meeting you.'

'Oh, I see,' said Marylou. 'Well, if Julia's told you about me, that makes it a whole lot easier. Because that's why I came to see you, Mr Ragwort — because of Julia. Something rather terrible has happened to her and I didn't know who to come to. I don't know if you've heard anything?' She looked round at us again, her eyes wide with anxious but discreet enquiry.

'We understand,' said Selena, 'that a guest in the same hotel has been the victim of an act of violence, unfortunately fatal, and that the police have asked Julia to remain in Venice while the matter is resolved.' She spoke with a certain coldness, due, I fancy, to a feeling that Marylou had somehow accepted responsibility for Julia's welfare while they were in Venice: there was in her man-

ner towards the American girl something of the fond
mother to the negligent nursemaid.

Having evidently imagined Julia friendless and forgotten, left indefinitely to languish without trial in a Venetian dungeon, Marylou seemed relieved to discover that
anyone in England was aware of her difficulties. Lacking
particulars of Julia's next-of-kin, she had been uncertain
who should be informed of them.

'But then I remembered her talking about you, Mr
Ragwort, and I somehow felt that you and Julia really had
a very sincere and valid relationship, even if — well, that's
just what I felt.'

'We are all,' said Ragwort, 'in our various ways, and for
more or less comprehensible reasons, quite fond of Julia,
really.'

'And I already had your address, because it was in the
guide book to Verona. Julia lent me that on our last day
in Venice. I hope you don't mind about that, Mr
Ragwort — she told me it was yours and to take great care
of it.'

She opened her canvas-coloured shoulder-bag.
Ragwort watched this with some anxiety; but she took
from it nothing more dangerous than a slim volume neatly
covered in brown paper. She laid it on Ragwort's desk. 'I
guess Julia'd want me to give it back to you, anyway,' she
said.

The tone to adopt, I felt, was one of sympathetic
encouragement, as to undergraduates when they are
explaining how the complications of their private lives
have prevented them from writing an essay. It is my
custom, on such occasions, to offer a small glass of sherry;
but the only sherry in the Nursery is that kept by Timothy
for the refreshment of his more eminent clients. Quite
apart from any ethical objection to taking it without his
permission, I feared that he might thoughtlessly have
locked it away before leaving for Venice.

'My dear Marylou,' I said—the reverence she had shown for my professorship seemed to sanction the use of her Christian name—'we know little or nothing of the circumstances leading to Julia's detention. It would be most helpful if you could give us any details. Have you any idea, for example, who discovered the murder?'

'Why yes,' said Marylou. 'I guess I did.' Selena looked at her in deep reproach. 'I mean, I was with my husband and a guy called Kenneth Dunfermline—it was a friend of his who was murdered—we found him in their room. I'm sorry, Professor Tamar, I'm not telling this too well.'

'Why don't you,' I said kindly, 'begin at the beginning?'

'Well,' said Marylou, 'I guess that means Friday afternoon. Stanford—that's my husband—Stanford and I went on a visit to Verona. In a group with quite a lot of people, but we really didn't know anyone except Graziella—that was our courier—and this guy Kenneth Dunfermline. He's a sculptor—quite well known, I think. We'd been in the same hotel all week, but we hadn't had a lot of inter-personal contact—Kenneth never seemed to be around much except at dinner-time. I'd got to know Ned better—that was his friend—Ned and Julia and I all went to the Lido one day. Well, Kenneth sat next to us on the coach out to Verona and he was really fascinating—he told us all about Venetian art and the Roman and Byzantine influence and everything. It was a wonderful experience, Professor Tamar, having someone like that to explain it all—we really appreciated it. Well, I really appreciated it—Stanford isn't too much into visual creativity.'

'But so far as you were concerned,' I said, 'the visit to Verona was one of unqualified pleasure?'

'Oh yes,' said Marylou. 'It's a really enchanting city, Professor Tamar.'

'And then, I suppose, you all came back together on the motor-coach?'

'Yes—we must have left Verona around half-six and got back to Venice about a quarter of eight. Then we took the launch back to our hotel and it was just about dark by the time we got there. We stood around for a minute or two after we arrived, talking to Graziella and thanking her for everything she'd done for us, because she'd really been an excellent courier.'

'Yes,' I said, hoping that no one else would appear in her narrative whose merits required tribute, 'and then?'

'Well, it had been pretty hot all day, so we all wanted to shower and change before dinner. We stopped at reception to collect our keys and Kenneth's wasn't there, so he said that Ned must still be in their room. So we all walked back together—our rooms were right opposite each other, not in the main part of the hotel, we had to go across a little bridge to get to them—and Kenneth and I were still talking about things we'd seen in Verona. When we got there, Kenneth went to open the door to his room and it was locked. Then he knocked and called out to Ned to let him in, but there wasn't any answer.'

'Was it the kind of door,' asked Selena, 'which could have been locked from the outside by someone who didn't have a key?'

'Oh yes—all the bedroom doors lock automatically—I guess they figure it's better securitywise.'

'I'm sorry,' said Selena. 'I shouldn't have interrupted you—do go on.'

'Well, Kenneth seemed a bit concerned, because Ned hadn't been feeling too good at lunch-time—he was nervous about the plane flight and Kenneth was afraid he might have passed out or something. I thought Kenneth was over-reacting, because I figured Ned had just gone out and forgotten to leave the key at reception. Well, either way, I didn't think it made too much sense just standing round in the corridor looking at the door and saying "Open Sesame". So I looked round and there was a chambermaid just coming out of our room — I guess she'd been turning the sheets down — and I asked her if she could let the Signor Dunfermline into his room, because his friend seemed to have gone out and taken the key with him. And she said perhaps his friend was still there but sleeping, because he was very tired perhaps. And she kind of giggled — I don't know why.'

'The Italians,' said Selena, 'have a very odd sense of humour.'

'I said maybe he was, but he'd have to stop sleeping now, because the Signor Dunfermline wanted to shower before dinner. So she kind of giggled again and shrugged her shoulders and unlocked the door. Kenneth started to go in and he turned the light on and he was still talking to us, you know, looking over his shoulder, saying he wouldn't be long and he'd see us at dinner. Then he stopped and said "Oh, my God," and I said "What's the matter, Kenneth?" and he just said "Oh, my God" again. So I went in to see what was wrong. There wasn't too much light in the room and at first I thought Ned was just sleeping. I kind of remember thinking, "He doesn't look too comfortable lying that way, I don't know how he can breathe with his face in the pillow like that." And then I saw the blood.'

Respect for property cannot always be paramount. I remembered moreover that Cantrip had acquired at an early age a fair expertise in the art of lock-picking — I suppose it is one of the options in the Cambridge law syllabus.

'Cantrip,' I said, 'could you get the sherry from Timothy's room?'

'Absolutely,' said Cantrip.

It was not only Marylou who required some stimulus to fortitude. Selena, in particular, was disconcerted by the removal from suspicion of Kenneth Dunfermline — Timothy's opinion that he was the person most likely to be accepted by the Italian police as an alternative to Julia had carried weight with her. She began to look through the guide book lying on Ragwort's desk.

'According to this,' she said, as Cantrip returned successful and began to pour sherry, 'Verona is 124 kilometres from Venice. That, I believe, is about 75 miles. It appears, moreover, that there is easy communication between the two cities by bus, train and motor-car. It sounds, therefore, as if it might be possible, if one arrived in Verona at about three o'clock, to return to Venice and get back again in time to catch the motor-coach at half past six. We know, of course, Marylou, that you remember Kenneth Dunfermline being on the motor-coach. You have told us, however, that when you reached Verona you were deeply absorbed in the artistic and architectural glories of the city — "enchanted", I think, was the word you used — and in those circumstances you might perhaps hardly have noticed, indeed not noticed at all, whether he was still in your company?'

'Not all the time,' said Marylou. 'But we had tea right around four o'clock at the Café Dante, and Stanford and I shared a table with him.'

'When you got back to the hotel,' I asked, 'you're sure Kenneth could not have gone up to his room ahead of you and then come back to cross the bridge with you for the second time?'

'Quite sure, Professor Tamar,' said Marylou. 'It was the way I told you — we were all together the whole time. If you've been hypothesizing that Kenneth might have done it — well, I'm sorry, but that's just totally nonviable in terms of the time-space factor.'

We devoted ourselves with some despondency to our sherry — its excellence was no more than a marginal consolation.

'Reverting,' I said, 'if it is not too painful for you, Marylou, to the discovery of the murder — there seem, from your description, to have been no signs of a struggle? Nothing to suggest that the unfortunate young man was stabbed in the course of a quarrel or anything of that nature?'

'No,' she said, 'I guess not. It didn't look like there'd been any kind of confrontation. It just looked like Ned had been lying face down, sleeping maybe, and if someone had come up quietly—well, Ned wouldn't have known too much about it.'

'Have you any idea,' I asked, 'why the Venetian police suspect Julia?'

'That's what I don't understand, Professor Tamar—I thought Julia was right out of it. You see, after we found Ned the way I told you, it was a pretty confused situation. I wanted Stanford to go get the Manager but Stanford was very resistant to leaving me. And I wasn't about to leave Kenneth alone in the state he was in—he was in a really bad way, Professor Tamar. He was just kneeling by the bed with his arm round Ned's shoulders and—well, I guess he was crying. Stanford said afterwards he didn't think the British behaved that way. I pointed out to Stanford that that was simply a nonempirical prejudgment and had no validity whatsoever—but Stanford swallows nonempirical prejudgments the way athletes swallow vitamin pills. So in the final event it was the chambermaid who went to get the Manager.'

It was clear, at any rate, why suspicion had so soon attached itself to Julia: the chambermaid was one of those, no doubt, who had observed Julia going into the annexe with Ned and later leaving without him. Assisting shortly afterwards at the discovery of the corpse, it would have been natural for her simply to inform the Manager that the English gentleman in Room 6 had been murdered by the English lady in Room 8. 'Was there,' I asked, 'so far as you know, anyone else in the annexe?'

'Mrs Frostfield and Major Linnaker—they were in the

same group we were — they came out into the corridor to
see what was going on. I guess the chambermaid had
screamed some — I guess I had, too.'

'Did you happen to notice,' asked Ragwort, 'whether
they had changed for dinner?'

'Mrs Frostfield certainly had — she was wearing a long
skirt and evening slippers. It's hard to say with Major Linnaker — he dressed pretty informally most of the time.
Well, when the police came they searched all the rooms in
the annexe but they didn't find anyone. I don't figure
that means too much, though, because if someone
wanted to get away it wouldn't have been too hard to slip
out of the window into the canal. Maybe it wouldn't smell
too good — but, I guess it's what I'd have done if I'd just
committed a murder and wanted to get away.'

'And then?' I said.

'Well, the police made us all wait in the corridor.
Except Kenneth — Kenneth wouldn't leave Ned and they
just let him stay. Then they got a stretcher and brought
Ned out with a sheet over him and took him down the
stairs. They'd got the police motor-launch right up next
to the entrance, so they didn't need to take him across the
bridge. There's only one light there and they stumbled a
bit getting into the launch, but it was all right. And Kenneth just went right along with them and they didn't stop
him.'

I thought of the heavy-shouldered sculptor following
the body of his friend; and easily imagined, for I too am
familiar with the city, how little the single light and the
fragments of its reflection in the black surface of the
canal would serve to penetrate the Venetian darkness.

'Well,' said Marylou, 'that was about it. They took
statements from all of us through an interpreter, but it
didn't take long and it was all pretty informal. Then we
had dinner in a private room — the Hotel Manager said
we wouldn't feel like eating in the dining-room after what

had happened. It was very considerate of him — additionally to which, maybe he thought having a guest murdered on the premises wasn't the best kind of publicity and he didn't want us talking to anyone else about it. But Julia wasn't there and I just figured she wasn't involved any way at all because she hadn't been in the annexe. That was kind of simplistic maybe, because she could have been in the annexe and come down again. But I just assumed she'd got back late and gone straight to the dining-room.'

'That seems,' said Ragwort, 'a very reasonable assumption.'

'So I didn't see Julia again that evening and I wasn't really feeling concerned about her. I mean, I was concerned because I knew she'd be upset, but not for any other reason. Well, next morning, when we were all meant to be at the landing stage to take the launch over to the airport, Julia wasn't there. But even then I just figured she was having problems with her packing and maybe I'd better go and help her.' Prompted, if not caused, by the pitiful image of Julia attempting unaided to pack her suitcase, two large and evenly matched tears began to roll down in perfect parallel on either side of Marylou's charming nose.

'My dear girl,' said Ragwort, 'don't cry.'

'Cheer up, old thing,' said Cantrip.

'Have some more sherry,' said Selena.

'I'm sorry,' said Marylou, 'I guess it's just a biochemical reflex. Well, that's when Graziella told us Julia wasn't coming, because the police still wanted to question her about the murder.'

Her first inclination, it seemed, on receipt of this intelligence, had been to remain in Venice until Julia could be extracted from the clutches of the police. Stanford, however, characteristically opposing this course of action, she had allowed herself, with a weakness which she now felt culpable, to be prevailed upon to return to London: she appeared to be seriously considering whether she ought not to make good this default by going straight back to Venice and persuading the Italian police of the absurdity of their accusations. We comforted her with assurances of the steps being taken to protect Julia's interests; with promises to let her know of any further developments; and with two more glasses of Timothy's sherry.

'It's a bit much,' said Cantrip, when she had gone. 'Losing three suspects all at one go.'

'I suppose,' said Ragwort, 'that she could be lying.'

'No,' said Selena. 'She must be telling us the same thing she told the Italian police. And that must be the same thing that Stanford and Kenneth Dunfermline told them. If it were merely a question of her evidence corroborating her husband's, one might not take much notice. But conspiracy between all three—no, Ragwort, I really don't think it'll do.'

Timothy rang soon afterwards to tell us the bad news. We told him we knew. He told us it was worse.

CHAPTER 12

It does me no credit—save in showing how little this chronicle is written in any spirit of self-advertisement—to admit that even now I was unable to identify the murderer and the motive for the crime. All the essential evidence was available: except to confirm an hypothesis already virtually assured no further investigation should have been necessary. Certain of my colleagues in the world of Scholarship would perhaps not scruple to omit all reference to their subsequent enquiries, preferring to set forth immediately the conclusions to be drawn from the evidence and to veil in silence their own delay in reaching them. The true scholar, however, should disdain such paltering.

To excuse my slowness, I say only that the Nursery is no place for quiet contemplation: and, as I have mentioned, the process of reflection was interrupted by Timothy's telephone call.

I have been exercised in my mind how properly to deal with this, since Timothy shortly afterwards wrote a letter to Selena containing an account of his progress more detailed than he had thought economic to convey by telephone. I have debated whether it would be permissible, to avoid the tedium of repetition, to reproduce that letter immediately, rather than at the point in my narrative at which, by chronology of receipt, it ought in strictness to appear; and have concluded that it would.

> As from Palazzo Artemisio
> Venice.
> Monday 12th September.

Dear Selena,

As I promised on the telephone, I am writing to let you know in more detail what has happened since my arrival in Venice. I hope, of course, that it will prove a wasted effort and that Julia will have been restored, before it reaches you, to the safety of Lincoln's Inn; but I am afraid, as things stand at present, that that is optimistic. I am writing this, by the way, in the dining-room of the Hotel Cytherea—feeling that it might be sensible to see the place where everything is supposed to have happened, I decided, after ringing you, to have lunch here.

After I left you all on Saturday, there were various delays before the plane finally took off, and by the time we landed it was already dark. Instead of going by boat across the Lagoon, I took a taxi across the Causeway to the Piazzale Roma and went from there by *vaporetto* down the Grand Canal to Saint Mark's, which is the nearest station to the Palazzo Artemisio.

I found I was feeling uneasy, almost apprehensive. I had forgotten how much darker Venice is at night than other cities. The darkness is broken here and there by the white silhouette of a floodlit church or palazzo; but its brightness is cold and disquieting—the building itself seems nothing but a clever lighting effect. Indeed, the whole city seems somehow illusory, like a stage set for a death-and-daggers melodrama. One feels the designer has overdone it rather—the water is too black, the alleyways too narrow, the silence of the gondolas too improbably sinister for anyone to believe they are real. But I remembered that a man really had been murdered.

If Julia had still been in custody, I should have felt obliged to take some immediate step on her behalf, though what I could usefully have done at that time of night I have no clear idea. As it was, I felt justified in going straight to the Palazzo Artemisio. I was admitted by the housekeeper, who clucked round me very amiably, apologizing on Richard Tiverton's behalf for his not being well enough to welcome me in person. The Palazzo itself, though, is not exactly what I would describe as comfortable. The late Miss Tiverton seems to have had a fancy, which I do not share, for living in a museum: I hardly dare move for fear of damaging something.

On the following morning, Richard Tiverton joined me for breakfast. He told me with many apologies that he did not yet feel able to give his mind to discussing his tax affairs. Having chosen to come to Venice by sea rather than air, he had found uncomfortably late that the sea did not suit his digestion: he was still feeling very unwell—looking it too, poor boy.

Wanting to begin as soon as possible to do something about Julia's problems, I did my best to encourage him to a leisurely recovery.

'I was intending,' I said, 'to add a few days' holiday to

the end of my stay in Venice. I should be quite happy, if you don't feel I'm imposing on your hospitality, to take it at the beginning rather than the end.' I meant, of course, that the fee for my services would not be increased by the delay; but that is hardly something, even in these permissive days, which one can say outright to the lay client.

'Thank you,' said Richard, 'that's very kind.' Whether he understood the financial implication of my remark or had expected, on the basis of his memory of public school, that I would tell him to pull himself together and face up to the Finance Act like a man, I am not entirely sure.

Not wanting to disclose to him that there was any competing claim on my professional energies, I decided to make any telephone calls relating to Julia from the nearest bar rather than from the Palazzo, where the only telephone is just by the front door—not at all a convenient place from the point of view of privacy. After breakfast, therefore, I went out, saying that I intended to spend the day wandering round Venice.

It was a frustrating morning. I wanted, of course, to talk to Julia as soon as possible; but the travel agents had been unable to tell me exactly where she was staying in Chioggia. Graziella, obviously, would have known; but there was no answer from the number they had given me for her. The police, presumably, would also have known; but to telephone them without introduction and knowing nothing of the case seemed hardly calculated to impress them with my professional standing.

At last, through the emergency number for the British Consulate, I managed to track down a Signor Vespari, whose duties during the weekend had included receiving the news that one of those under the Consulate's protection had been murdered and another was suspected of the crime.

Signor Vespari agreed to join me for lunch at

Montin's—the restaurant in the Dorsodouro which Ragwort likes. He told me what little he knew about the murder—that is, about the Finance Act and the unfortunate impression made by Julia's denial of any acquaintance with the victim—and we discussed at some length the steps to be taken to protect her interests. We agreed that after I had seen her I should talk to the police officer in charge of the case—Signor Vespari undertook to arrange this for me. We both felt, at this stage, that the case against Julia was so slight that the police must be doubtful whether to pursue it.

After lunch he was kind enough to invite me back to his flat and to allow me to make my telephone calls to Julia and yourself. He is, perhaps, quite enjoying the excitement of having a murder on his hands—generally speaking, it seems, the British in Venice do nothing worse than get drunk in Saint Mark's Square.

It was in a mood, therefore, of reasonable optimism that I took the *vaporetto* across the Lagoon to Chioggia. I made my way to Julia's hotel and was greeted, as I approached the reception desk, with the familiar words, 'Hello, Timothy, come and have a drink.'

Physically, at any rate, her recent difficulties seemed to have done Julia no harm. There has been, it is true, some increase in her customary dishevelment: she looks like one of Priam's daughters after a more than usually trying rape—but one, all the same, who during the Siege of Troy has eaten well, slept well and done plenty of sunbathing.

The trouble was that she knew nothing about the murder. I mean not merely that she is innocent of any complicity, but that she had no idea how or when it was discovered, or why suspicion had fallen on herself. There she was, she said, peacefully eating spaghetti in the dining-room of the Cytherea, doing no harm to anyone, when she was summoned to the Manager's office. The peremptory terms of the invitation led her to expect a rebuke of some kind; but she supposed it to have something to do with an episode earlier in the day, of which I gather she has already written to you, involving one of the waiters.

In the Manager's office she found, in addition to the Manager himself, two police officers. This, she felt, was making altogether too much of the matter, since after all, she said, the waiter had been perfectly willing. It did cross her mind, however, that he might have been even younger than he looked and that she did not know precisely what age, under Italian law, was regarded as that of consent. When, therefore, the police officers told her that they were enquiring into the death by violence of Mr Edward Watson, it was with some relief that she told them she knew no one of that name.

'That, Julia,' I said, 'was really rather a pity.'

'If you,' said Julia, 'had recently shared a bed with a young man of ethereal beauty, would it occur to you that his surname was Watson?'

'The contingency,' I answered, 'is in my case remote. I should have thought, however, that it was a perfectly respectable name, such as anyone might have.'

'Precisely so,' said Julia, sadly.

It had not been until Graziella arrived that anyone made it clear to Julia who it was who had been murdered. Fortunately, Graziella had conceived of the duties of a courier as including the protection of her clients during any interrogation by the police. She had accompanied Julia to the police station and had remained with her while she was questioned by the Vice-Quaestor—that is the title of the officer in charge of the case. The questioning had continued until after midnight, delayed by occasional disputes between Graziella and the official interpreter about the precise shade of meaning to be attributed to Julia's answers.

Following, I gathered, some rather forceful represen-
tations from Graziella, Julia was released, on terms,
however, of surrendering her passport and remaining in
the Veneto. She had spent the rest of the night on
Graziella's sofa.

The account she had given the police of Friday afternoon is the same as is contained in her last letter to you:
there is no point in my repeating it. After hearing it, I still
felt that the field of suspects was entirely open. Not only
the Art Lovers but almost anyone else, it seemed to me,
could have been in the annexe on Friday evening. In particular, though, I still thought there had been time, after
Kenneth came back from Verona, for a short but violent
quarrel between him and Ned.

I felt more troubled about the lowering effect which
the affair had had on her spirits. She attaches great significance to the signs of nervousness displayed by Ned on
the morning of his death, attributing them to a fear of a
murderous attack. She is persuaded that he was relying
on her presence to protect him, and concludes that she is
much to blame for leaving him asleep and defenceless.

'My dear Julia,' I said, 'no one in their senses would
choose you as a bodyguard.'

Since, however, she seemed unconvinced of this, I
thought I had better change the subject by telling her of
the professional reasons for my being in Venice: the idea
of anyone incurring a £400,000 tax liability which could
be avoided by a simple change of domicile was sufficiently
shocking to divert her mind. There is, I think, nothing
else in our conversation which needs to be reported to
you.

This morning, taking breakfast again with my client, I
was as sorry as circumstances permitted to find him not
yet fully recovered. I am not, I suppose, taking quite so
firm a line with Richard as my instructing solicitor would

hope. Well, the Italian lawyer dealing with his great-aunt's estate is joining us for dinner this evening—that will be soon enough to begin making him realize the seriousness of his position.

Having arranged with Signor Vespari that I would call at the Consulate at ten o'clock, I found when I arrived that he had already made an appointment for me to see the Vice-Quaestor later in the morning. He had also telephoned Graziella, to tell her of my being in Venice: this had the agreeable result that she had offered to meet me at the Consulate and to act as my interpreter in the interview with the Vice-Quaestor.

Graziella spoke indignantly on the way to the police station, of the absurdity of suspecting 'the little Signorina Julia.' There being nothing in their relative sizes to justify the epithet—Graziella is delicately built—I take it to be a term of endearment.

'The little Signorina Julia,' she said, 'is of course a most charming girl, most intelligent and serious'—Julia's attentiveness to her lectures on the Gothic and the Byzantine has evidently made a good impression—'but as for committing murder—no, Signor Shepherd, she would not know how to.' Graziella shrugged her shoulders, as if admitting some minor defect in an otherwise admirable character—she herself, no doubt, would, if she thought it necessary, commit a very competent murder. 'To stab a man—if one has seen the Signorina attempting to slice a peach—'

I agreed that Julia's dexterity would be tested to its limit by such a task.

'I have tried,' said Graziella, 'to explain this to the Vice-Quaestor. But he will take no notice, because he wants everyone to say how clever he is when there is a murder to catch the murderer ten minutes afterwards. So he has continued to question the little Signorina half the night, hoping she will say something foolish. Finally I have explained to him that we are not living in a police state, thank God, and that it is not permissible for him to do this. So at last he has agreed that I shall arrange for the Signorina to stay in Chioggia, but he will not let her go home to London.'

'Julia told me,' I said, 'how kind you had been.'

'It is nothing,' said Graziella. 'But you will understand, Signor Shepherd, that perhaps the Vice-Quaestor will not be so very pleased to see me again.'

The Vice-Quaestor, a man of sad and operatic appearance, did indeed give the impression, when we were shown into his office, of being a police officer who had his troubles and did not find them alleviated by the reappearance of Graziella. 'My own English is poor,' he said — with, as it turned out, undue modesty — 'but I have two officers both very competent to interpret. The Signora need not have troubled herself.'

'It is no trouble, Signor Vice-Quaestor,' said Graziella serenely. 'I am most happy to assist Signor Shepherd in anything he can do to help the little Signorina Julia.' Looking round his office, she evidently found it wanting in neatness and elegance. Before accepting the chair offered to her, she carefully dusted it with a paper hand-kerchief. Then, seeing that I was about to sit down without any similar precaution, she jumped up again, saying 'Excuse me, Signor Shepherd, just a moment —' and dusted my chair as well. The Vice-Quaestor began to look harassed.

But in spite of the psychological advantage of making the Vice-Quaestor feel that his office was a pigsty, it was in the course of this interview that I first began to feel seriously worried about Julia's position. It became clear, you see, that he really does think she did the murder.

It seemed at first that what impressed him was simply the sequence of events: Julia had been with the young man in his room; she had left alone; two hours later he had been found dead there — if there were an innocent explanation, it was for her to offer it.

'With respect,' I said, 'that is a little unreasonable. It is precisely on the assumption that she is innocent that she will not be able to offer an explanation.' Graziella translated this with approval; but the Vice-Quaestor looked as if he thought it a piece of sophistry. 'If she had any motive,' I continued, 'then the circumstances might appear suspicious. But what conceivable reason could she have for doing such a thing?'

'Ah, Signor Shepherd,' he answered in English, without waiting for a translation, 'who knows what a woman will do for the sake of love?' The man not only looks operatic — he thinks operatically as well.

'We are not speaking,' I said, 'of a grand passion, but of a very brief and casual liaison.'

'Ah, for him, perhaps,' said the police officer. 'But for her — consider, Signor, she has loved this man, she has given herself to him. And afterwards, if he tells her that he does not love her, that she has been a mere amusement to him — who knows what she might do then?'

'Miss Larwood,' I said, 'is not a schoolgirl, but an intelligent and sophisticated woman who has been for several years in practice at the Bar.' This statement is perfectly true — I cannot really see what there is about it to make it seem so peculiarly misleading.

The Vice-Quaestor found English inadequate to express his answer. There was a rather sharp exchange of Italian before Graziella translated it.

'The Vice-Quaestor is of the opinion,' she said, 'that it is just such a woman, a woman who has known nothing of love but has lived the cold life of the intellect, such a woman, when she believes that at last she has found happiness, who would respond with particular violence when she found she had been deceived. You must understand, Signor Shepherd,' she added, looking coldly at the police officer, 'that when the Vice-Quaestor refers to happiness he means marriage—that, in the opinion of the Vice-Quaestor, is the greatest happiness that any woman could hope for.'

'Yes, I see,' I said. 'And was there something further?'

'The Vice-Quaestor has also invited me to tell you that if the little Signorina Julia were to admit quite frankly, as he says, that that was what happened the Court would no doubt be very sympathetic. I have explained, however, to the Vice-Quaestor that the little Signorina Julia is a very nice girl, a very kind-hearted girl, who likes to please people, but she is not so foolish as to admit to a crime she has not committed in order to play even a most sympathetic part in the drama which he has invented.'

I nodded. It did not seem prudent to offer a different account of Julia's character from that at present entertained by the Vice-Quaestor. A man who sees life in operatic terms no doubt divides women into the virtuous, who will commit murder for the sake of their honour, and the wicked, who will do so for no reason at all. I suggested instead that if the crime were thought to be one of passion it was surely more probable that Kenneth Dunfermline, whose relationship with the victim seemed to have been more intimate than that of a mere travelling companion—

'No, Signor Shepherd,' said the police officer. And even Graziella shook her head.

It was at this stage that I learnt for the first time the exact circumstances in which the crime was discovered. Since Marylou has already given you a full account, there is no point in my repeating it—what she told you seems to be exactly the same as she told the police and it was confirmed, of course, by her husband and Kenneth Dunfermline. Well, it established, as you know, that Dunfermline is out of it.

It was rather a setback: I had been quite optimistic

about persuading the police that he was the most likely person to have committed the crime. Still, though he and the Americans were excluded from suspicion, there were any number of other people who would have had the opportunity.

'No, Signor Shepherd,' said the Vice-Quaestor again.

It was at this point that things began to be difficult. What made them so was the evidence of the chamber-maids. There are, apparently, four chambermaids. Their rooms are on the second floor of the annexe; but in the afternoons, instead of resting there, they prefer to sit in the entrance-way, talking and enjoying the sunshine. On Friday afternoon, they settled down as usual just after lunch—that is to say, about quarter past two—and remained there until dusk, when they dispersed to turn down the beds. From time to time one or another of them would have been briefly absent, making coffee and so forth; but there were always at least three of them there.

Questioned on Saturday morning by the Vice-Quaestor, they were all prepared to swear that the only people who had entered or left the annexe during that time were the following: Julia and Ned, going into the annexe together a few minutes after they themselves had settled down there; Julia, leaving again at about quarter past six; Mrs Frostfield, who returned at about seven; and Major Linnaker, who arrived shortly afterwards. They had not actually seen the return of the other Art Lovers; but it was only a minute or two after they had dispersed that one of them was asked by Marylou to unlock the door to the room shared by Ned and Kenneth and so became a witness to the discovery of the crime.

I have no doubt that they are all charming girls; but I did rather wish there had not been so many of them. I pointed out, however, that they had been taking, by their own account, something in the nature of a siesta. In the heat of the afternoon, it would have been natural for them to become drowsy. There would surely have been several occasions when someone waiting for an opportunity to slip unnoticed into the annexe—

'No, Signor Shepherd,' said the Vice-Quaestor, becoming, I felt, repetitive. He had questioned them closely about this possibility and they had been sure that none of them had slept—they had been taking it in turns to read aloud from a book which they found most interesting.

'Ah well,' I said indulgently, 'if they were deeply absorbed in some romantic novel—'

The book which had engaged their attention was not, as it turned out, a romantic novel: it was 'The Origin of the Family, Private Property and the State' by Friedrich Engels.

'Two of them are graduates,' said the Vice-Quaestor, spreading his hands in a gesture of despondency. 'What can one expect?' He went on to make one or two further comments, which I thought injudicious, on the higher education of women. They provoked a rather heated response, in Italian, from Graziella—for the next ten minutes I was quite unable to follow the conversation, which appeared to cover a wide range of political and economic issues. At the end of it the Vice-Quaestor looked more despondent than ever.

'I am sorry, Signor Shepherd,' said Graziella, 'you have not come here to talk about the difficulties of our poor country—you were saying?'

'I was saying,' I said, 'that if these girls were deeply absorbed in a work of political philosophy—'

But it was no use. Interested as they were in their reading, they might not have noticed anyone who simply came on to the bridge and returned to the terrace; but they were physically so disposed about the entrance-way to the annexe that no one could have entered it without disturbing them.

'Of course,' I said, 'we have been considering only the

orthodox means of access. It would have been possible, I suppose, for someone travelling by boat along the canal to climb up to one of the balconies and to leave by the same route? The bedrooms of such a hotel as the Cytherea must present an attractive target for robbery.'

Physically, the Vice-Quaestor agreed, it was a possibility: but only, of course, under cover of darkness — and the murder had been discovered a mere five minutes or so after night had fallen. There were thieves in Venice, he did not deny it, as in other great cities. But they would not be so foolish as to break in when darkness had only just fallen and people were still in their rooms changing for dinner: they would wait until the early hours of the morning, when everyone was asleep and the English and Americans had left their windows open.

'So you see, Signor Shepherd, the only persons who had any opportunity to commit the crime, apart from your friend the Signorina Larwood, are the Signora Frostfield and Major Linnaker. They are both persons of the highest respectability. Moreover, they were only slightly acquainted with the murdered man and had no reason to wish him harm.' The Vice-Quaestor's increasing confidence in his command of English seemed ominous. I decided I had better begin looking pleased and grateful.

'Yes, I see,' I said. 'Thank you, that's most helpful. The preliminary enquiries made in London on Miss Larwood's behalf do, as it happens, suggest that Major Linnaker may be rather less respectable than he seems and that Mrs Frostfield's connection with the murdered man may be less slight than she would like you to suppose.' I eased my conscience by remembering that business with the holdall at Heathrow and the conversation which Julia overheard between Eleanor and Kenneth. 'But such enquiries do, of course, involve a certain amount of time and expense. If there had been a large number of other potential suspects, I should have felt hesitant about allowing them to continue. But I now feel justified, in the light of what you have told me, in authorizing them to proceed.'

You will gather, from the absurdity of these remarks, how entirely I was at a loss. Still, the Vice-Quaestor did seem a little impressed by the notion of enquiries being made in London on Julia's behalf: at any rate, he has asked me to pass on to him any information which they may elicit.

He has also agreed to take no action so far as Julia is concerned until the forensic report is available— he is expecting this to reach him some time on Thursday morning. He is hoping, evidently, that it will shed some light on the precise nature of the weapon used: no weapon has been found— he believes that it is at the bottom of the canal and it would be useless to search for it. Still, this is, I think, one point which troubles him about his case against Julia: even he does not imagine that she would keep a stiletto in her underwear.

That, I think, is all there is to tell you about the interview. Afterwards I offered Graziella lunch— it seemed the least I could do. She declined, however, being pressed for time: she is leaving Venice this evening to spend a week in Rome. She had been wondering, it seems, if she should defer her holiday, in case Julia required her assistance; but she expresses herself satisfied, now I am here, that the matter is in safe hands— I wish I felt equally confident.

And so, after telephoning you from the Consulate and giving Signor Vespari a brief account of my interview with the Vice-Quaestor, I came, as I told you, to have lunch at the Cytherea, hoping, I suppose, for some sudden inspiration. I have had an excellent lunch, but no inspiration.

I am finishing this on the terrace, in the same corner, I think, where Julia used to write to you. The four chambermaids are still sitting in the entrance-way to the annexe. I suppose they are the same ones whose evidence is so troublesome, though today they are not reading anything, but conducting a flirtation with one of the waiters. At least, that is what it looks like — I suppose, for all I know, that it may be a seminar on political economy. I have been wondering whether it is possible that they are not telling the truth: if there were only one or two of them, it would be feasible — but four?

As a lunch-time customer, I could think of no excuse for going into the annexe; but I went and stood for a while on the bridge, from which, I am told by the waiter, one can see Byron's house. I stood looking at the view down the canal, still vaguely hoping for inspiration; but none came

It is possible, I suppose, that someone was already in the annexe when the chambermaids took up their position and afterwards escaped by way of the canal. But if there were such a person his purpose cannot have been murder — no one could have known that Ned would go back to his room. And if his object was merely theft, why commit murder? He could have slipped out easily enough while Ned and Julia were sleeping.

So it really does look as if it must be Eleanor or the Major. If you can find out anything to their discredit, it will be, I need hardly say, most helpful in my dealings with the Vice-Quaestor. As I said on the telephone, I would prefer any messages to go to the Consulate — I shall be calling in there every morning and Signor Vespari will make sure that any news is passed on to me.

I am sorry not to write more optimistically.

Yours affectionately,
Timothy.

CHAPTER 13

'Properly regarded,' said Selena, having replaced the telephone receiver, 'it's most encouraging to find that it must be either Eleanor or the Major. We shall pursue our enquiries with every confidence that we are not chasing red herrings.' She resumed her place in the secondhand armchair.

'My dear Selena,' said Ragwort, 'you speak airily of pursuing our enquiries. What, precisely, do you propose that we should do?'

'Easy,' said Cantrip. 'We'll go and question them—we've got their addresses.'

However things may be done in Cambridge, in the metropolis it is unfortunately not possible for one private citizen to arrive unannounced on the doorstep of another and to submit that other to a rigorous interrogation, using, if necessary, rack and thumbscrew. I asked if any of them might know anyone sufficiently acquainted with either suspect to enable us to make a more sophisticated approach.

'I suppose,' said Selena, 'that we must know someone.'

'Certainly you must,' I said. 'The whole object of an Oxford education is to ensure that when you want to know someone you know someone who knows them.'

'I expect,' said Ragwort, 'that Benjamin Dobble would know something about them.'

Both Selena and myself are acquainted with Benjamin Dobble; but neither of us sufficiently well to be able at sudden notice to summon him to our assistance.

'I suppose if I asked him,' said Ragwort, with an expression of rather complacent self-sacrifice, 'he'd probably agree to have dinner with us. At Oxford, he used to think . . .' Ragwort did not specify what opinion Benjamin had held of him at Oxford; but a brief consultation of the looking-glass over the mantelpiece seemed to reassure him that it was likely to be still entertained.

Benjamin joined us in the Corkscrew promptly at six o'clock. He is a large young man, whose smooth brown hair appears to be cut by the pudding-basin method: this combines with a certain roundness of feature to give the impression of a farm hand of the less intellectual type. It may, indeed, be not altogether misleading: I have heard it said that he had to work quite hard for his First in Economics — well, that may be mere malice; but there is no doubt that in the year he obtained his Fellowship of the College of All Souls the competition was unusually weak. Still, whatever reservations one may have about his intellectual capacity, if one wants to know anything about the world of art and objects, Benjamin is the man to ask. He combines the duties of his Fellowship with the post of Saleroom Correspondent to an investment periodical: there is little he does not know of such matters.

'My dear Benjamin,' said Ragwort, 'how charming of you to join us.'

'My dear Desmond,' said Benjamin, 'how sweet of you to invite me.'

Ragwort pulled an extra chair into the convivial radius of light created by the candle on our table, filled another glass with Nierstein and effected introductions between Benjamin and Cantrip.

'I gather,' said Benjamin, 'that I am expected to make myself useful. Are you proposing to invest in antiques?'

'No,' said Ragwort, 'not at the moment, Benjamin.'

'Silver?'

'Not just at present,' said Ragwort.

'My dear Desmond,' said Benjamin, 'you really had better come to the point, or I shall begin to think that you love me for myself alone.'

'But of course we do, Benjamin,' said Ragwort. 'Still, since you insist — do you happen to know a woman called Julia Larwood?'

'Woman who knocks things over?' Ragwort nodded. 'Yes, of course I do. I would go so far as to say that we are twin souls. The last time I saw her was at a party in

Balliol—we both got very drunk and sat on the stairs all evening, talking about you, Desmond. We began by talking about your virtues and went on to talk about your vices.'

'But Benjamin,' said Ragwort, 'I have no vices.'

'It was,' said Benjamin, 'our mutual regret in reaching that conclusion which established that we were twin souls.'

'Well, since you have so much in common, you will be sorry to hear that she is at present detained in Venice on suspicion of murder.'

'Dear me, how disagreeable for her. Has she, as a matter of interest, actually murdered anyone?'

'It appears,' said Ragwort, 'to have been, as murders go, a perfectly tidy, competent murder.'

'Oh, in that case, certainly, Julia can't have done it. Well, who is the victim?'

'Do you happen to have heard of a sculptor called Kenneth Dunfermline?'

'My dear Desmond, of course. He's rather important. I have gone so far as to advise my readers that they might have a little flutter on him. But Dunfermline can't have been murdered—people would have told one.'

'Not Dunfermline himself. The young man he was travelling with.'

'Oh dear,' said Benjamin. 'Oh dear—not the lovely Ned?' This notion of twin souls seemed to have something in it. Ragwort nodded. 'Oh dear, how sad, how very sad. Because he really was lovely, you know, one of the loveliest things anyone ever saw. Present company excepted, of course. But if anyone was going to murder him, I'm afraid one would rather have expected it to be Kenneth.'

'It seems,' said Selena, 'that it couldn't have been.'

'Still,' I said, 'it would be interesting, Benjamin, to know why you think so.'

'Oh—Kenneth takes things so seriously. He's a Scotsman, you know, from Ayrshire or somewhere like that. I think his father was a miner. There are certain hardships to which such a background does not, I suspect, inure one. In particular, to having one's most tender feelings made the object of mockery and contempt by heartless young men with charming profiles. Now, when that happens to someone like, say, Julia or myself, who is well accustomed to it—'

'Do have some more wine, Benjamin,' said Ragwort.

'Yes, thank you, Desmond, how kind. As I was saying— Julia and I, being used to that sort of treatment, can take it philosophically. Not so, I fear, Kenneth Dunfermline. For Kenneth, the affair with Ned was the grand passion, the real thing, the first and last, the once and for always.'

'And Ned,' asked Selena, 'did not reciprocate?'

'Well, I don't quite say that, exactly. But at parties and so forth, when people started telling Ned how beautiful he was and wondering if he might be free for lunch sometime, he didn't altogether give the impression of being unavailable due to prior commitments. On the contrary, he showed a tendency, on such occasions, to blossom like the rose and be fairly free with his telephone number. And Kenneth would stand there looking all sombre and Celtic, like the Grampians in a thunderstorm.'

'In short,' said Ragwort, 'you would be inclined to describe young Ned as something of a flighty piece?'

'My dear Desmond, what a flair you have for the *mot juste*. "Flighty" is the very word. So if Kenneth had got peeved to the point of violence, one wouldn't really have been too surprised. Still, I'm glad you say he didn't do it—he's an awfully good sculptor. And he hasn't had much luck since he came South, poor boy, what with falling for Ned and getting mixed up with Eleanor Frostfield. Just a minute, I'll get another bottle of Nierstein.'

In Selena's cry of protest, as he rose and moved to the

bar, there was more anguish than is commonly inspired by the sight of a guest contributing to the expenses of the evening; but Benjamin failed to perceive it. He became lost, to communication if not to view, among a little crowd of journalists from Great Turnstile and lawyers from Old Buildings.

'Now,' he said, returning at last to our table, 'tell me about poor Ned and why people think Julia did it.'

'In a moment,' said Selena. 'You tell us first what you mean about Kenneth being mixed up with Eleanor Frostfield. Do you mean they're married to each other?'

'Good God, no,' said Benjamin. 'What a horribly bizarre idea, Selena. No, I simply meant that he's under contract to her. Frostfield's, as you doubtless know, is a long-established firm of dealers in art and antiques. Since her late husband took refuge in mortality, Eleanor has been the majority shareholder and guiding spirit. Well, Frostfield's gave Kenneth his first exhibition — not all to himself, but as one of a group of promising young artists just out of art school. Part of the contract for the exhibition was that Kenneth shouldn't sell his work except through Frostfield's for — well, I don't know how long exactly, but it's certainly got several years to run.'

'That, I suppose,' said Selena, 'would be the usual arrangement, when a gallery exhibits the work of a particular artist.'

'An arrangement along those lines, yes, naturally. In the particular case, however, I understand that the percentage taken by Frostfield's is unusually high. And that the contract extends over an unusually long period. Well, when people are just out of art school, they'll sign anything to get an exhibition, or even a little bit of one. A few years later, when your work's selling rather well and you find the gallery is still taking the lion's share of the proceeds, it must get rather galling. Particularly, I imagine, if one is trying to retain a hold on the affections of someone like Ned.'

'Are you suggesting,' asked Ragwort, 'that the unfortunate young man was of a mercenary disposition?'

'Oh, I wouldn't say that. But fond of nice things, you know — silk shirts and good seats at the theatre and doing the shopping at Fortnum's. These, you will agree, my dear Desmond, are not unreasonable expectations for a young man with a charming profile — but a trifle expensive.'

'This contract of Kenneth's with Eleanor,' said Selena. 'I should have thought that arguably it involved an abuse of superior bargaining power. I rather think, you know, that on a good day, with the right Court of Appeal, one might give oneself a fair chance of getting it set aside.'

'Oh, my dear Selena,' said Benjamin, 'I don't doubt if Faust had had the good sense to consult you about his contract with Mephistopheles you'd have thought of a way of getting him out of it. But it's not the sort of thing Kenneth would have thought of — it's only lawyers, you know, who think that contracts are things you can get out of. And Kenneth wouldn't even know any lawyers.'

'Except Ned,' said Selena, looking dreamily at the dark ceiling.

The notion that Eleanor had done away with Ned to prevent him advising Kenneth on the possibility of breaking his contract seemed to me, if anything, rather more far-fetched than the theory that she had done so in order to secure a marginal tax advantage. Still, the discovery of any connection between her and the murdered man was a matter for some satisfaction.

'One doesn't like,' said Benjamin, 'to appear vulgarly inquisitive. But if everyone one knows has suddenly started murdering everyone else, it would be terribly nice to know about it.'

'My dear Benjamin,' said Ragwort, 'of course. You shall have a full account.'

Regret for Ned, sympathy for Kenneth, solicitude for Julia—all these seemly and appropriate sentiments Benjamin expressed and no doubt entertained. But the mind, like the compass, swings back to its centre of attraction: in the whole of Ragwort's narrative, what chiefly engaged his attention was a casual reference to the purpose for which Eleanor and the Major had been in Venice. Miss Tiverton's collection of antiques and objects had been, since her death, the subject of much speculation; and yet Benjamin had had no idea that it was available to inspection. He was at a loss to know how they could have learnt of it; and wounded in his professional pride.

'The most likely explanation, surely,' said Selena, 'is that Frostfield's had been instructed to value the collection for the purposes of probate, or whatever they have in Italy.'

'No,' said Benjamin, 'no, I don't think so. If Frostfield's were doing the valuation, Eleanor wouldn't have been doing it herself. She'd have sent some downtrodden employee to sort things out first and make an inventory.'

'Well, perhaps Kenneth was doing the donkey-work. Or wouldn't he know how to?'

'He couldn't do a professional valuation, of course. He'd probably be a good person to go through the Collection and sort out what was important—he's rather erudite artistically. If he'd been on very good terms with Eleanor, he might have done that for her as a favour and for the fun of the thing; but, for the reasons I have indicated, relations between them are thought to be strained. Besides, it still wouldn't explain how Bob Linnaker knew about it. No one in their senses would ask Bob to value a collection—well, not unless they wanted it to be much smaller after the valuation than before. Oh dear, I suppose you'll all tell me that's slander or something.'

'Benjamin,' I said, 'when you make these remarks reflecting on the probity of Major Linnaker, are we to take it that they have some basis in fact?'

'Hilary,' said Benjamin, large-eyed with reproach, 'we are colleagues—fellow scholars—I hope I may say, friends. Do you think me the sort of man to say such things if they were not true? Or at least partly true? Or at least widely believed to be at least partly true?'

'No, of course not,' I said. 'But which?'

'Ah,' said Benjamin, taking a deep draught of Nierstein. 'Now that, I am bound to admit, is a little hard to say. Bob's military career was spent for the most part in North Africa and the Middle East. Various places where the British used to have a military presence. When he first went into the antique business, the bulk of his stock consisted of things more or less looted by himself and his friends from those parts of the world. And oddly enough, quite a lot of what they'd picked up was very nice indeed. So the word got round that if you wanted something rather good for a reasonable price and weren't too fussy about provenance, Bob was the man to go to. It's a reputation he's rather traded on ever since.'

'You are surely not suggesting,' said Ragwort, 'that an antique dealer might actually wish to have a reputation for dealing in stolen goods?'

'Well, yes, Desmond dear—a certain kind of antique dealer. You see, what people like best—that is to say, what collectors like best—is to think they're getting a bargain. Now, if you see something that looks nice going terribly cheap—let us say, since we speak of things Venetian, a piece of furniture made by Andrea Di Brustolon or a Cozzi teapot for £1,000 or so—then the obvious conclusion is that it's a fake.'

'Cheap?' said Cantrip. 'A thousand quid? For a teapot?'

'Oh, certainly—after all, a Cozzi coffeepot made £17,000 at Christies a few months ago. So the obvious conclusion, in such a case, is that the thing's not genuine. But another possible explanation is that it's been come by dishonestly—and that's what the collector wants to believe, because that means it's a bargain. So that's the belief that Bob sets out to encourage. He doesn't actually say, of course, that anything is stolen — just looks mysterious about where it came from and uses a lot of phrases like "nod's as good as a wink" and "no names, no pack drill".'

'I see,' said Selena, 'and if, after all, it turns out simply to be a fake, the purchaser can hardly bring proceedings under the Trade Descriptions Act on the ground that the goods were falsely represented to have been stolen.'

'Quite so. And I would guess that a good seventy per cent of what Bob sells is quite simply fake. On the other hand, I hardly think he could maintain his reputation in the trade unless some of it were genuinely stolen. Besides, the reputation is to some degree self-fulfilling — I mean, if I'd acquired something in dubious circumstances and wanted to dispose of it, I suppose I'd probably go to Bob.'

'Really,' said Selena, 'this is all very encouraging. We have established a connection between Ned and Eleanor; and we have learnt that the Major is by no means respectable. Benjamin, you are a most admirable witness — where shall we take you for dinner?'

'Of course,' said Cantrip, 'we already knew the Major was a jolly suspicious character. Because of him stealing the holdall.'

'As it happens,' I said, 'what is suspicious is that he didn't steal the holdall.'

It was, I readily admit, an enigmatic remark: I should have been happy, if asked, to offer an explanation. Engrossed, however, in making arrangements for dinner, they did not ask for one.

In the event, we again dined at Guido's. It took some time to order the meal: the waiter who served us being of decorative appearance, Benjamin chose to prolong the process. When it was concluded, he gave his mind once more to considering how, without arousing suspicion, we might be introduced to Eleanor and the Major, with a view to their discreet interrogation.

'As far as Bob's concerned,' he said, 'I think you should just turn up at his shop on Wednesday, pretending to be ordinary customers.'

'Why not tomorrow?' asked Selena.

'Closed,' said Benjamin.

'Bother,' said Selena.

'And when I say ordinary customers—it would perhaps be useful to suggest that you were interested in something particular. Something which could not be acquired by methods altogether above board, or at any rate, not without great expense. I'll try to think of something suitable.'

'Benjamin,' I said, 'could we make it that painting that was stolen in Verona last week?'

'What painting?' said Benjamin. 'I haven't heard about it.'

I had, as I have mentioned, spent part of the previous day in reading through copies of the past week's *Times*. There had been an item in the Wednesday edition which I had thought, even then, of sufficient interest to cut out. I took out the cutting and laid it on the table.

LITTLE-KNOWN PAINTING STOLEN IN VERONA—
INTERNATIONAL ART GANG NOT SUSPECTED

Police in Verona are puzzled by the theft yesterday from the Church of Saint Nicholas of an undistinguished Madonna and Child by a little-known nineteenth-century artist. The international gang believed responsible for the recent wave of major art thefts in Italy would certainly, it is thought, have chosen one of the many more valuable paintings on view in the Church.

It is accordingly assumed that the theft is the work of a crank.

'Oh yes,' said Selena, 'I saw that in *The Times* last week.'

'I know you did,' I replied. 'You referred to it as one of the instances of the Italian crime wave. That's why I looked for it. It struck me at the time as curious — it's quite usual, of course, for people to steal valuable paintings; but to steal one of little value seems decidedly eccentric.'

'My dear Hilary,' said Ragwort, 'are you not being a little over-adventurous in your reasoning? I know the Major was in Verona on the day that the picture seems to have been stolen, but so, if you'll forgive my mentioning it, were some quarter of a million other people, not counting tourists — it is, as you know, a large and populous city.'

'Besides,' said Benjamin, 'I can't see why Bob Linnaker should steal a valueless painting any more than anyone else.'

'All the same,' I said, 'to please me, Benjamin, can you try to think of some convincing reason, before we go and see him, why that particular painting might, after all, be of interest to a customer?'

'My dear Hilary, to please you, of course I'll try. But I really do think it's a very long shot.'

I had supposed that to arrange any interview with Eleanor might prove more difficult: it was hardly to be expected that she would attend personally to the day-to-day running of Frostfield's Gallery. We were fortunate, however: the private viewing of the annual exhibition by Frostfield's of the work of promising young artists — 'alas, all heedless of their doom' said Benjamin sadly — was to take place on the following evening. Benjamin, by virtue of his professional position, had naturally received an invitation. Plainly, he could not take us all; but he could, he believed, by a little innocent deception, secure admission for Ragwort and myself.

'I shall say, Hilary, that your College has decided to invest a proportion of its substantial funds in works of art and has chosen you, with my assistance, to explore the market. As a potential purchaser, you will need no invitation. And Eleanor will be so pleased with me for bringing custom in her direction that I shall get away with bringing Desmond as well. Of you, Desmond, I shall say simply that you are a young friend of mine who was very anxious to come to the private viewing and to whom I can refuse nothing. And in that, my dear Desmond, there is no deception at all.'

'If I am to be represented,' said Ragwort, 'as a young man of dubious morals and importunate disposition, there could be no deception more gross. Still, I suppose I shall have to put up with it.'

We arranged, therefore, that Ragwort and I would call for Benjamin at his flat in Grafton Street and from there proceed with him to Frostfield's Gallery and Showroom, a few minutes' walk away, just off New Bond Street.

CHAPTER 14

It is a mistake to take Ragwort anywhere near Bond Street.

Having reflected much on the best use to be made of our meeting with Eleanor, I had concluded that certain questions could discreetly be asked only by Benjamin. I was anxious, therefore, to arrive at his flat in good time to explain to him what he was to say and to ensure that he was properly rehearsed. Leaving New Square at half past four should have given us ample time for this purpose.

I had forgotten, however, that our route from Green Park Underground station would lead us past so many establishments displaying in their windows silver, jewellery, antiques, porcelain, crystal and other luxurious merchandise. Though I made frequent reference to the harmful effects on the profile of keeping the nose pressed continually against plate glass, it took us nearly half an hour to reach Grafton Steet.

In the time remaining before Benjamin felt that we should be on our way, I was able to explain to him only once, and that in less detail than I could have wished, what he was to say to Eleanor. There had been not even the most perfunctory rehearsal. It was accordingly in a mood of some disquiet and remembering gloomily the rumours of his painstaking First that I accompanied Benjamin and Ragwort along New Bond Street, to arrive in due course at Frostfield's Gallery.

The circular blue and gold emblem on the plate-glass doors announced to the public at large that Frostfield's was a member of the British Antique Dealers' Association and to the Latin-speaking portion of it that Art has no enemies but Ignorance: a saying attributed to Benvenuto Cellini. In the marble-floored entrance hall there was no ornament but a single sculpture, about four feet high, in metal on a stone base, in a style which one would describe, I suppose, as figurative with abstract overtones.

'That's one of Kenneth's things,' said Benjamin. 'How sensible of Eleanor to have it there. People will remember, you see, that at just such an exhibition as this one some five years ago they could have snapped up something by Kenneth for a mere £500 — and now just look at the sort of price his work is fetching.'

Interested by the connection, I looked at the piece more closely. It was called 'The Death of Adonis'. My readers will remember the story from Ovid and Shakespeare — the young Adonis, beloved of Aphrodite, meets his death while out hunting and is transformed into a flower. I could not tell if Ned might have served as the model—the artist had disdained portraiture; but he had suggested persuasively the notion of the young man becoming rooted to the place where he fell, sinking perpetually down towards the earth, while the spiky-blossomed flowers pushed upwards among his limbs. The price set by Frostfield's on this achievement was £15,000.

'Kenneth's rather fond of that sort of subject,' said Benjamin. 'You know—Daphne turning into a bay tree and Narcissus turning into a narcissus and so forth.'

'What kind of flower is it supposed to be?' asked Ragwort.

'Traditionally,' I said, 'Adonis is reputed to have been transformed into some kind of anemone. I think, however, that the artist has preferred to believe that it was a species of amaranth. The flower called in English love-lies-bleeding.'

Our spirits a little clouded, we went into the room which contained the exhibition. Eleanor, it seemed to me, had not dealt so meagrely with the promising young artists as accounts of her had led me to expect: the catalogue was attractive if not luxurious; the distance between the paintings was less, perhaps, than might have been insisted on by an established artist, but only fractionally so; the effervescent white wine which was offered to the guests was one of the more respectable substitutes for champagne.

'My dear Hilary,' said Benjamin, shrugging his shoulders, when I remarked on these matters, 'what less could she do? This is, after all, Frostfield's.'

As for the assertion he had made on the previous evening that it was pointless to hold an exhibition in September, because no one would be there—it was all too false: the long room was crowded to the point of discomfort with artists and potential customers. The artists, said Benjamin, were the ones in suits; the ones in jeans and flowered shirts were the customers—solicitors and stockbrokers and so forth. Eleanor herself was at the far end — the chances of any conversation with her seemed pitifully remote.

'She is moving round the room,' said Benjamin, 'in a clockwise direction. Unless you have any superstitious objection to our moving widdershins, we ought to coincide with her somewhere near that picture of the Doges' Palace, which will make an excellent starting point for the conversation you want me to engage in.'

Following the course which he suggested, we seemed unlikely to reach the point of coincidence with Eleanor in much less than an hour. I wondered if Benjamin could remember so long the lines I had allotted him; and I observed anxiously that he gave no sign of being engaged in silent rehearsal, but allowed himself to be led into gossip by almost everyone we met on our anti-clockwise progress. I recalled dismally that the rumours of his diligent First had come from a usually reliable source.

My mind was a little distracted from these anxieties by our encountering a singularly beautiful girl. I should mention, perhaps, lest I be thought in any way to have misled my readers, that her figure was pudgy, her complexion sallow and her hair a rather drab shade of brown. These possible defects, however, pass unnoticed in a young woman whose expression is that of a medieval saint after a particularly satisfactory vision of the Eternal City. She smiled ecstatically at Benjamin. She smiled ecstatically at me. She smiled ecstatically at Ragwort.

'Congratulations, Penelope,' said Benjamin.

'Thank you,' said the girl. 'Yes, it's nice, isn't it?' Those who think the adjective inadequate to describe the joys of Paradise have not heard it spoken in such a tone.

'What,' asked Ragwort, when she had drifted blissfully away, 'was that about?'

Benjamin pointed to a small brown and grey abstract hanging a few feet away. A little red star had been stuck to the corner. 'That's hers, you see. And the star means it's sold. For rather less, I dare say, than she could earn with a fortnight's temporary typing—and Frostfield's, in any case, will be taking the lion's share. These consider-ations, however, do not weigh much with an artist who has just discovered, for the first time, that a total stranger may care for their work enough to pay hard cash for it.'

Our path at long last crossed Eleanor's, under, as Ben-jamin had calculated, the picture of the Doges' Palace. His estimate of the welcome which would be accorded me, as one commanding substantial funds for investment in works of art, proved well founded. Eleanor was charm-ing. That is to say, her manner seemed designed to merit that description: she displayed towards us a sort of girlish archness, such as a doting father might have found cap-tivating in an only daughter at the age of eight. The ef-fect was as of attempting to camouflage an armoured tank by icing it with pink sugar: a stratagem, in my view, doomed to failure.

I was wondering how I could discreetly prompt Ben-jamin to his first line, which I now felt sure he had forgot-ten, when the girl Penelope, pursuing some more erratic course than ourselves, came floating again towards us. There being in rapture no discernment, she smiled ecstatically at Eleanor.

'Ah, Penelope, my dear,' said Eleanor, 'I see we've sold your little painting. How very nice. Have you had a word with the buyer yet?'

'No,' said Penelope. 'Should I have done?'

'Well, my dear,' said Eleanor, 'I do think it would be rather a good idea, don't you? Of course, it's a very nice little picture. But knowing that particular purchaser as one does, one can't quite believe that the purchase had nothing at all to do with the fact that the artist was a rather attractive young lady. So I think it would be sen-sible if you had a little chat to him, Penelope dear.'

'Oh,' said the girl, her rapture growing dim. It was at this stage, I suppose, that I actually observed those possible defects of the face and figure which I have previously mentioned. I began to think Cellini had underestimated the enemies of art; and to wonder whether Eleanor might not, perhaps, have murdered Ned in a spirit of mere vandalism.

'Surely, my dear Mrs Frostfield,' said Benjamin, 'you speak in jest. From what one knows of that particular purchaser, it would only be if the artist were a charming young *man* that one could suspect an ulterior motive.' Benjamin has since admitted to me that there was no basis for this suggestion. He is, however, a kind-hearted fellow, always to be relied on to sign petitions and give donations to good causes.

'What a delightful picture that is,' he went on, 'of the Doges' Palace. Always a popular subject, of course, but that one is charmingly done. By the way,' he continued, looking at Eleanor with an expression of rustic innocence, 'I gather, dear Mrs Frostfield, that you've been in Venice quite recently?'

I felt a little relief from my anxieties: Benjamin had spoken his first line with admirable smoothness.

'Venice?' said Eleanor, waving her jewelled knuckles in a gesture of repugnance, 'Venice? Oh, my dear Benjamin, please don't ask me to talk about Venice.'

Upon being invited, however, to explain her distaste for the subject, she appeared willing to tell us at some length of the appalling experience which she had lately endured in that city. I do not set out verbatim her account of the murder, for it differed in no material respect from what we had heard already from Marylou. The emphasis, certainly, was a little different: Eleanor seemed to regard the matter principally as demonstrating a gross neglect on the part of the management of the Cytherea of their duty to ensure her own comfort and well-being. She

concluded by saying dramatically that she would never
stay there again.

Though her news was not in truth new to him, Benjamin managed to show on hearing it all proper signs of
amazement and distress. For myself, as one not
acquainted with either Ned or Kenneth, more general
expressions of outrage seemed appropriate, mingled with
a natural curiosity.

'Have they any idea who did it?' I asked.

'Oh yes. A girl travelling in the same group as ourselves. They arrested her almost at once. She'd been having some sort of affair with poor Ned apparently, and I
suppose they must have quarrelled. I must say, I wasn't at
all surprised about that—I always thought her a rather
unstable type: always drinking too much and falling over
things. I never cared for her.' Poor Julia—so much for
Ruth and Naomi.

Ragwort did splendidly. He lavished on Eleanor a
generous mixture of sympathy (for her appalling experience), admiration (for her fortitude in surviving it) and
indignant outrage (at the failure of the hotel to protect
her from it). There were moments when I felt that he
might be overdoing it; but he assures me that with women
such as Eleanor this is not possible.

'And you were actually interrogated by the police? Oh,
Mrs Frostfield, how perfectly disgraceful. Surely someone
could have done something?'

'My dear boy, the Manager was simply hopeless. And
the Graziella woman, who was supposed to be our
courier, wasn't even there. One was obliged to submit.'

'Dreadful,' said Ragwort, 'quite dreadful. And refusing
to find you a room in some other part of the hotel—I find
that completely unforgivable. To expect you to spend the
night in the same room, almost next to the one where
you'd found this unfortunate young man lying
murdered—'

'It wasn't I who actually found him, of course,' said Eleanor. If, as Ragwort afterwards maintained, her disclaimer came more promptly than was natural, it was by a fraction of time too minute for my own perception. 'But I had seen him carried out on a stretcher, only a few feet away from me. With a sheet over him, thank God. But that was quite dreadful enough, I do assure you.'

'Appalling,' said Ragwort. 'I do think it's wonderful of you to be here, Mrs Frostfield, so soon after such a frightful experience.'

'One has one's responsibilities,' said Eleanor heroically. 'I couldn't let down my young artists, you know — it means so much to them to have me here in person. By the way, Benjamin, you naughty man, how did you know I'd been in Venice? I thought it was quite my own little secret.'

I almost began to feel a measure of good will towards her: she could not have offered Benjamin a better cue if she had read my script herself.

'That's the extraordinary thing,' said Benjamin, now looking so innocent as to be practically half-witted. 'I had a postcard from Venice, you see, from someone who said they'd seen you there. And they simply signed themselves Bruce and said they were looking forward to seeing me. Which is really rather embarrassing, because I can't think who they are. I've been racking my brains to think who it could be. So I'd rather been hoping, Mrs Frostfield — this frightful news about Ned made me forget all about it — I'd rather been hoping, as it's obviously someone who knows you, that you might be able to work out who it is and save me from some unspeakable *faux pas* when I next meet them.'

I was filled with relief. Benjamin is a dear, good, intelligent young man: I do not doubt that the rumours about his First are inspired entirely by malice. 'Bruce?' said Eleanor. 'Bruce? How very mysterious, Benjamin. I certainly didn't meet anyone called Bruce in Venice. In fact,

I don't think I know anyone at all of that name. I'm afraid I can't help you.'

There was nothing in her gunmetal-blue eyes to suggest that she was lying; though, if Julia's account of her conversation with Kenneth was to be relied on, it seemed certain that she must be.

'Benjamin,' I said, 'about this painting that was stolen in Verona.' After leaving Frostfield's, he had hospitably invited us back to his flat for another glass of wine. 'Have you been able to give any further thought to the matter?'

'Yes,' said Benjamin, looking rather pleased with himself, like a man about to put on an amateur conjuring performance at a village fair. 'Yes, I have. You believe, Hilary, as I understand it, that Bob Linnaker has the picture but doesn't believe it has any particular value. Which, indeed, so far as one knows, it hasn't. In order, however, to persuade him to admit he has it, you wish to pose as a customer anxious to acquire it.'

'That,' I said, 'is an admirable summary of the position.'

'Well, the obvious thing, of course, would be to say that there's a Tiepolo or something painted underneath it. But it's difficult to see how you'd know about something like that — and anyway, that would just make Bob start scraping away at the thing himself. So I thought of something else, which I hope may quite appeal to you. May I invite you to entertain an hypothesis?'

'Certainly,' said Ragwort, 'we shall be delighted to.'

'Well,' said Benjamin, 'I should like you to suppose that at some time round the turn of the century the Committee, or whatever it is, in charge of the Church of Saint Nicholas in Verona had a meeting. And that one of the members pointed out that on one of the walls they had a rather boring blank space, which would look much better with a picture over it. And that another, while agreeing that this was the case, said it wasn't on, because all round the space were a lot of nice pictures by Bassetti and other great Masters of the seventeenth century and it'd have to be something that fitted in with them, and they didn't paint pictures the way Bassetti did any more. To which the first speaker replied that in the next village but one there was a young man, called, let's say, John Smith—or, since my hypothesis is set in Italy, Giovanni Fabbro—who could paint, if called on to do so, just like Bassetti, or indeed like any of the other great Italian Masters. Who could produce, in short, the sort of thing that the speaker, while not professing to be an expert in such matters, would personally be prepared to call Art, which was more than could be said for any of this Impressionist and Cubist rubbish. Will you accompany me so far in my hypothesis?'

'Certainly, Benjamin,' I said. 'Do proceed.'

'Good. So Giovanni is instructed to do a nice Madonna in the style of Bassetti, being reminded no doubt, when it comes to agreeing the price, that the work is for the greater glory of God and that only limited funds are available. His reputation spreading, he is commissioned to do similar work by other churches and by private patrons with the occasional gap between Old Masters on the walls of their villas and palazzos. I should like you now to assume the First World War.'

'By all means,' said Ragwort. 'We shall be happy to oblige you.'

'Desmond, how kind. Well then, the First World War. And as a result of it, many strange vicissitudes and reversals of fortune, leading to the disposal of a number of valuable collections. And when the collection of the Barone di Cuesto or the Conte di Cuello comes up for auction, and it is well established, on the best possible authority, that the Barone's ancestors had commissioned a number of paintings by Veronese, it is unlikely to occur to anyone that out of six paintings which all look like the work of Veronese one is actually the work of Giovanni Fabbro. Assume now, however, the passing of the years and the development of more sophisticated technologies in the authentication of paintings: so that various collectors gradually discover that some of the great Italian Masters which they are proud to possess are in fact the work of an unknown twentieth-century copyist. What,' asked Benjamin with the air of a conjuror demonstrating to his audience that the hat is completely empty, 'do you think happens then?'

'Much crossness, I should think,' answered Ragwort. 'Demands for money back. Letters to newspapers about the decline in standards in the art trade. Lawyers of two continents brushing up on the law of misrepresentation.'

'Ah yes, certainly.' Benjamin looked gratified, as if receiving confirmation that the hat was indeed empty. 'Certainly, all of that. But then. Then, my dears, when the dust has settled a little and the National and the Met are selling off these impostures for what they can get, it occurs to people that old Giovanni must have been rather a clever chap to do these convincing imitations, which have taken in all the experts for such a long time. So they start thinking that if they can't afford a real Titian or Veronese, a genuine forgery by Giovanni Fabbro might well be the next best thing. With the result, dear children,' said Benjamin, with the benevolent satisfaction of the conjuror actually producing the rabbit from the hat, 'with the result that among a certain section of collectors forgeries by Fabbro become rather sought after and, in consequence, valuable.'

'Benjamin,' I asked, 'is all this probable or merely possible?'

'It is not,' Benjamin answered, 'improbable. It's more or

less exactly what happened with Van Meegeren. With whom, indeed, the point has now been reached at which people are forging Van Meegeren forgeries.'

'Meanwhile in Verona?' I said.

'Meanwhile in Verona, as you so astutely say, Hilary, everyone knows that the third picture on the left after the first transept is not one of their valuable Old Masters but just a rather nice picture by a comparatively modern local artist. Which would be, no doubt, what they would tell the police when it was stolen.'

Ragwort was rather carried away by the story: he asked Benjamin if he really believed that the painting stolen from Verona might be valuable as a forgery. Benjamin found this a sufficient pretext to pat him indulgently on the shoulder.

'Desmond dear, I don't think anything of the kind. I haven't the faintest idea why that particular painting should have been in the Church of Saint Nicholas and I have no reason whatever to suppose that it is the work of a celebrated copyist or forger. Giovanni Fabbro is entirely my own invention. My hypothesis is a meretricious little thing, hired out to you, as it were, for half an hour's casual diversion: it is only Bob Linnaker, we hope, who may be sufficiently persuaded of her virtue to take her in marriage.'

Back in Islington, feeding the cats, I reflected on the possible significance of Eleanor's denial that she knew anyone called Bruce. One wondered if she had suspected, after all, that the story of the postcard was a fabrication, and it crossed my mind that she might, if so, telephone my College to seek confirmation of my *bona fides*. Had she done so, she would not, of course, have found anyone to confirm that I was authorized to invest the College funds in the purchase of works of art; on the other hand, in view of the happy indifference of most of my colleagues to the financial affairs of the College, she was equally unlikely to have found anyone to deny it. Remembering the chillness of her gunmetal-blue eyes, I found this a remarkably comforting thought.

CHAPTER 15

'Bags I do the Major,' said Cantrip.

Over coffee on the following morning, that is to say on the Wednesday, I had added my own impressions of Eleanor to the account already given by Ragwort. We were considering what was next to be done.

'It is to be remembered,' said Selena, 'that we are assuming the Major to be a possible murderer. If we were not making that assumption, there would be no point in seeing him. If we are making it, I am not quite happy about any of us seeing him alone.'

'If you're going to go and buy a load of stolen goods,' said Cantrip, 'you can't take a whole crowd of friends with you. The presence of third parties reduces the prospective seller to a clamlike condition.'

'Well,' said Selena, 'couldn't Benjamin go with you, as a professional adviser?'

'No,' I said. 'I asked him last night. He's flying to New York today for some exhibition or other.'

'Bother,' said Selena. 'How very heartless of Benjamin.'

'So one of us'll have to go alone,' said Cantrip. 'And why I bags it's me is because I'm the only one that knows karate. If the Major cuts up rough, I shall leap upon him with panther-like swiftness, crying "Hoocha"—old Japanese war-cry—and stun him with a single blow of incredible precision. Oh, I say, frightfully sorry, Ragwort.'

Attempting to demonstrate the proposed movement in the confined space provided for our accommodation by the coffee-house, Cantrip had brought his left elbow into abrupt contact with Ragwort's shoulder, at a moment when Ragwort was raising his cup to his lips.

'That's quite all right,' said Ragwort, 'don't worry for a moment. I had rather been hoping that this suit might last another week or so before it had to go to the cleaners; but no doubt I was wrong. In referring, however, to karate, are you quite sure that you're not confusing it with some new kind of dance?'

'Just because you're miffed about your suit,' said Cantrip, 'there's no need to be offensive about my karate. I'm jolly well up on it. I knew a chap at Cambridge who was a Black Belt and he showed me how to do it, one weekend when it was raining.'

Proficiency in the ancient art of the Samurai requires, as I understand it, some years of rigorous training. It even involves, I have been told, a certain cultivation of the soul: the question whether Cantrip has such a thing is a matter, as my readers may recall, of some dispute. Still, he has a good deal of agility and natural aggression—it did not seem to me that it would be seriously irresponsible to allow him to interview the Major alone. I nonetheless felt obliged to raise an objection.

'Cantrip,' I said, 'it won't do. He saw you at the airport, when you were looking at the luggage. He might recognize you.'

'Well yes, I expect he will,' said Cantrip. 'And if he doesn't, I'll remind him. I've got it all worked out. I'll go into his shop and pootle around for a bit, the way you do in antique shops. And after a while he'll come up to me and ask if I'm looking for anything in particular. And then I shall give a tremendous start of surprise.'

'Cantrip,' said Selena, 'you won't overdo it, will you?'

'I shall give a tremendously natural and convincing

start of surprise and say, Good heavens, wasn't he at the airport on Saturday when I was making such a frightful ass of myself? And he'll say, Good Lord, aren't you the frightful ass who couldn't find his suitcase? And I shall say, Yes, what an extraordinary coincidence. And then I'll go on to say what a frightful ass he must have thought I was. And he'll say yes, as a matter of fact, to be perfectly frank he did think I was rather a frightful ass.'

'And when,' said Ragwort, 'a *consensus ad idem* has been reached on this point?'

'Well, then I'll go on to say that why I was in such a stew was because I was supposed to be meeting my Uncle Hereward for lunch and my plane was late. I'll try to get the idea across that I'd been in Paris with a girl my uncle didn't approve of and I didn't want him to know I'd been away at all—it'll add what we in Fleet Street call human interest.'

'Is your Uncle Hereward,' asked Selena, 'the one with eccentric ideas about pure womanhood?'

'That's right. Anyway, I'll tell him that my Uncle Hereward has a tremendous thing about punctuality, being an ex-military man. And the Major, hearing that I'm related by blood to a brother officer, will fall on my neck and embrace me. Metaphorically, I mean, because I see this as a jolly English and manly sort of scene.'

'Quite so,' I said, 'but how are you going to get in the business about the picture?'

'Well, after we've chewed the fat a bit about regiments and brigades and so forth, I'll slip in something about my uncle being interested in collecting pictures and antiques.'

'That,' said Ragwort, 'will certainly carry more conviction than any claim that you yourself are an amateur of the fine arts.'

'Right. And I'll go on to say that my uncle is specially interested in forgeries, like things by this Van Megawatt chap. I'll tell the Major that if he ever comes across anything in that line I'd be jolly grateful if he'd let me know about it, because if I can put my uncle on to it it'll put me in good with him.'

'You will imply, I suppose,' said Ragwort, 'that you have expectations?'

'Yes. Subtly, though. It'd sound a bit off to say outright that I thought the old boy was going to leave me a packet. Not that he is, of course, because he thinks I'm the generation that's betrayed his ideals—but the Major's not to know that.'

'Cantrip,' I said, 'about the picture—'

'Don't flap, Hilary. What I'll say is that last week my uncle was frightfully miffed because he read in *The Times* that someone had swiped a picture he'd specially have liked to get his hands on himself. I'll say he was in Verona on holiday last year and identified this painting as something by this February chap.'

'Fabbro,' I said anxiously.

'Don't worry, Hilary—it'll be all right on the night. And the thing that miffs him most, I'll say, is that if he'd realized they didn't know its value and hadn't got it wired up to alarm bells and things, he'd have swiped the thing himself. Jolly subtle, don't you think?'

'You mean,' said Selena, 'that this will indicate to the Major, should the picture in fact be in his possession, that your uncle would have no moral objection to acquiring stolen property?'

'That's right,' said Cantrip. 'Of course, if he actually knows anything about my uncle, he'll know that anyway. But I suppose there must be people in the Army who've managed never to hear of the old boy.'

Selena remained uneasy about allowing Cantrip to go alone. Eventually we reached a compromise. We would all go together to Fulham. When prudence required, the rest of us would separate from Cantrip, but only to the extent of walking on the other side of the road. We would find a vantage point opposite the Major's antique shop and keep Cantrip under careful observation. Cantrip for his part undertook that he would avoid, if at all possible, being lured from the front of the shop into any rearward den in which a murderous attack upon him might pass unobserved.

'The only thing is,' said Cantrip, 'it may take me a bit of time to get the Major to break down and confess everything and if the solicitors for the Duke of Whatsitsname or someone like that suddenly need the services of a Chancery Junior, it won't do them much good asking at 62 New Square. Henry's not going to like it.'

'My dear Cantrip,' said Selena, 'if you are prepared to engage in a solitary interview with a possible murderer, it will be a poor thing indeed if Ragwort and I lack the courage to tell Henry that we are all going to a most important lunch and may be gone some little time.'

'Quite so,' said Ragwort. 'Besides, with any luck, Henry will leave for lunch before we do and we can leave a message with the temporary typist.'

Remembering the tedious complexities of reaching the New King's Road by public transport, Selena, that morning, had prudently brought her motor-car to Lincoln's Inn. At the hour when the members of 62 New Square would usually have gone to lunch, we set out in it for Fulham. Having negotiated, with that brisk insouciance on which I have previously commented, the complexities of the one-way system between Lincoln's Inn and the Thames Embankment, she drove westwards through Chelsea.

Ragwort, because he has a house there, contends that Fulham is going up in the world. I do not quite like to argue with him about it. I must confess, however, that the New King's Road, at any rate, always gives me the impression of moving in the reverse direction. Those substantial terraced houses can never, I suppose, have been intended for occupation by the indigent; but the state of their paintwork and pointing suggests that they were acquired some years ago in a period of actual or expected affluence which afterwards proved short-lived or illusory.

There are, in this part of London, numerous establishments dealing in second-hand merchandise, declining, with more or less regularity as one proceeds westward, from antiques to bric-à-brac to junk. The premises occupied by Major Linnaker were in the doubtful no-man's-land between the first and the second. We observed with satisfaction that his shop was situated almost directly opposite a public house whose landlord had had sufficient confidence in the warmth of the September weather to place outside on the pavement a wrought-iron table and chairs.

Selena drove past the shop. Turning right, some hundred yards beyond it, she brought her motor-car to a halt in a quiet side-street.

'On leaving,' she said, as she locked the vehicle, 'I think, Cantrip, that it might be prudent—'

'I am not,' said Cantrip, 'a complete imbecile. If a chap's going east and stops casually to look in an antique shop, it's definitely fishy if he turns west again when he comes out of it. I'll turn left, left and left again and rendezvous here. When I leave—'

'We'll give you two minutes' start,' said Selena, 'to make sure you're not being followed.'

'Roger,' said Cantrip. 'Over and out. See you all later.'

'Cantrip,' said Selena, 'you will be careful?'

'Absolutely,' said Cantrip.

He left us and began to stroll back along the New King's Road. Crossing to the other side, the rest of us

maintained an even pace with him and, as we hoped, an
equal appearance of *nonchaleur*. Reaching the public
house, we sat down at the wrought-iron table and watched
him. As if his eye had been caught by some object of interest in the window, he paused outside the Major's
antique shop.

The Major, in displaying his wares, had made no
attempt at uncluttered elegance. He had evidently been
happy to surround a Jacobean sideboard with a set of
Sheraton chairs—I supposed, in the light of what Benjamin had said, that they were all faked; but close beside
them there was a china umbrella-stand in a sort of willow
pattern, which I thought must be genuine—it seemed too
hideous for anyone to have wished to copy it.

'Our presence here,' said Ragwort, 'would appear more
natural if we were drinking something. Shall I get some
beer?'

'Excellent,' said Selena. 'And some sandwiches. It may
be all we'll get for lunch.'

Ragwort went indoors in search of food and drink.
Selena and I, remaining seated in our chairs on the pavement, saw Cantrip enter the antique shop and begin to
pootle. There emerged in due course from the interior a
figure whom we readily identified, even with the width of
the road between us, as the Major: his bristling white
moustache and bronzed complexion were easily recognized. We saw him approach Cantrip, asking him, presumably, whether he was more particularly interested in
the Sheraton chairs or the china umbrella-stand. Cantrip
looked up.

'Ah,' said Selena, 'that's Cantrip's start of surprise.'

Ragwort returned, carrying three pints of beer and a
plate of sausage rolls: the barman had greeted with de-
rision his request for sandwiches, reminding him, in a
manner which Ragwort had found offensive, that the
bread delivery men were on strike. Sipping the beer and

nibbling cautiously at the sausage rolls, we continued to observe the forefront of the antique shop.

'Agreement has now been reached,' said Ragwort, 'on the question whether Cantrip is a frightful ass.'

The sausage rolls were even nastier than the sandwiches would probably have been. I began to wish that the sausage roll deliverers had also been on strike.

'I think,' said Selena, 'that the moment has now been reached at which the Major metaphorically falls on Cantrip's neck in a metaphorical embrace.' I agreed that this seemed a reasonable conclusion—the Major had produced from some cupboard or other a bottle and two glasses.

'I suppose,' said Ragwort, 'that there's no danger of him trying to poison Cantrip?'

'I hardly think,' I said, 'that Cantrip can have said anything so far to provoke him to such extremities. Besides, he is drinking from the same bottle.'

The relaxed and convivial attitude of those in the antique shop suggested that their conversation was concerned rather with military anecdote than with any overtures for the purchase of stolen property. We could not in fairness blame Cantrip for taking his time—we had warned him to be slow and subtle. I confess, however, that I began to feel that he was taking longer than was altogether necessary: comfortably ensconced and drinking at the Major's expense, he had become, it seemed to me, a little forgetful of the tedium and discomfort endured by those watching over him.

On account of the bread strike it was the time, as my readers may remember, when the exchange of recipes for baking at home had displaced the Economy as the chief topic of light conversation. Ragwort had a recipe, obtained from his grandmother, infinitely superior to any which had appeared in the public press. Selena asked him to write it out for her. Watching him engaged on this task and listening to his lecture on the importance of accurate measurement, we forgot for several minutes to take any notice of what was happening in the antique shop.

When we next looked the Major was holding a gun.

Julia is no doubt right in attributing Ragwort's unconquered virtue to the expression of aloof disapproval which he adopts when confronted with anything in the nature of a proposition. It is also true, however, that he can run extremely fast: on Sundays during the cricket season he is in great demand in his native Sussex village on account of his speed between the wickets. While Selena and I were still waiting impatiently at the kerbside for a safe passage through the traffic, Ragwort, with no worse mischief than might befall his immortal soul from the curses of a startled lorry driver, was across.

Selena's impatience was, I confess, rather greater than my own. Little as I liked the prospect of the evening newspaper containing the headline 'Barristers Shot in Fulham Fracas', I did not think it would be improved by the insertion of the words 'and Oxford Don'. This seemed to me precisely the sort of moment at which the proper course is to summon a constable. Unfortunately, there was none at hand; and Ragwort and Selena, with the impetuous enthusiasm of youth, seemed unlikely to wait until one arrived. I could not, I felt, with any semblance of decorum, remain on one side of the New King's Road while the junior members of 62 New Square struggled with an armed maniac on the other.

For a few moments our view of the antique shop was obscured by the passage of an articulated lorry. When we could again see the interior, the scene had changed dramatically: it was now Cantrip who was holding the gun. I perceived that I must have wronged him in doubting his skill at karate. With a movement of amazing swiftness, he had disarmed the Major and would now lead him forth into the New King's Road; and would keep him

covered while Ragwort, now standing slightly disconcerted outside the shop, summoned assistance from the
appropriate authorities.

Nothing of the sort occurred. After a few moments,
Cantrip put down the gun. He turned so that his back was
towards us. Ragwort continued to stand outside, apparently lost in admiration of the umbrella-stand. A driver
who had slowed down to let Selena and myself cross the
road banged impatiently on his horn: we waved apologet-
ically and stepped back from the kerbside—there no
longer seemed any point in crossing.

What one so much admires in Selena is her instinct for
what the moment requires: she went straight to the bar
and came back with three large Scotches.

Ragwort, returning to us at a more prudent pace than
he had left, was unable to explain the incident. Cantrip,
it seemed, observing his presence, had turned away from
the window, put his hands behind his back and pointed
both thumbs upwards: this had been construed by
Ragwort as meaning that all was well. He had then
spread his palms and made a pushing gesture: Ragwort
had taken this to indicate a desire to continue undisturbed his *tête-à-tête* with the Major.

We continued to watch the window of the antique
shop. Cantrip and the Major had both sat down again
and were engaged in apparently amiable conversation.
We saw the Major open another bottle.

After two hours or so Cantrip came out. He turned left
as arranged. His step, I thought, was rather less brisk
than usual. We waited, as we had promised, for two
minutes to make sure that he was not being followed.
Satisfied that he was not, we rose and went back to the
car. Cantrip was leaning wearily against it, pitifully pale,
poor boy.

'Cantrip,' said Selena, 'are you all right?'

'No,' said Cantrip, 'actually, I think I'm dying. But if

we can go and have some coffee at Ragwort's, I suppose I'll probably survive.'

I was at a loss to account for the poor boy's condition. He had drunk, certainly, a rather large quantity of whisky, unaccompanied by any solid food; but I would not have thought, on the basis of my knowledge of him, that this alone would have had so marked an effect. The incident which had alarmed us had apparently left him unmoved, and the rest of his interview with the Major had seemed to pass off peacefully enough; yet we saw that it had left him exhausted in mind and body.

'Cantrip,' said Selena, 'what was all that business with the gun?'

'What gun?' said Cantrip.

I reminded him gently—for he seemed to be suffering from some kind of amnesia—that at an early stage in the interview the Major had evidently been threatening him with a firearm.

'Oh,' said Cantrip, 'that wasn't a gun exactly. That was a Baker flintlock rifle—one of the ones they issued to the Corps of Riflemen in 1800. Jolly interesting—I saw it hanging on the wall and asked if I could have a look at it. I say, you didn't really think he was threatening to shoot me with it, did you?'

'Yes,' said Selena. 'Anxiety was entertained.'

'Oh, come off it,' said Cantrip. 'You'd have to be a complete lunatic to try and shoot anyone with a flintlock rifle in this day and age.'

'We didn't know that, Cantrip,' said Selena.

'Oh,' said Cantrip. 'Frightfully sorry.'

'Did you manage,' I asked, 'to tell him about the picture?'

'Oh yes,' said Cantrip. 'I told him all about my Uncle

Hereward being frightfully keen on forgeries and things and specially this February chap.'

'Fabbro,' I said.

'Right,' said Cantrip. 'Well, I told him all about that and about that painting that got stolen in Verona. And he's promised to ask around a bit among one or two pals of his—mum's the word, he said, no names, no pack drill—to see if he can find out anything about it. And if he does, he'll let me know about it right away, so that I can tell my Uncle Hereward and get in good with him. Oh yes, that bit all went all right—I got it all in quite quickly, actually.'

'In that case,' asked Ragwort, 'what were you talking about for the remaining two hours?'

'Women,' said Cantrip.

'Cantrip,' said Selena, 'if you're going to tell me that while we were sitting outside that beastly pub eating beastly sausage rolls and worrying about whether the Major was going to try to shoot you, you were simply engaged in an exchange of schoolboy scurrilities—' but the look of exhaustion returning to Cantrip's eyes silenced her reproaches.

'Was it really only two hours?' he said. 'It seemed longer than that. Much longer. Much, much longer. The Major's known a lot of women. English women, Italian women, Arab women, Serbo-Croatian women. The right sort of women, the wrong sort of women. Women who would, women who wouldn't, women who might have. He told me about them all. Are you sure it was only two hours?'

'Couldn't you make him stop?' said Ragwort.

'No,' said Cantrip.

'Why did you let him start?' said Selena.

'Well,' said Cantrip, 'I thought if I got him talking about women he'd be bound to say something about Julia sooner or later. After all, it's only a week since he asked her to marry him.'

'And did he?' I asked.

'Yes,' said Cantrip. 'In the end, he did. Not by name—but he said he'd had an unhappy experience very recently when he thought he'd found the right woman at last and she turned out to be the wrong sort. Frightfully brainy girl, he said, who'd been to Oxford, so she could run rings round a simple soldier like him. She had him completely fooled, he said, and he only found out in the nick of time that she was a wrong 'un.'

'Really,' said Selena, 'what frightful cheek. For a man who makes his living from selling stolen antiques to refer in those terms to a member of Lincoln's Inn—'

'Yes, that's what I thought,' said Cantrip. 'Anyway, I asked him how he'd found out about her being the wrong sort and he clammed up on me and said it was too painful to talk about. Well, I thought that was pretty suspicious, because up till then he'd been as unclamlike as you could get. So what I reckon is that he thought if he talked any more about it he'd give himself away—I mean, about having found out about Julia and the chap from the Revenue and done the chap in in a frenzy of jealous passion, like I've always said he did.'

'I hope,' I said, 'that you have told him how to get in touch with you if he finds out anything about the painting?'

'Yes, I gave him my phone number in Chambers. So the next time he wants to tell someone about some Outer Mongolian woman of the wrong sort who wouldn't, I suppose he'll ring me up.'

'I suspect,' I said, 'that you may hear from him very soon. But I don't think,' I added, seeing the hunted look in the boy's eyes, 'that he'll want to talk about women.'

CHAPTER 16

I awoke on Thursday morning with an unshakable conviction, not sufficiently accounted for by any knowledge of my conscious mind, that matters were moving towards a crisis — a conviction so powerful that I felt compelled yet again to disregard the call of Scholarship: delaying my departure from Islington to make one necessary telephone call, I made my way directly to 62 New Square.

Knocking on the door of the largest room of the Nursery and being invited to come in, I found Ragwort and Cantrip reading a letter, which I perceived to be in that clear, careful hand in which Timothy, when my pupil, had written his always conscientious essays. It was the letter which I have already set out in Chapter 12 of this volume. Ragwort handed it to me, saying, however, as he did so, that it added nothing to what we already knew. I settled down in the large leather armchair and began to read.

'Hilary,' asked Ragwort, 'are you thinking of staying long?'

'Am I,' I asked, 'unwelcome?'

'My dear Hilary, of course not,' said Ragwort. 'But we're having a certain amount of difficulty with Henry. He's just a little put out that none of us returned to Chambers after lunch yesterday.'

'Miffed as a mongoose,' said Cantrip.

'If I am right in assuming,' said Ragwort, 'that a mongoose is even more miffed than the maggots which are the usual standard of comparison, that is certainly the case. Your presence, Hilary, has been noted and is regarded as contributing to our delinquency. If Henry finds you here again this morning—'

I assured them that my entry to 62 New Square had been unobtrusive and that if Henry's footstep should be heard outside I would conceal myself, with all swiftness, behind a curtain.

Hoping to appease Henry's indignation, they had undertaken not to go out for coffee. Selena, however, foreseeing the need for such a gesture, had brought with her to Chambers a jar of instant coffee and her electric kettle.

She seemed downcast, a thing unusual with her. She felt that our enquiries had been ineffectual: they had established, she said, that I disliked Eleanor and that Cantrip was bored by the Major—neither of these facts, she felt, would be sufficient to persuade the Vice-Quaestor to transfer his suspicions from Julia.

'More than that, surely,' said Ragwort. 'We know there's a definite connection between Eleanor and Kenneth Dunfermline, and therefore between Eleanor and the dead man.'

'Yes,' said Cantrip. 'And we know the Major deals in stolen goods. I mean, if the Italian fuzz think that's respectable—'

'He hasn't got a criminal conviction,' said Selena. 'The Vice-Quaestor is going to say it's mere gossip.'

'Well,' said Cantrip, 'there's always the holdall. We know he pinched that.'

I pointed out that if Cantrip had been listening to me on Monday evening he would have heard me mention that the Major had not stolen the dead man's holdall.

'I was listening, Hilary,' said Cantrip. 'But I thought you were just having a loopy spell, due to spending too much time in the Public Record Office or something, so I thought I'd do the tactful thing and not draw attention to it.'

'The Major,' I repeated, 'did not steal the dead man's holdall.'

'He jolly well did,' said Cantrip. 'I saw him do it. You've got first-hand evidence from a member of the English Bar and if you're going to start casting aspidistras on its reliability—'

'My dear Cantrip,' I said soothingly—for one knows that he is inclined, when heated, to start throwing books at one—'my dear Cantrip, I am not for a moment doubting your word. I am saying merely that in interpreting the evidence you have considered it in part, rather than as a whole. It is a pitfall not easily avoided save by the trained scholar.'

'Hilary,' said Selena, handing me a cup of coffee, 'we are supposed, as you are very well aware, to be working. You have now, however, aroused in us a curiosity which will prevent our doing so until you have explained your theory, whatever it may be, about the holdall. Please be kind enough to do so with all expedition.'

'Do you remember,' I asked, not resenting her asperity, for I knew her to be under strain, 'Julia's first letter?' They nodded. 'You will recall, then, that Julia identified the Art Lovers among her fellow passengers by looking at the labels on their hand luggage. Including—indeed, beginning with—the Major. From which we may conclude that on the journey out the Major had something with him which the airline was prepared to regard as hand luggage. It was not a day, as we know, on which a broad view was being taken—they had disallowed Julia's suitcase. Now, when we saw them returning to Heathrow, the Major had two pieces of luggage: one was a large suitcase, which even the most permissive airline would not have permitted him to have in the passenger compartment; the other was the holdall believed by Cantrip to be the property of the murdered man.'

'Well,' said Cantrip, 'if the Major had another case with him, he must have left it behind in Venice and taken the holdall instead.'

'Why in the world should he do that?' I asked.

'Whatever you say, Hilary,' said Cantrip, 'it had the dead chap's name on the label.'

'From which we may conclude,' I answered, 'either that the Major had stolen the holdall; or that he had stolen the label.'

They sipped their coffee and looked thoughtful.

'Why,' asked Ragwort, 'should he do that?'

'Let us suppose, my dear Ragwort, that you have an object which you wish to take through Customs and the discovery of which will occasion a certain embarrassment. Would it not be prudent, in those circumstances, to ensure that if the case containing it happens to be opened by a Customs official the name on the label is that of someone other than yourself? Someone, naturally, travelling in the same group, so that it will remain with your own luggage and can easily be reclaimed at the end of the journey if nothing untoward has taken place.'

'Yes,' said Ragwort. 'Yes, I can see that it might be. But why do you assume that the label is stolen, Hilary? Why not simply get a blank label and write someone else's name on it?'

'You would want to use one of the labels supplied by the travel agents, who generally give only two to each passenger. Yours, it is to be assumed, already have your own name on them. Besides, you would have the difficulty of forging the handwriting. No, I am fairly sure that you would want to steal the label. And that, I suggest, explains the Major's surreptitious visit to Ned Watson's room on Friday morning.'

'It's quite ingenious,' said Selena. 'And I'm perfectly prepared to believe that the Major had something he wanted to smuggle out of Italy. What I don't understand, Hilary, is why you think it's that painting that was stolen in Verona. When an antique dealer of dubious character has been rummaging round in Venice for a week, there are surely a great many other things—'

The telephone on Ragwort's desk emitted the bad-tempered buzz which indicates a desire to attract attention on the part of someone in the Clerks' Room. Answering, he was told by Henry, in tones of the utmost gloom, that the young American lady was here again and on her way up to see him.

'It seems,' said Ragwort, replacing the telephone, 'that Marylou is paying us another visit. I wonder why.'

'Possibly,' I said, 'because I asked her to.'

'Hilary,' said Ragwort, 'that really is a bit much.' But the girl's arrival precluded further protest: he was obliged instead to express his pleasure at seeing her again; to offer her a chair; and to ask Cantrip to find another cup.

'My dear Marylou,' I said, 'how kind of you to come so promptly.'

'Please don't mention it, Professor Tamar,' she answered, with the charming deference which she had shown at our first meeting. 'If there's anything I can do to help Julia—have you any news of her?'

'Not yet,' I said, 'but we are expecting further developments very shortly. Did you manage, I wonder, to find the book I spoke of?'

'Why, certainly,' said Marylou, taking from her large and expensive shoulder-bag a guide book to the city of Padua.

'Oh,' asked Ragwort, looking surprised, 'did Julia lend you that as well?'

'No,' answered the girl. 'It's one we got on the visit to Padua. But Professor Tamar called and asked me—' she paused, looking at me as if seeking my permission to disclose what had been said.

'I was anxious,' I said, 'to have a brief glance at the guide to Padua. It is almost impossible in London to obtain individual guide books to the smaller Italian cities, and your copy, Ragwort, so far as I know, is still with

Julia. Since Marylou was the only other person I knew who had recently visited the city, I rang her to ask whether by any chance she had acquired a guide book. She told me that she had and has now very kindly brought it round.'

'Hilary,' said Cantrip, in a tone which he seemed to believe soothing, 'you're having another of your loopy spells. Nothing happened in Padua. Verona was the place where the picture got stolen.'

'Thank you, Cantrip,' I said, 'I am well aware of that.' I began to look through the index to the guide book.

There was another irritable buzz from the Clerks' Room, answered again by Ragwort. 'There's a telephone call for you, Cantrip,' he said. 'I'll say you'll take it in Selena's room, shall I?'

The index proving less informative than I had hoped, it took me some little time to find the passage I required and to confirm my expectation of its content. I had just done so when Cantrip returned.

'That was the Major,' he said. 'He says he's got the painting.'

Or something, at any rate, which seemed to the Major, from the works of reference he had consulted, to be remarkably like it. As he had promised, he had asked around among his mates about the stolen picture; none of them knew anything about it; but one, by an extraordinary coincidence, had discovered a virtually identical painting while clearing out his attic the previous week. It was not for the Major to disbelieve his friend's story. Still less was it for the Major to tell Cantrip that it was in fact the painting stolen in Verona—if that had been the case, and if the Major had known it to be the case, it would of course have been his duty to inform the police. On the other hand, strictly between Cantrip, himself and the gatepost, he thought, if Cantrip's uncle were to come and have a look at it, that he might be very struck by the resemblance.

'Congratulations, Hilary,' said Selena. 'You seem to have guessed right.'

'My dear Selena,' I said, 'the careful process of reasoning by which the Scholar advances from established premise to ineluctable conclusion is hardly to be described as guesswork.'

'My dear Hilary,' she said, 'of course it was guesswork. The painting might have been stolen by anyone — well, anyone who was in Verona on that day.'

'I do not dispute,' I said, 'that there would have been a large number of people in Verona on Tuesday of last week. Among them, however, I suspect there were only three who believed that the Church of Saint Nicholas there contained a Madonna by the younger Tiepolo. And two of them were talking about Catullus.'

I picked up again the guide book brought by Marylou and turned to the passage I had been reading when Cantrip returned from his telephone call. 'It is a misapprehension, you see, likely to be entertained only by someone going round Verona with the assistance of a guide book to Padua.'

There was a brief silence, which ended with Selena saying, 'Nonsense, Hilary. Julia did very well in Verona.'

I read to them the paragraph in the guide book to Padua in which reference was made to the Madonna by Tiepolo in the Church of Saint Nicholas. Then I picked up the guide to Verona, still lying on Ragwort's desk, and read them the description of the Church in that city dedicated to the same Saint — it made no mention of any work by that particular Great Master. I spread out the maps folded inside the cover of each guide book, pointing out that in each case the name of the town was shown only on the upper right-hand corner, so as to be invisible if the map were folded for convenient study of the central portion. I showed them how easily the blue line which represented the canal half-encircling Padua could be taken to represent the river which embraces in similar manner the city of Verona. I demonstrated that every street, square and building identified by Julia in Verona with the aid of her guide book had its counterpart in Padua.

Selena, for some reason, was rather put out about it all. Julia, she said, had been doing her best; if the Italians were so inconsiderate as to call all the streets by the same names in different towns, that was not Julia's fault; if people were foolish enough to treat her casual remarks as the cornerstone for a full-scale art robbery, still less was that Julia's fault.

'Furthermore,' she went on, apparently regarding me as in some way to blame, 'whatever you say, Hilary, it was still pure guesswork. Until you saw the guide book to Padua this morning, the whole idea was the merest conjecture.'

'By no means,' I said. 'It was always, at the very least, highly probable. My dear Selena, let us be a little realistic. If one sends Julia off to Italy with four guide books, all wrapped in brown paper covers, what are the odds against her having the right one in the right place every time?'

'Oh, really,' said Ragwort. 'One knows, of course, that Julia is a complete half-wit, but even so—'

'I don't think you should talk that way about Julia, Mr Ragwort,' said Marylou, her customary diffidence qualified by indignation. 'Julia is a very intelligent and highly educated person.'

'Quite so,' I said. 'With a dim and illiterate half-wit the odds against are about 250 to 1. With a highly intelligent and educated half-wit such as Julia they are astronomical. I thought from the start that there was something un-natural about Julia's success in Verona. And on Monday I realized that it must have been the wrong guide book. Julia, you will recall, was using in Verona a guide book written in Italian. But on Monday, when Marylou brought back the guide to Verona which Julia had lent her, you picked it up, Selena, and read from it, quite easily and without hesitation, an account of communications between that city and Venice. Remembering that your many talents do not include any fluency in Italian, I knew without even looking at it that it was not the one Julia had been using in Verona.'

'Oh,' said Selena. There was a further silence.

'I'm sorry, I guess I'm a little confused,' said Marylou. 'Is it your hypothesis, Professor Tamar, that Major Linnaker stole a painting because Julia had used the wrong guide book?'

'It is our view,' said Ragwort—the principle of giving credit where it is due has few adherents in Lincoln's Inn—'that Major Linnaker was responsible for the theft of a painting reported stolen last week from the Church of Saint Nicholas in Verona. We also believe that he brought the picture back to England in a holdall labelled with the name of the murdered man.'

'Does that mean,' asked Marylou, 'that the Major did the murder?'

'Well—' said Ragwort, and looked at me. I said nothing.

' 'Course it does,' said Cantrip. 'The chap from the Revenue found out what he was up to and the Major bumped him off. I always said it was the Major that did it.'

'It must mean, at any rate,' said Selena, 'that the Vice-Quaestor can no longer treat the Major as a person above suspicion. And the Italians, I believe, take a rather dim view of people stealing their works of art. When Timothy tells the Vice-Quaestor that the Major goes in for that kind of thing and can be shown to have done so during his recent holiday—I really do think, you know, that on the strength of that we might have some more of Timothy's sherry.'

Confident of the satisfaction that our news would give

him, we drank his sherry with a clear conscience. We explained to Marylou that we were expecting him to telephone very shortly, to tell us the result of the forensic report; and assured her that she was welcome to stay until he did so. Nearly an hour had passed, however, and we had consumed a very fair part of a bottle, by the time Henry, still lugubrious, announced that Mr Shepherd was calling from Venice and wished to speak to Miss Jardine. Gathering round the telephone, we were able, without excessive difficulty, to make out what Timothy was saying.

'Timothy,' said Selena, 'we have some news for you.'

'I rather think you'd better hear mine first,' said Timothy. Despite the intervening distance, his anxiety was perceptible. 'The Vice-Quaestor has just told me the result of the forensic report. It's rather disturbing.'

'Yes,' said Selena, 'yes, all right.'

'The doctor who examined the body says that Ned Watson was killed some time in the early afternoon. Not later than three o'clock. He'd be inclined to think it was earlier; but three o'clock is the outside limit.'

An expensive ten seconds of silence on the international telephone line was followed by Selena saying, 'Dear me. Does that mean that neither Eleanor nor the Major could have done it after all?'

'Yes,' said Timothy. 'Yes, it seems to. And it also means, you see, if Julia's evidence is accepted, that she must have spent most of Friday afternoon sleeping beside a corpse. It's all rather unsatisfactory.'

CHAPTER 17

It was, as Selena said, a pity, because the medical evidence had been in other respects most helpful. It had shown that the blow which killed Ned Watson had been one of great power and accuracy, which had driven some long and pointed blade at a single thrust into his heart. Save that the young man had evidently cut himself while shaving, there was no other wound of any kind.

The Vice-Quaestor had admitted that it was not a blow which would easily be inflicted by a woman; but women, he said, were strange creatures—in moments of passion they found amazing strength. Not, however, Timothy had suggested, even at their most passionate, an instant knowledge of anatomy—a subject of which Julia was entirely ignorant.

The Vice-Quaestor had said again that women were strange creatures. It was, he agreed, remarkable that she should have achieved such a blow. Less remarkable, however, than the suggestion that some entirely unknown person, with some altogether mysterious grudge against the Signor Watson, had entered the annexe on Friday morning, had lain in wait there on the uncertain chance of his victim returning unaccompanied, had stayed patiently in hiding while Julia and the Signor Watson enjoyed their pleasures and Julia fell asleep, had struck the fatal blow without disturbing her and had then remained hidden for a further five hours until darkness permitted him to escape by way of the canal. The Vice-Quaestor felt that this would be a very remarkable course of conduct. Quite apart from the unusual circumstance—as it seemed to the Vice-Quaestor, though if Timothy were to say that such a thing would in England be quite commonplace the Vice-Quaestor would naturally be obliged to believe him—the, as it seemed to him, unusual circumstance of a lady having risen from the side of her lover without observing that he was now a corpse.

'One would think,' said Ragwort, 'that even Julia—'
'Yes,' said Cantrip. 'Yes, one would.'
We went uncheerfully for lunch, Marylou remaining

with us. We again made our way to the Corkscrew, where at lunchtime they offer quite an agreeable salad. Selena bought a bottle of Nierstein; but the meal lacked festivity. It was impossible to talk of anything but Julia's difficulties; equally impossible to do so with any optimism.

'Well,' said Cantrip, 'we're left with the Bruce chap. I always said it was the Bruce chap.'

'No,' said Ragwort, 'you said it was the Major.'

'What I always said was,' said Cantrip, 'that if it wasn't the Major, then it was the Bruce chap. And it wasn't the Major, so it is the Bruce chap. This chap Bruce,' he added, for the enlightenment of Marylou, 'was trying to nick something from Kenneth Dunfermline — we don't know what it was, but something jolly valuable. So the way I see it is this. Bruce knows Friday's his last chance, because everyone's going back to London next day, and he weasels into the annexe at lunchtime, when he thinks the coast's clear. But Dunfermline's hidden this thing pretty carefully, and Bruce is still looking for it when Ned and Julia come back unexpectedly. So he hides in the wardrobe. When he thinks they're both asleep, he comes out of the wardrobe with a view to making a swift getaway. But he stubs his toe against the bed or something and Ned wakes up again. So Bruce stabs him.'

'Why?' asked Ragwort. 'Surely it would be more sensible simply to run away?'

'Right, the natural thing would just be to scarper. So what I reckon is that Bruce is someone Ned knew, and he's got to stab him because he's been recognized. He doesn't need to stab Julia, because she's asleep. Anyway, then he nips downstairs and sees all these chambermaids sitting round in the doorway and decides he can't risk going past them. So he holes up somewhere in the annexe till it gets dark and then he swims for it.'

'Properly regarded,' said Selena, turning her wine glass between her fingers, 'it is a by no means unconvincing theory. The difficulty is that we can't find out who Bruce is. Well – I suppose the accuracy of the blow must suggest someone with a medical qualification: if we could persuade the Italian police to make a list of medical men registered as guests in hotels in Venice last week –' but the unlikelihood, on the present state of the evidence, of securing the Vice-Quaestor's cooperation in such an enterprise discouraged even Selena.

Wearying of the sense of being at a funeral breakfast, I began to reread Timothy's letter, at which earlier I had had time to glance only briefly. There continued round me a subdued discussion of ways of discovering the identity of Bruce; but I paid little heed to it. I imagined instead the terrace of the Cytherea, where Timothy, and earlier Julia, had sat and written their letters to Selena. I tried to imagine the passage and re-passage on Friday morning of various people across the bridge to the annexe. There was something about it, I knew, which my unconscious mind had already recognized as rather curious. I gave all the attention of my conscious mind to identifying what it was.

By the time I had drunk my second glass of Nierstein, it was clear to me what must be done.

'Marylou,' I said, 'can you go back to Venice?'

Asked, perhaps, a trifle suddenly, the question briefly bewildered her. It took a little time to explain at greater length that I wished her to take the next available flight back to Venice. I realized, I said, that I was asking her to incur considerable trouble and expense without offering an explanation of its purpose; but the time for an explanation was unfortunately not yet ripe.

'Well,' said Marylou, 'if you think it's necessary, Professor Tamar –'

'I think that it is,' I said, 'extremely desirable.'

'Then of course I'll go,' said the admirable American girl. 'I'll go call the airline and find out when the next

flight is.' She rose from her chair and moved towards the
telephone. The little crowd of journalists who surrounded
it parted in admiration of her elegance.

'Hilary,' said Selena, 'have you the slightest idea what
you're doing? You're asking that girl to spend a very large
sum of money—'

'My dear Selena,' I said, 'if Ragwort's judgment is to
be relied on, the fare to Venice is rather less than she
would pay for a dress; and she has worn a different dress
on every occasion that we have seen her.' I dissuaded
Selena with some difficulty from any quixotic suggestion
that we should contribute to the cost.

Marylou returned from the telephone to say that a seat
was available on the plane leaving for Milan at six o'clock.
From there she could go to Venice by train, either that
night or on the following morning. She asked me anxiously
if that would be all right.

'Excellent,' I said. 'Spend the night in Milan. You
should arrive in plenty of time to find accommodation. I
should like you to be in Venice by eleven o'clock next
morning; but the Italians have an excellent train service—there should be no difficulty. When your train gets
to Venice, don't take the *vaporetto*—just walk across the
bridge outside the railway station, the Scalzi Bridge, and
then go left till you get to the Accademia. There's a café
there—do you happen to know it?'

'Yes,' said Marylou, 'Julia and I had a Campari soda
there.'

'Sit down there and wait for Timothy. I shall send him
a telegram, explaining where you will be. You have not, I
know, met Timothy; but he will recognize you from my
description. After that, simply do whatever Timothy tells
you. The main thing is, until he arrives, to stay in the café
by the Accademia Bridge. If he's not there by two o'clock,
there has been a breakdown of communications and you
should go to the British Consulate—you'll find it easily,

it's only about twenty yards away. But don't on any account go back across the Grand Canal—stay in the Dorsodouro until Timothy is with you.'

The American girl, when I said this, looked at me with a certain apprehension; but said nothing.

It was agreed that she should return home, pack a small suitcase with such items as seemed necessary and return to 62 New Square, whence Selena would drive her to the airport. It was, Selena had said, with a rather severe glance at myself, the least she could do.

'What,' asked Ragwort, 'will you tell your husband?'

'Well,' said Marylou, 'there's not too much empathy between Stanford and Julia. If I told Stanford I was going to Venice to help Julia, I guess his reaction might be somewhat negative. So I figured I'd just leave a note saying my mother's cousin Alice was very sick and I had to go to her. My mother's cousin Alice is very into ecology and she lives in a farmhouse in Brittany, France, and doesn't have a telephone.' She looked round anxiously, as if this proposed deception might incur censure. It did not.

'I say, Hilary,' said Cantrip, when she'd gone, 'you aren't having another of your loopy spells, are you? You're sure it'll do some good sending the poor grummit back to Venice?'

'No,' I answered, too preoccupied to take offence at the form of the question. 'No, Cantrip, not entirely sure. I am assuming, you see, a fact for which there is no direct evidence.'

'Hilary,' said Ragwort, 'do you mean to say that you have persuaded this girl, whom we hardly know, to deceive her husband and travel halfway across Europe merely on the basis—'

'My dear Ragwort,' I said, 'I do wish you wouldn't fuss. I am quite reasonably sure. To be entirely sure, however, I should need a further piece of information, and the only person from whom I might obtain it is Kenneth Dunfermline. I'd really prefer to avoid seeing him—it seems likely, in the circumstances, to be a depressing interview. Still, as you say, Ragwort, it would be irresponsible — would you be kind enough to come with me?'

Murmuring of wild geese and mare's nests, Ragwort nonetheless consented.

'I am, of course, delighted,' said Selena, standing beside us on the pavement outside the Corkscrew as we waited for a taxi, 'to know that you have a theory, Hilary. Does there happen, by any chance, to be the smallest scrap of evidence for it?'

'Oh yes,' I said. 'Yes, the evidence is almost conclusive. There is one point, you see, on which I agree with Julia — I attach great importance to the signs of nervousness displayed by Ned Watson on the morning of the murder.'

Kentish Town, though not far from my temporary home in Islington, is an area of London with which I am unfamiliar. The driver of our taxi, however, found the street without difficulty. It was a terrace of small Georgian houses — a little shabby, but nice enough. Or not, perhaps, quite nice enough for a young man of such delicate tastes as Ned.

'Sure you've got the right number?' said the taxi driver, turning to address us through the glass partition. 'This one looks as if they're all away.' The house did have, certainly, an unoccupied appearance: on a golden afternoon, the windows were blank with shutters. 'Or as if someone had died.'

'Yes,' I said, 'I think it's the right place.'

My first ring at the doorbell brought no answer. After a minute or so, I rang again.

'He's not there,' said Ragwort.

But the door did open. Framed between the doorposts, Kenneth Dunfermline looked large enough to carry them, lintel and all, like a yoke across his shoulders. He had evidently been working, for he was naked to the waist: I perceived that his bulk was not due to any surplus of flesh but to the massive development of his chest and the powerful muscles of his shoulders and upper arms. Not Julia's sort of thing, certainly; but to any taste less morbidly aesthetic he might have seemed a rather magnificent figure, had it not been for the drab pallor of his skin — whatever occasions there had been that summer for sunbathing, Kenneth Dunfermline had not taken them. And his face — I would have thought, looking at his face, though I understand such a thing to be physiologically impossible, that in the five days since we had seen him he had not slept at all.

He stood looking from one to the other of us under the continuous line of his thick black eyebrows, as though dazed, like a bull sent suddenly from darkness into the harsh sunlight of the arena.

'Mr Dunfermline?' I said.

'Yes,' he answered, as if doubtful about it.

'I really must apologize,' I said, 'for intruding on you without warning like this. I have only a short time in London and I was most anxious to meet you. I saw some of your work at Frostfield's Gallery and Mrs Frostfield was good enough to give me your address. I simply came round on impulse — it's quite unforgivable, I'm really very sorry.'

'Not at all,' said the sculptor, vaguely, as if it were a phrase learned by rote as the appropriate response to an apology, but repeated without confidence that it was right. 'It doesn't matter.'

'My name, by the way, is Hilary Tamar. Professor Hilary Tamar, of St George's College, Oxford. This is my friend Desmond Ragwort, of Lincoln's Inn.'

'You'd better come in,' said Kenneth. It sounded less grudging than the words might suggest: he knew, it seemed,

that there was something he was supposed to do about
people standing on the doorstep, but could not with cer-
tainty remember what it was.

We followed him through a little entrance hall and into
his studio. Running the width of the house, it had windows at the back as well as the front; but those at the back
were also shuttered. It was lit by fluorescent tubes, which
hung by chains from the ceiling. The walls, never
papered and for some years not whitewashed, had
darkened to the colour of putty, the ceiling and wood-
work to a similar but deeper shade. The floorboards were
unpolished and uncarpeted.

The film of whitish dust which lay over everything and
the diversity of the objects which the room contained—
stacks of clay, coils of copper wire, bottles of turpentine—
obscured, at first impression, its extraordinary tidiness;
but after a moment or two one perceived that the tools
and materials of the sculptor's craft had been arranged in
meticulous order on the rows of metal shelving which
covered most of the wall space—he would not be delayed
in his work by any difficulty in finding the right chisel.

There was no decoration. Even the photographs which
covered one section of wall—some close-up studies of the
hand, a series of still shots of a young man diving—
seemed intended rather as *aides-mémoires* to the struc-
ture of the human body. There was a set of landscape
photographs—views from various angles of a place surrounded by olive trees—which served, at first sight, no
utilitarian purpose. Looking, however, at the trestle table
in the middle of the room, I saw laid out on it a model of
the same scene, but with the addition of a fountain, its
waters represented by blue polystyrene. I concluded that
the landscapes also were intended to assist work in progress.

At least there was somewhere to sit—the studio couch
near the front window had presumably been provided for

the benefit of any live model whom the sculptor might have to employ. Upholstered in dark red velvet, it had been covered over with an old blanket — perhaps to protect it from the dust, but more probably, I thought, because Kenneth was irked by the intrusion of the splash of colour. Suspecting that it might be some time before he thought of inviting me to sit down, I did so without invitation. Ragwort followed my example. The sculptor, despite his evident weariness, remained standing.

'Do you,' he asked, 'want anything?' He seemed to find the words with great effort, as if the language of human discourse were one foreign to him, in which he had laboriously acquired a small vocabulary.

'Yes,' I said, with a smile which I hoped was disarming, 'and having intruded on you in this appalling way, the least I can do is to come to the point as quickly as possible. The position is, you see, that my College has conceived the notion of erecting a work of sculpture in the Quadrangle. Something in harmony with our existing buildings, but a distinguished piece of work unmistakably of our own time. The idea, I must emphasize, is in its infancy, I might almost say its gestation period. We are, I fear, a sadly dilatory lot. But people have suggested that I should explore the possibilities.'

'I don't think—' said the sculptor, and stopped without my having interrupted him, but making a downward movement of his large hand which seemed to signify rejection of this and any other offer that the world might make to him.

'My dear Mr Dunfermline, I am not for a moment suggesting that you should commit yourself at this stage. As I have indicated, we ourselves are by no means in a position to do so. We are simply trying, at present, to discover what would be involved in such a project — we are as children in such matters. We have very little idea, for example, of what it might cost.'

The massive shoulders rose slightly in a gesture of indifference and bewilderment.

'Depends what you want.'

'Yes, naturally. Much, no doubt, would depend on the material selected. We ourselves do not know what material an artist would consider suitable.'

'Stone,' said Kenneth, as if it were a credo that he would not, in the utmost weariness, forget. 'Stone's best.'

'A work in stone would, of course, harmonize admirably with our existing buildings. The design we would wish to leave very much to the judgement of the artist.' I looked towards the trestle table and received inspiration. 'Some of my colleagues, however, have suggested that it might be agreeable to have a fountain. I perceive that you have been working on something of that kind. It looks, if it is not impertinent of me to say so, as if it would be a most impressive piece.'

The heavy shoulders rose again in the same gesture of indifference: he had wearied, it seemed, of the effort to find words. I looked rather desperately at Ragwort, sitting demurely beside me like a well-behaved schoolboy.

'Yes, it is most impressive,' said Ragwort. 'But rather sombre, if you don't mind my saying so.' It was true that there was something mournful about it. The central figure seemed to be that of a woman, whose flowing hair, however, covered her face and melted into the folds of the garment which enveloped her, so that one could not be certain which way she might be facing; round her, a dozen or so smaller figures, of children, girls and young men, were represented as lying, as if asleep, on the parapet round the fountain. I could see no particular reason for finding it a sorrowful scene; but Ragwort was right in saying that it was. 'In the final version, I suppose,' continued Ragwort, 'the figures would be lifesize?'

'Yes. A little over.'

'And is it intended,' said Ragwort, 'for a particular client?'

'It was. I shan't make it. He's leaving the place I was going to make it for.' I felt that I had been right to draw Ragwort into the conversation: three consecutive sentences was a considerable achievement.

'What a shame,' said Ragwort. 'I hope you hadn't spent a great deal of time on the preliminary work?'

'About a year,' said Kenneth, without resentment. 'I'd done all the drawings and models. That on the table, that's how it would have been. You've got to get it right, before you start cutting the stone. You can't change your mind after that.'

Reluctant as I was to interrupt the flow of conversation, I felt able to delay no longer the question I wished to ask.

'I suppose,' I said, off-handedly, 'that your client was Richard Tiverton?'

Ragwort made no exclamation; but he could not restrain a look of surprise. The possibility that Timothy and Kenneth might have a mutual client had plainly not occurred to him.

'Yes,' said the sculptor, his heavy eyebrows gathering in slow perplexity. 'How did you know?'

'As I mentioned,' I said, 'Desmond and I were at Frostfield's the other day. Mrs Frostfield was talking about the Tiverton Collection and she mentioned that you had been helping to sort it out—so I knew that Richard Tiverton was a client of yours. And she also said something, I think, about him having to leave Cyprus. For tax reasons, I gather.'

Ragwort now looked both surprised and severe—no doubt at my untruthfulness.

'Eleanor does talk,' said the sculptor, as if, had he had energy for such an emotion, the fact would have irritated him.

'Oh dear,' I said, 'perhaps I shouldn't have mentioned it. If it's confidential, you may rely on my discretion.'

'It doesn't matter,' said Kenneth.

'I had no idea,' I went on, 'that there was any secret about it. I would rather have imagined, if there had been, that Mrs Frostfield herself would be as anxious as anyone to keep it. It must be rather an advantage to have information on such a matter not known to one's competitors, and she did not strike me as the kind of woman who would readily forgo an advantage. Indeed, she gave me the impression of being rather ruthless. One would not put it past her, for example, to have suggested that you should sell her some of the more valuable items at a favourable price and share the profit.'

'She did,' said Kenneth. 'Stupid — I wouldn't do down Richard to please Eleanor. She's quite stupid, really.' He spoke without indignation — though I remembered, from Julia's account of the conversation on the terrace, that the proposition, when first made, had roused him to considerable anger.

'How ridiculous of her,' said Ragwort. 'She must have known you were doing it as an office of friendship. One can hardly suppose, if I may say so, that an artist of your standing would undertake such a task on a purely professional basis.'

'An office of friendship,' repeated Kenneth, turning the phrase over like a piece of stone that pleased him. 'Yes, that's right.'

'It must be a great responsibility,' I said, 'to have in one's care a collection of such value. I gather from Mrs Frostfield that it attracted interest from some rather unscrupulous characters. What was the name she mentioned? Bruce something — I can't remember the rest of it, but you know who I mean, Mr Dunfermline.'

'No,' answered Kenneth, with blank indifference, 'I haven't heard of anyone called Bruce.'

Neither Ragwort nor myself venturing to touch more closely on the subject of his grief, nothing further was said of any significance. I urged him, before we left, if he should receive an invitation to come to Oxford and consider the artistic possibilities of our Quadrangle, not to reject it out of hand.

'Are you,' asked Ragwort, in the kind but severe tone in which he sometimes reminds Julia to buy enough food for the weekend, 'going to be all right?'

'Yes,' said the sculptor, 'I'll be all right,' and smiled — whether at the absurdity of Ragwort's question or the conventional untruthfulness of his own answer — a surprisingly beautiful smile.

The interview had left me feeling dispirited, for I perceived now that the sculptor's attachment to Ned had been one of great intensity and passion, such as one rarely sees. One could not wish, for oneself or for one's friends, any first-hand experience of such extremity of feeling — it is not conducive to comfortable living. And yet there is about it, when observed, something curiously touching and attractive, so that one almost, absurdly, regrets one's own inability to entertain it.

Ragwort could not be persuaded that our expedition had been a success. Kenneth, he said, was plainly too dazed to remember anything not of great importance to him. We had told a great many lies and learnt nothing.

'We have learnt,' I said, 'that Kenneth was the person in charge of the Tiverton Collection last week.'

'It's an interesting coincidence,' said Ragwort, 'but it can't have anything to do with the murder.'

'Don't you think so? You are surely forgetting, my dear Ragwort, that it is a very valuable collection and that Eleanor, in particular, is most anxious to acquire certain items in it. We know she is not unduly scrupulous. When Kenneth refused to cooperate, do you think it impossible that she employed her friend Bruce to acquire them by more direct methods? And if Ned found out about it and threatened to tell his friend, would that be an insufficient motive for murder? Using the same accomplice, and ensuring that it was committed while she herself was safely elsewhere?'

Ragwort looked sceptical; but agreed to stop at the first post office we passed and telephone Selena to tell her that all was well and that Marylou should proceed with her journey. In the meantime I took the opportunity to send those telegrams which I thought necessary to ensure that on the following day everyone would be in the right place at the right time.

'This idea of yours about Bruce and Eleanor,' said Ragwort afterwards, 'is it what you really believe, Hilary?'

'I would suggest,' I answered, 'that it is not unworthy of your consideration.'

It is very wrong to tease Ragwort; but one cannot always help it. My readers will not have doubted for a moment that the theory was pure moonshine; I mentioned at the beginning of Chapter 6 that the designs of Eleanor and the Major on the personal effects of the late Miss Tiverton had not caused or contributed in any way to the murder, and my readers will not suppose that I would deceive them in such a matter.

'I take it,' said Ragwort, as he left me at Islington, 'that we shall be seeing you in Chambers tomorrow?'

'Yes,' I said. 'But not unduly early. Nothing can happen before eleven o'clock.'

CHAPTER 18

Nothing could happen before eleven o'clock. The instructions in my telegram to Timothy had been clear: whatever time Marylou arrived at the café beside the Accademia, he was not to approach her until eleven-thirty—it would then, by English time, be half past ten. After that, it could scarcely take less than half an hour for people and events to move towards the point of resolution; and if things fell out as I expected, there would be some further delay before Timothy was able to telephone with news of them. Timothy does not always show that unquestioning acceptance of my judgement which one would hope to see in a former pupil; but I had relied on him to think it prudent, presented with a *fait accompli*, to abide to the letter by my instructions. Nothing, therefore, could happen before eleven o'clock. All the same—

At half past nine on Friday morning I found myself climbing the stone stairs which lead to the second floor of 62 New Square. The members of the Nursery were already gathered in the largest of its three rooms, Ragwort and Cantrip at their desks, Selena in the large leather armchair. Ragwort had been explaining, it seemed, the theory I had suggested to him on the previous afternoon. It was not going down well—they all looked despondent.

'If I was advising a client,' said Cantrip, 'I'd say that if that's our case we jolly well ought to settle.'

'I understand,' said Ragwort, 'that one cannot dispose of a criminal charge by way of compromise. I suppose one can offer to plead guilty to manslaughter if they'll drop the more serious charge.'

'I dare say,' said Selena, 'that one would so advise a client. But this is not a matter where we should allow our professional judgement to interfere with our personal feelings.'

I assured them that there was no need for anxiety and that matters were proceeding satisfactorily.

'Well, I'm glad you think so, Hilary,' said Cantrip. 'As far as I can see, they're proceeding with total loopiness. Even if there's anything in this idea that Eleanor's in cahoots with the Bruce chap—and personally I think it's a dead loss—it still wouldn't get us anywhere, because we don't know who the Bruce chap is. And why on earth you think he's still in Venice—'

'And even if he is,' said Ragwort, 'why you think Marylou's going to recognize him—'

'I don't,' I said.

'But Hilary,' said Selena, with something less than her customary composure, 'you have led Marylou to believe—'

'Nonsense,' I said. 'I have done nothing of the kind.'

'But we were discussing,' said Selena, 'how we could find out who Bruce was and you asked Marylou if she could go to Venice.'

'Ah yes,' I said. 'I remember now that you were discussing something of that kind. It was, however, mere coincidence; I was paying but little attention. No, I don't expect her to recognize Bruce. My dear children, it is surely clear to you by now that Bruce does not exist?'

They were rather cross with me, on two alternative grounds, apparently; that Bruce did exist and I was wantonly deceiving them; or, if he did not, that by some remarkable alchemy I had mischievously caused his non-existence. Such expressions as 'frivolous dilettante' and 'irresponsible academic' were freely used. They quietened at last, however, to the point of demanding an explanation.

'I suppose,' I said, 'that none of you have ever studied the science of textual criticism and that you are all, therefore, unfamiliar with the principle of the *lectum difficillimum?*'

'You suppose,' said Selena, 'correctly.'

'Very well. I shall begin accordingly with a brief exposition of that principle.'

'I say, Hilary,' said Cantrip, 'do you absolutely have to?'

'Yes. I must begin by reminding you that a great part of Scholarship consists of the study of ancient or medieval documents. It is but rarely, however, that we are fortunate enough to have available the original manuscript in the hand of the author. The older the document, the more probable it is that we shall have to rely on a copy. Or a copy of a copy. So multiplies the possibility of error, through the carelessness or ignorance of the copyist. The reconstruction in such cases of the original — the discovery of the correct reading — that is the art of textual criticism.'

'A moment ago,' said Ragwort, 'you called it a science.'

'It is both an art and a science. It demands the exercise, to the highest degree, of every aspect of human genius. It requires the most rigorous logic, the most diligent application of experience, the most heroic flights of creative imagination.'

'Yes, Hilary,' said Selena. 'I'm sure it does. Could we return to the point?'

'Certainly. As I would by now have explained, if Ragwort had abstained from captious interruption, there have been developed by scholars versed in the art or science of textual criticism certain principles. Among the most important of these is that of the *lectum difficillimum* — that is to say, that the most difficult reading is to be preferred. Suppose, to take a simple case, that you have variant readings between two copies of the same manuscript, one using a very common word and the other an unusual one. You may conclude without hesitation that the version using the rarer word is correct. The mistake in the other can be explained by a copyist misreading an unfamiliar word for one which is known to him — that is the most natural thing in the world. The reverse, on the other hand, is inconceivable.'

'Hilary,' said Selena, 'please — '

'The same phenomenon, of course, occurs in the context of the spoken word. We all know, for example, that Cantrip, being, due to the deficiencies of his education — for which, as I have always said, he is rather to be pitied than censured — unfamiliar with the term "rococo", is under the impression that there is a style of architecture known as rocky cocoa — after, I suppose, some beverage of popular consumption in Cambridge.'

'What,' said Ragwort, 'has all this to do with Julia?'

'It has everything to do with Julia. And everything to do with Bruce. For you will remember that the only evidence of Bruce's existence is a conversation between Eleanor and Kenneth as overheard by Julia.'

'But there is,' said Ragwort, 'no alternative reading. We have no other account of the conversation.'

'No direct account, no. There is, however, secondary evidence which conflicts with Julia's, in that both Eleanor and Kenneth deny knowing anyone called Bruce. We must consider, therefore, the possibility of an error in Julia's account. Reporting the conversation in *oratio obliqua*, she tells us that Eleanor said that Bruce had stolen an armchair and a rococo mirror which she rather liked. The precise words, presumably, which Julia thought she heard were, "Bruce stole an armchair and a rococo mirror which I rather liked." '

'Well?' said Selena.

'One of the most celebrated makers of furniture in Venice in the seventeenth century was Andrea di

Brustolon — Benjamin, you may remember, mentioned him the other evening. Julia, however, has probably never heard of him — she is not well up on the baroque and rococo periods.'

I cannot say that they yielded gracefully; but I eventually persuaded them that a mention by Eleanor of a 'Brustolon armchair,' as an item in the Tiverton Collection which she would like to acquire, was more probable than any reference to some unknown larcenist; that the person against whom she had warned Kenneth in the earlier part of the conversation was almost certainly, in the light of what we had since learnt about him, the Major; and that what had to be kept under lock and key was not some mysterious object of value kept by Kenneth in his room, but the Collection itself, Eleanor having inadvertently disclosed to the Major Kenneth's connection with it.

'But if Bruce doesn't exist,' said Selena, 'what's Marylou doing in Venice?'

'That,' I answered, 'I am expecting to learn very shortly. But nothing can happen before eleven o'clock. It's now only just after half past ten — there's plenty of time for someone to make some coffee.'

There was, while we drank our coffee, an absence of conversation rare in Lincoln's Inn. My companions kept looking warily at the telephone, as if it might spontaneously deliver some Delphic utterance.

'Selena,' said Ragwort, at about quarter to the hour, 'did you tell them downstairs that any calls for you should come through to this room?'

'Yes,' said Selena. 'Of course.' And at ten to rang the Clerks' Room to remind them.

We drank more coffee. The clocks within earshot of Lincoln's Inn began to strike the hour.

'From your statement, Hilary,' said Ragwort, at five minutes past, 'that nothing would happen before eleven, we have been assuming that something would happen after that time. You are now going, I suppose, to explain to us the fallacy in our reasoning.'

'My dear Ragwort, I would not dream of such heartless casuistry. Something will certainly happen — but how long after eleven, I cannot definitely say. Timothy may have difficulty getting in touch with us.'

At twenty past eleven the telephone emitted a buzz. Ragwort stretched out his hand towards the receiver.

The door, at the same moment, was thrown open with such intemperate violence as caused it to bang against the skirting-board and there irrupted into the room a young man of threatening aspect. I recognized, from seeing him at Heathrow, the belligerent thrust of the shoulders and the pugnacious jut of the wide jaw.

'Which of you,' asked our visitor, glaring furiously about him, 'is Desmond Ragwort?' His accent was similar to Marylou's, but his tone far less agreeable.

'I am,' answered Ragwort, without hesitation. He was, after all, among friends, and divided from the visitor by a substantial oak desk. 'May I ask who you are and how I can assist you?'

The interruption had stayed his hand in its movement towards the telephone. Selena, sitting on the floor beside the kettle, contrived to amalgamate in a single movement of great rapidity the act of rising to her feet and that of crossing the room: most graceful and attractive if one had leisure to observe it. She lifted the receiver.

'My name,' said our visitor, 'is Stanford Bredon and I want to know where my wife is. I want to know what the hell's going on round here. I want to know—'

'Yes, Henry, of course I'm here,' said Selena. 'Do please put Mr Shepherd through as quickly as possible. No, Henry, I know you don't know what it's about. But I do, and it's a matter of some urgency. Please, Henry.'

'I want to know,' continued Stanford, 'why when I got

home last night I found a note from my wife saying she'd had to go stay with her mother's cousin Alice, because Alice was very sick. And when I called my wife's mother in New York, because Alice is not on the telephone but I figured if something was wrong with her my wife's mother would know about it—'

The resonance of his indignation prevented me, though I was now standing next to Selena and within twelve inches of the telephone, from hearing the other end of her conversation.

'She told me that her cousin Alice was right there with her in New York on a visit and had never felt better in her life.'

'Mr Bredon,' said Ragwort, 'the good health of your wife's relative is a matter for rejoicing rather than condolence. If, however, it displeases you, you should surely address your complaint to her doctor, rather than myself.'

'Hilary,' said Selena, 'there seems to be some difficulty with the police. Timothy says he must talk to you.' She handed me the receiver, relieving my frustration at being unable to hear what Timothy was saying—only partially, however, for Timothy also seemed to be speaking against a background of considerable noise, including, in particular, a baritone voice, which I took to be that of the Vice-Quaestor, complaining indignantly about the English.

'For heaven's sake, Hilary,' said Timothy, 'will you please explain to me what to tell the Vice-Quaestor?'

'Timothy,' I said, 'what exactly has happened?'

'The English,' said the background baritone. 'Always the English, always they make trouble. We are quiet, peaceful people in Venice, we do not have crimes, we do not have scandals. And then the English come—'

Stanford was now leaning across Ragwort's desk, disposed, it seemed, if he could reach him, to throttle

Ragwort with his bare hands.

'Ah,' said Selena, in her most placatory manner, 'you must be Marylou's husband. We've heard so much about you.'

'My dear Hilary,' said Timothy, 'what has happened is that on your instructions I have diverted half the police force of Venice from its proper duties—'

'We have no murders,' continued the baritone, 'and then the English come here and murder each other—'

'And why,' said Stanford, 'when I look in our address book, which is a joint address book, because Marylou and I believe that marriage is a relationship of absolute trust—'

'And that the Vice-Quaestor,' continued Timothy, 'has noticed an alarming rise in the number of violent deaths within his jurisdiction—'

'And corrupt the morals of our young,' said the baritone.

'I find in that address book,' said Stanford, 'a name and address which were not there before, of a person whom I do not know—'

'And the Vice-Quaestor,' said Timothy, 'would, quite naturally, like to know how I knew what was going to happen. And since, as I have explained to the Vice-Quaestor, I have been acting entirely on your instructions, Hilary, and have no idea—'

'And eat sandwiches,' said the baritone, in tragic crescendo, 'in the Piazza San Marco.'

'And that name,' said Stanford, 'is Desmond Ragwort and his address is 62 New Square.'

'I say,' said Cantrip, 'if you don't take your hands off my learned friend Mr Ragwort—'

'And the Vice-Quaestor is not prepared to let any of us leave Venice—'

'And I am not leaving this room—'

'Until he has a complete explanation.'

'Until I have a full explanation.'

'Hoocha!' cried Cantrip — poor boy, he had been long-
ing for days for an opportunity to demonstrate his karate.

> Palazzo Artemisio.
> Friday afternoon.

Dear Hilary,

Since my telephone call this morning was made in
rather difficult conditions and apparently coincided with
the outbreak in Chambers of some sort of riot, I was
unable to give you as full an account of the morning's
events as you would no doubt have liked. Well, I suppose
you are entitled to one, and I have ample time for the
task: the Vice-Quaestor declines to let any of us leave
Venice until the whole affair is clarified to his satisfaction; and he does not expect this before Monday.

I called at the Consulate, as usual, a little after ten
o'clock, to see if there were any messages for me and to
discuss with Signor Vespari, in view of the unfavourable
forensic report, what arrangements should be made for
Julia to be represented by an Italian lawyer experienced
in criminal matters. I found him waiting for me with great
impatience, being curious to know the contents of your
telegram, which he handed to me as soon as I arrived. I
read it, I must confess, with considerable irritation.
Though not noticeably brief, it gave me, of course, no
indication of what you were hoping to prove; I thought it
highly probable that you were introducing unnecessary
complications to gratify your taste for amateur
theatricals. On the other hand, not knowing what other
arrangements you might have made, I could not be sure
what the consequences might be if I failed to comply.

My first impulse was to telephone and demand an
explanation. I was not sure, however, where to find you at

that time, and you had left me with less than an hour and a half in which to secure the cooperation of the Vice-Quaestor. I resigned myself with the utmost reluctance to acting blindly on your instructions. I decided, moreover, since you had gone into such detail, that I had better follow them to the letter—though the only thing that really seemed to matter was that Marylou and I should be outside the Basilica San Marco at twelve o'clock and that we should then be under discreet observation by the police.

You do not seem to realize, Hilary, that it is unusual for a senior police officer to be peremptorily summoned by a foreign lawyer to attend with two of his men at a particular time and place at an hour's notice and without explanation. I am still not sure how we managed it—or rather, how Signor Vespari managed it, since he did all the talking. He told the Vice-Quaestor that my 'investigations in London' had been conducted by three members of the English Bar, under the personal supervision of a scholar of international repute—meaning, God help us, yourself—and added, rather grandly, that if your instructions were not carried out he could not be answerable for the consequences. Whether because he was really impressed by all this nonsense, or out of mere curiosity, the Vice-Quaestor eventually agreed to do as we asked.

Leaving the Consulate at twenty past eleven and walking towards the Accademia Bridge, I saw that Marylou was already sitting at one of the tables outside the café. It seemed absurd to delay approaching her; but since you had insisted that I should not do so until exactly half past, I spent the next ten minutes pretending to choose postcards from the newspaper stall ouside the Accademia Gallery. Out of the corner of my eye I could see the Vice-Quaestor and two other policemen standing near the door of the Gallery, making rather a success of looking as if they had nothing to do.

At exactly half past, I went up to Marylou and asked if she was Mrs Bredon. Although I had recognized her easily from seeing her at Heathrow, I assumed that you would not have mentioned that occasion to her. She acknowledged that she was, but invited me to call her Marylou. After I had briefly explained to her what you wanted us to do, we set forth across the Accademia Bridge. She suggested that it would be more convenient to go by *vaporetto* across the Canal straight to St Mark's. I told her, however, that you had specifically directed me to go on foot, and that I did not think it prudent to depart from your instructions.

Your insistence that once we had met I should on no account leave her side until speaking to you on the telephone made me extremely nervous. It was not clear to me whether I was there to prevent her escape or to guard her against attack. But having come to Venice of her own free will, I could not imagine why she should suddenly run away. I concluded that my function was protective. All the way to the Piazza, I kept looking over my shoulder for some lurking assailant: the narrowness of the crowded streets seemed dangerously restrictive of movement in any emergency. I was a little, but not much, comforted by our retinue of policemen.

We reached the Piazza at about ten to twelve. I found it at first a relief to be in an open space; but half way across I began to think that the centre of the Piazza was a singularly exposed and vulnerable place, and to wish that I had kept Marylou in the shelter, however illusory, of one of the colonnades at the side. Still, we arrived without misadventure at the entrance to the Basilica. We stood there, among the tourists and the pigeons, wondering what was going to happen, Marylou looking round for a face she might recognize, I still apprehensive of some attack on her.

The mechanically operated bronze figures at the top of the Orologio, which mark the hour by striking on the bell, began to emerge from their places, raising their hammers. The other tourists in the Piazza looked up to watch the little spectacle; the street photographers and sellers of souvenirs continued about their business; Marylou and I went on searching for a familiar face or a threatening gesture, but counted, as we did so, the alternate strokes of the hammers against the bell. The last stroke sounded and was lost in the blue sky above the Piazza; and nothing happened.

'What do we do now?' asked Marylou.

'According to our instructions,' I said, 'we go straight home—that is to say, to the Palazzo Artemisio, where I am staying—and telephone Professor Tamar to report progress. We control as best we can our irritation at being involved in this fiasco.'

I had been, as you very well know, reluctant to make any telephone calls from the Palazzo, not wishing Richard Tiverton to be aware that I had been concerned, while in Venice, with other affairs than his own. I felt, however, a residual unwillingness to depart from your instructions; besides, it was easier to telephone from there than to trail back to the Consulate. I hoped, in any case, that I would be able to make the telephone call without attracting Richard's attention, since he was still not feeling well enough to leave his room much. I would, I thought, express as succinctly as possible my opinion of the little pantomime you had organized; I would then tell the policemen, with grovelling apologies, that I no longer required their attendance; I would then take Marylou to lunch at Montin's.

I was a little embarrassed, therefore, on entering the Palazzo, to find my client already in the entrance hall, himself engaged in a telephone conversation. The more so since it seemed to be acrimonious—he was saying, irritably, 'But you must have done — who else would have sent it?' As we came in, however, he looked up and broke off the conversation.

'I'm so sorry, Richard,' I said, 'please don't let us disturb you.'

He did not, however, resume his conversation. I saw, as my eyes adjusted to the comparative darkness of the interior, that he was paying no attention to me, but was staring at the girl beside me.

Looking again at her, I saw that she was staring back at him, with an expression of great amazement.

'Why, Ned,' said Marylou, 'I thought you were — ' for reasons of euphony or otherwise, she did not complete the sentence, but began to scream.

'I'm sorry,' said the young man, speaking calmly into the telephone receiver. 'It's the American girl. She's recognized me. And there are some policemen.' The Vice-Quaestor's subordinates, drawn by the scream, had come to the door, still open, of the Palazzo. 'I'm afraid that's the end of it. Goodbye.'

He left the receiver hanging and ran for the marble staircase. The two policemen ran in and after him. I followed, with some notion, I think, that he was still my client and I should be on hand to protect him.

In spite of his delicate appearance, he must have been quite athletic. With only a few yards' start he reached the fourth floor, the top floor of the Palazzo, a flignt and a half ahead of the policemen.

There is a window on the landing: he leapt for the sill and pushed the shutters open. He stood there, suddenly golden in the sunlight: I saw for a moment what Julia meant about Praxiteles and Michelangelo; and the two policemen — sensible, solid men, no doubt, with wives and families the two policemen were checked in their pursuit.

'Oh no,' he said, smiling down at us, 'no, I don't think

so, thank you.' And turned and jumped.

'The canal,' said one of the policemen, turning to run back. 'He's escaping by the canal.'

'No,' said his colleague, 'not the canal.' Getting his bearings more quickly than the other, he had realized that that window did not face on to a canal, but on to a stone-flagged campiello: it is thus a surer escape than by water from the hands of any police force.

When I eventually managed to give the Vice-Quaestor some kind of explanation, he got in touch, of course, with the police in London, to ask them to go and talk to Kenneth Dunfermline. By the time they got there, though, it was too late—he had stabbed himself through the heart.

I remain, in spite of all this,

Your affectionate pupil,
Timothy.

PS. The Vice-Quaestor has received by telex from London copies of three letters found beside Dunfermline's body, the last in his own handwriting, and never posted. These he has kindly made available to me, and I enclose them. Also a copy of a telegram found here at the Palazzo, lying on the table beside the telephone.

CHAPTER 19

Villa Niobe
Paphos.
Republic of Cyprus.
20th August.

Dear Kenneth,

I can't tell you how pleased I am you can come to Venice. Not just because of having you to cast an expert eye over Aunt Prissie's antiques, you know—though it's marvellous of you to do that for me and I feel a b   guilty about taking you away from more important things — but far more just because I'm looking forward so much to you being there. I don't know anyone at all in Venice — and even if I did, there couldn't be anyone like you to go and look at things with.

You'll be getting there a week before me, so you'll have all that time to rummage round the Palazzo Artemisio — if it really is something you'll enjoy doing — and see if there's a lost Titian in the broom cupboard or anything like that. You'd rather stay in a hotel, I expect, until I arrive — you'd be a bit miserable staying on your own in the Palazzo with no one but the housekeeper — you must let me pay the bill, of course, and all your other expenses. I hope you're not going to be difficult about it — I want to set up as a patron of the arts, you know, and earn myself a footnote in your biography, so please don't go all Scots and uppity on me.

My boat docks in Venice on the morning of the 9th — that's a Friday — and that'll be the end of your peaceful rummaging. You must come and stay with me at the Palazzo, and I'll drag you all round Venice, making you tell me about painting and architecture.

The only boring thing I have to do is to talk to all these lawyers — well, two of them. I knew I'd have to talk to the Italian one, who looked after things for Aunt Prissie — but my trustee in London is insisting on sending an English one as well. My trustee thinks that I 'don't appreciate the adverse fiscal consequences of the present situation.' So he wants to instruct Counsel — that's another sort of lawyer, it seems, who uses even longer words than a solicitor — to come and explain them to me. He's making such a fuss, I'm going to have to let him — and I'll have to invite the poor man to stay at the Palazzo — it would be a bit mean not to, wouldn't it? So I'm afraid he'll be popping up all over the place, talking about fiscal consequences. It's all a complete waste of time, because what they want me to do is leave Cyprus, if you please — seriously, just sell the Villa and the farm and clear out. Leave Cyprus indeed—as if I would! Aren't lawyers ridiculous?

Anyway, I shall tell them that my friend Kenneth Dunfermline, the distinguished sculptor, is personally designing a most beautiful fountain especially for the Villa Niobe, so I can't possibly leave. And they'll be so impressed, they'll go away and leave us in peace.

You don't seem to understand, Ken, that it really is quite something for me to have made friends with someone like you—you're so completely different from anyone else I know. And I could so easily not have met you at all—if you hadn't decided to come to Cyprus last year, or even if you'd decided to stop for lunch in some different village. The really extraordinary thing, though, is that you put up with me at all, considering how hopelessly ignorant I am about painting and sculpture and everything, and can't talk about anything except Cyprus politics and how the olives are doing—it's simply astonishing that I don't bore you to tears.

Well, I shan't talk about anything like that in Venice— just look at paintings and read a lot of Byron and ask you silly questions about art. Will you find me a nuisance? Yes, I expect so, and be too soft-hearted to tell me.

Till the 9th, then—

Yours
Richard.

Palazzo Artemisio.
Saturday 10th September.

It's appallingly dangerous writing to you, but I've got to—I must know what's happening, Ken. Except from you, I've no way at all of finding out anything that's happened since I went into the canal last night from the balcony of the Cytherea. I'm like a prisoner in this place — I daren't go out in case I meet someone who knows me. I've told the housekeeper I'm ill — I really am ill, too, no pretence about it.

For pity's sake, Ken, can't you understand that I never thought you were serious? I thought it was all a sort of joke — well, not a joke, exactly, but make-believe, a sort of game. Yes, all right, it was a pretty morbid game and I joined in and played it too, practising his signature, and so on — but I never thought you meant it, I never thought you really meant to kill him.

Most of the things you did that you said were part of it, like going to Cyprus and finding him and making friends with him — I thought you were really doing them for quite ordinary, sensible reasons, because it did make sense, after all, to find someone with plenty of money who liked your work and could commission you to do things.

So that morning when he was due to arrive in Venice — yesterday, I suppose, it doesn't seem possible — I just expected, when I went back to our room — I swear, Ken, I just expected to find you talking to him and showing him the drawings of the fountain and him saying how good they were. And I thought you'd introduce me to him and we'd probably like each other and all be friends. It's so much what I expected and I can imagine it so clearly, there are moments I can make myself believe it's what really happened, and that the other thing's just a nightmare.

Only not for long, because I know the nightmare is what really happened — going back and finding you'd killed him. I feel sick when I think about it. You say you did it for me, because you love me — but I don't understand that; if you really cared about me you couldn't want me to go through such a horrible experience.

When we came downstairs again, I was in such a panic I hardly knew what I was doing. All through lunch I kept wondering what would happen if someone went into our room and found him. You hadn't really hidden him, you know, Ken, not properly—think of all those chamber-maids—just suppose one of them had wanted to clean the room—she'd have moved the beds, wouldn't she?

So I knew, when you'd gone, that I'd have to do it the way you said—go back to that room and stay there until it was dark. On my own for six hours with a dead man, thinking about what had happened. And I couldn't do it—I just couldn't, Ken, I don't know how you could expect me to.

So I took Julia back with me. You'll be angry with me, I suppose—and God knows it sounds a grotesque thing to have done, making love to someone on one bed with a man lying dead under the other—but I couldn't help it. I went on making love to her all afternoon, because it was the only way of not thinking about anything, and if I started thinking I couldn't bear it.

I kept telling myself that I mustn't fall asleep, but the terrifying thing is that I actually did; I can hardly believe it. I woke up and Julia wasn't there and the shadows were longer and for about half a minute I felt happy, really ter-ribly happy, because I thought I'd dreamed it all and now I'd woken up and everything was all right. Well, that passed pretty quickly.

The worst thing was putting him back on the bed. He was nearly too heavy for me—you hadn't thought about that at all, had you, Ken? And you'd said he wouldn't bleed much, because of the wound being straight to his heart—but he did, he'd bled quite a lot, and I had to clean the place on the floor where he'd been lying. And in spite of all the planning, you didn't manage to give me much time, did you? I was still waiting for it to get prop-erly dark when I heard you in the corridor—so I had to risk it and go straight into the canal.

After that, I suppose you'd say it all went quite well—I was horribly frightened and I'll stink of the canal forever — but I didn't drown and I didn't run into any sharp obstacles and I didn't lose my little bundle of clothes. I came out of the canal at the place you showed me — though God knows I never thought then that I'd really be doing it — and dried myself and dressed. I got to the Palazzo without anyone seeing me and presented myself to the housekeeper as Richard Tiverton. She didn't suspect anything, but she was very worried by me looking so ill — I was feeling very sick and couldn't stop shivering. And you say you did it because you loved me.

Now there are going to be all these lawyers — I'm terrified about it, especially the English one — suppose it's someone who knows me? Even if he does, I suppose he might not recognize me — I'm looking so frightful, I can't bear to see myself in the glass. Well, I've got to see them anyway, there's no way out of it.

After that I'll be able to leave Venice. I'll go at night by water-taxi to somewhere on the Lagoon and have a car ready to drive South somewhere. I expect I can get the Italian lawyer to arrange all that for me — now that I'm so rich, I suppose he'll be happy to indulge my eccentricities. I'll say I've accepted their advice about leaving Cyprus — that'll explain my not going back there. And they know about Richard hating England, so they won't expect me to go there, either. That means I can avoid the two really dangerous places without anyone thinking there's anything odd about it.

But there isn't anywhere that's really safe, is there? The world's a small place nowadays. I shan't be able to walk down a street in Paris or go to a party in San Francisco or eat in a restaurant in Melbourne and be absolutely sure of not meeting someone who says, 'Why, it's Ned Watson, isn't it?' Or 'But you're not Richard Tiverton.' So I'll have to be one of those reclusive millionaires, won't I? Staying indoors by myself all the time and not seeing anyone. The only person I can safely have anything to do with will be

you, won't it, Ken? You'll have me all to yourself for ever
and ever just as you've always wanted – how terribly
clever of you. My clever friend Kenneth, who turns stone
into people and people into stone.

I can't leave Venice until I've heard from you, of
course. Don't ring me, not unless it's urgent – the
telephone's terribly public and someone might overhear
something. But write as soon as you can, for God's sake.

I know we agreed that if I wrote to you I'd write as
Richard. But after a letter like this, there doesn't seem
much point in saying I'm anyone but

> Yours, whether I like it or not,
> Ned.

The studio. Night.
I don't know what day it is. I haven't been out since I
got home. Your letter came today. I'm sorry you're ill. It's
true, I didn't think properly how bad it would be for you.
I'm sorry. I thought I'd worked everything out right, but
I've got it wrong somehow and it's too late to change it.

But I don't understand about it not being serious. It
was always serious, Ned. Ever since you said you wished
you were him, I knew I had to do it for you. I saw it was
the only way of you having the kind of life you ought to
have and I knew I ought to give it to you. Because if there
was something I wouldn't do to give it to you it would
mean I didn't love you enough. And I did, Ned, because
you were so beautiful.

It all seemed to be going right to begin with. I found
Richard and he looked enough like you. Not really like
you, not beautiful like you, but enough. And it was easy
making friends with him, he liked me. I liked him, too,
but I saw he had all the things you ought to have and I
ought to give them to you. So I only had to wait for the
right time and place.

And even afterwards, I still felt I'd done everything

right and it was all working out properly. I felt sort of dizzy, but very clear at the same time, as if I were watching myself from outside doing all the things I had to do. I went on feeling like that all the time I was in Verona. I talked to the American girl, the one with nice clothes, all about Byzantine art. The way I used to talk to Richard — he liked me telling him about things like that.

But when I went back it all began to go wrong, because you were lying there and I remembered you were dead and I didn't know what to do anymore. I'm sorry, I'm getting confused, I mean that's how it seemed, I haven't slept much, I've been working on the fountain.

I remembered I mustn't let them see your face, I couldn't remember why, but I knew it was important. So I held you and people came and wanted to take you away but I wouldn't let them, not all alone without me.

You sound as if you don't want me anymore. I don't mind really, it doesn't seem to matter now. But you mustn't say I don't really love you, because I do, I really do love you, Richard.

RICHARD TIVERTON PALAZZO ARTEMISIO VENICE. PLEASE RING ME NOON EXACTLY ITALIAN TIME TOMORROW FRIDAY. IMPORTANT.

                                                    KENNETH

'And what troubles the Vice-Quaestor,' said Timothy, 'is, of course, the matter of the telegram. The one from Kenneth asking Ned to ring him.' Timothy's gaze was directed towards a point on the panelling of the Corkscrew some eighteen inches or so above my head: the tone, though not the syntax of his remark, suggested that he intended a question.

It was the following Tuesday. The Vice-Quaestor had felt matters sufficiently clarified to allow Julia, Timothy and Marylou to leave Venice. Julia's restoration to Lincoln's Inn was thought an occasion sufficiently auspicious to justify our lunching again in the Corkscrew. Selena had telephoned Marylou, inviting her to join us.

The arrangement required me to disregard yet again, for longer than I could have wished, the tender call of Scholarship. I felt it right, however, to make the sacrifice. It seemed fair and proper that all those involved in the affair should be given a full explanation of the process of reasoning by which I had arrived at the truth: I have no patience with obscurity.

I had not been able to enter immediately on my exposition. We had begun with an account by Julia of her experiences as a suspect. At the stage at which Julia thought it appropriate, for reasons obscure to me, to start quoting Jean-Jacques Rousseau, Selena reminded her that her Opinion on Schedule 7 of the Finance Act, at present being typed and promised by half past one, would require her signature.

Heeding the call of her professional responsibilities, Julia had said that it was very kind of us all to have gone to so much trouble on her behalf and we must allow her to pay for the next bottle of Nierstein. Then, pausing only to take from her handbag and give to Selena a sufficient sum for that purpose, retrieve from the floor the various articles involuntarily extracted from her handbag at the same time, and apologize to the man at the adjoining table for having spilt over him the remnants of her prawn salad, she had left us.

I was still not able to embark on my explanation. Timothy was urged by Ragwort to describe in greater detail the events of the previous Friday. He spoke with some feeling of the difficulties he had experienced in soothing the Vice-Quaestor and persuading him that neither Julia, Marylou nor himself could assist further with his enquiries.

It was at the end of this that he made his remark, tonally, as I have mentioned, though not syntactically, a question, about the Vice-Quaestor's mental disquiet on the matter of the telegram from Kenneth.

'Because of course,' continued Timothy, 'if Kenneth had not sent such a telegram, Ned would not have been talking to him on the telephone at the moment when Marylou recognized him and the Vice-Quaestor could have arranged for the police in London to arrest Kenneth before he knew anything was amiss. As it was — well, the Vice-Quaestor is not entirely pleased. He thinks it a very remarkable coincidence.'

'Timothy,' I said, 'were you now to learn that this was other than a remarkable coincidence, would you feel obliged to inform the Vice-Quaestor?'

Lowering his gaze to a point only six inches above my head, Timothy answered that he would not.

'In that case, my dear Timothy,' I said, 'I shall be quite candid with you. It was I who sent the telegram.'

'Yes,' said Timothy, 'I thought you did. It was taking a grave responsibility, wasn't it, to leave Dunfermline with that choice?'

'It would have been a graver one, surely,' I said, 'to leave him without one. Still, you will no doubt wish me to explain how I first came to suspect —'

'Well, not at the moment, actually,' said Timothy, drawing back his chair and rising from the table. 'I am instructed to advise in conference, as a matter of some urgency, on the devolution of the Tiverton Trust Fund, in the event, which must now occur, of the settlor having no descendant living on 19th December of this year. My solicitor is arriving at two o'clock — I really must leave you.'

I am very fond of Timothy and would never deny that he is, in some ways, a young man of some ability; but I have often felt, and did so now, that he lacks the intellectual curiosity which is the mark of the truly first-class mind.

'What I find curious,' said Ragwort, 'is the fact that they thought of this plan before Kenneth and Richard had even met. How did they know that Richard even existed? He had no friends in England.'

'The Tiverton trust,' I answered, 'was managed in England. Given the magnitude of the funds, there would no doubt have been considerable correspondence over the years between the trustees and the Inland Revenue. It doesn't seem very unlikely that Ned, being employed by that Department, should have at some time discovered that a young man of about the same age as himself, resident in Cyprus, was the heir to an estate in excess of a million pounds. So one day, I suppose, when Ned can't afford some small luxury he fancies, "I wish," he says, "I wish I were Richard Tiverton." '

'It was very wrong of him,' said Ragwort, 'to have mentioned it at all. Any information given to the Inland Revenue is supposed to be in the strictest confidence.'

'Yes, Ragwort,' I said, 'his behaviour, in that respect at any rate, was certainly most culpable. But you would no doubt like me to explain—'

'Could we make it some other time?' said Ragwort. 'It's most interesting, but I really must go. I have an appointment before the Master at two-thirty. And after telling him that it's urgent enough to be heard in the Long Vacation, I'd better not be late for it. You will all excuse me, won't you?'

It was all a little provoking. Still, looking on the bright side, it left more Nierstein for those of us who remained.

'I say, Hilary,' said Cantrip, when he had measured out equitably the contents of the bottle, 'what was it you were rabbiting on about on Thursday, last time we were in here, about the significance of Ned being nervous on the Friday morning? Or were you just having one of your loopy spells?'

'Cantrip,' I said calmly, 'I would be grateful if you would remember, for the first and last time, that I am not subject to what you term loopy spells, by which curious expression you mean, I suppose, intermittent bouts of insanity. It was the signs of nervousness displayed by Ned on Friday morning which would have enabled me, had I not allowed my mind to be distracted by irrelevant matters, to say immediately how the crime was done and who committed it.'

'Well,' said Selena, 'we know now that he had just become an accessory to murder. Enough, I imagine, to make anyone nervous. I cannot see, however, that an attack of nervousness is uniquely referable to such a cause.'

'My dear Selena,' I said, 'have you forgotten that he had cut himself shaving?'

'No,' said Selena, 'but I don't see anything very odd about that.'

'I do. Very odd indeed. Consider — what impression do you have from Julia's letters of the young man's appearance? Leaving out the rhetoric?'

'Well,' said Selena, 'that he was thin and had a good profile. And a nice complexion. And very fair hair.'

'Precisely so. And at nine o'clock on the morning of the murder Julia had seen him on the terrace of the Cytherea looking very much at his best and having evidently completed a full toilette. Can you really imagine, Selena, that a young man of his colouring and complexion would find it necessary to resort again to his razor before lunch-time?'

'Why, Professor Tamar,' said Marylou, 'that's really brilliant.'

'It's kind of you to say so; but to one trained in the

techniques of Scholarship, it's really very simple. But what followed from it?'

'I say,' said Cantrip, 'sorry to interrupt, but what did Ragwort say he was doing this afternoon?'

'He's got a Master's appointment,' said Selena. 'I thought he said this morning that it was something to do with that case you've got against each other about the washing-line. But as you're still here, I assume—'

'Strewth,' said Cantrip, leaping from his chair. 'The blighter, he might have reminded me.' By the time the door of the Corkscrew swung to behind him, he was no more than a blur of black and white on the other side of High Holborn, moving fast towards the Law Courts.

'Do please go on, Professor Tamar,' said Marylou. 'I think it's simply fascinating.' She is a delightful girl.

'Once I realized that the razor-cut must have been a fake, my mind turned immediately to the idea of an impersonation. At some stage later in the day, Ned was to impersonate someone who had sustained such an injury, or such a person was to impersonate him. But later in the day Ned had been a corpse. I was drawn irresistibly to the conclusion that the corpse was, as it were, an involuntary impostor. It was clear, Marylou, from your own account of the discovery of the crime, that Kenneth had not allowed anyone who knew Ned to look closely at the body. But he must have known, of course, that there would be a medical examination and that even such a trifling wound would probably be noticed. If none of those who had last seen Ned remembered him having suffered anything of the kind, it was possible that the police might begin to entertain some doubt, however small, about the identity of the corpse.'

'That's really brilliant,' said Marylou again.

'I should, as I say, have seen it all much earlier, without knowing the medical evidence. That, of course, was conclusive. Julia is admittedly unobservant '

'It's not exactly,' said Selena, 'that she's unobservant. It's just that she doesn't always notice what's happening.'

'I think,' said Marylou, 'that it's because Julia is a very intelligent woman and has her mind on other things.'

'Quite so,' I said. 'Well, I allow that Julia, with her mind on higher things, might not have noticed on waking that her room was littered with corpses. But if she had retired to bed with a young man at about half past two and he had been dead by three, I cannot think that the events occurring in the meantime would have roused her to such immoderate enthusiasm as was displayed in her last letter from Venice.'

'And when,' asked Selena, 'did you decide that the corpse was Richard Tiverton?'

'There, I confess, my reasoning was more speculative. But there seemed no reason to go to such lengths simply to fake Ned's death. Almost certainly, the purpose of the crime must have been to enable Ned to take over the identity of someone else — the identity of the corpse. And what kind of identity was it likely to be? Well, a man, certainly, probably English, and about the same age as Ned. But the main thing was that the alternative identity must be more attractive than his own — one naturally thought of money. We were looking, therefore, for a young man of substantial fortune, almost certainly in Venice for the first time. There may, I concede, be several people answering that description; but we already knew of one and it seemed worth pursuing. It was all quite speculative, however, until we established the connection between Kenneth and Richard Tiverton. Then I was sure.'

'Well,' said Selena, finishing her glass, 'I suppose you had some evidence for your theory, Hilary. I can't say I'd have cared to go into Court on it. I really must go now. I've promised Henry that my Opinion on the Settled Land Act will be ready by four o'clock.'

After exchanging with Marylou expressions of pleasure in having met and hopes of meeting again, she left us.

'Professor Tamar,' said Marylou, 'I'd be really honoured, if you don't think it's impertinent, if you'd permit me to buy another bottle of wine.'

When an invitation is couched in such terms, one can hardly refuse. I allowed her to order another bottle.

'There is just one point,' she said, rather timidly, as we settled to drinking it in the short time available under English licensing laws. 'I mean, I liked going back to Venice on my own and it was a very valid and wonderful experience for me. But wasn't there anyone nearer who could have recognized Ned?'

'Graziella,' I replied, 'was on holiday — I didn't know how difficult it might be to find her. Nor did I know which members of the staff of the Cytherea had seen enough of Ned to identify him with confidence — time was short and we could not afford mistakes.'

'Yes,' she said, 'I understand that. But Julia was staying just across the Lagoon and surely — ?'

'My dear Marylou, I hope you will not feel that I have spared Julia's feelings at the expense of yours. But Julia, in her own way, had been quite fond of Ned. And if she had identified him, she would no doubt have felt responsible for the consequent events. It would, I think, have distressed her considerably — Julia, as you will have gathered, is a sentimental woman.'